Chapter 1

Lieutenant Commander Mike James, F
newest and most secret ship, the HMS
the deck of the hydrofoil as it slowed to enter ...
the main town on the island of St Therese.

At 10AM, local time the heat from the sun was quickly climbing to its full intensity even more noticeable now the spray from the sea which had provided a welcome cooling had ceased when the vessel had slowed down.

"Bloody hell it's hot!" the Irish brogue of Lieutenant Sean 'Engines' Duffin, the Rapier's chief engineer exclaimed.

"Hmm? Oh, yes, it is." Mike replied shaken from his thoughts.

Duffin looked seriously at his friend "What's the matter, Mike, you've been mopping around since we left the base. Come on man we're on leave!"

"I was just thinking about the Captain, something she said just before we left got me worrying about her."

"Sure, she's always been a bit tightly wound. It's probably nothing and we're on leave man. Two whole days in St Therese! And God knows when we might get another, so I don't know about you but I intend to make the most o this one."

"And I suppose making the most of this one means hiding out of the sun in a bar so your delicate ginger complexion doesn't burn," Mike replied jokingly

"Listen apart from being magically attractive to women this can be a terrible curse in the Sun." his friend replied touching his red hair "And taking the piss out of it is racist!" he finished

Mike laughed "Well if the sun is such a problem, I'm sure I can arrange a transfer for you to Redemption base. I'm sure they'd jump at the chance to get the Rapier's chief engineer working on their ships."

"Hmm let me think, hiding from the sun in the Pacific Islands or Freezing my arse off in Antarctica. No sir I don't think I could possibly desert my shipmates at a time like this. I guess I'll just have to risk the sunburn."

Mike slapped his friend on the back "Well I'm sure the Admiral appreciates your self-sacrifice Lieutenant." He said laughing.

Duffin laughed back "Now no more mopping around."

"I'm ok Engines, now go and get the ratings together, the Admiral wants me to give them a final reminder before we dock," Mike replied smiling.

As he watched his friend go and gather the rest of the sailors going on leave his thoughts went back to the day he joined the Damocles project.

Mike waited patiently outside the Admirals office. He'd arrived at Damocles base earlier that morning. The base was situated on a small unnamed piece of land that was home to an extinct volcano in the Pacific Islands. When he was first told about the posting he'd been surprised the Navy had a base out here in this sparsely populated region, when he'd received the posting he'd tried to find some information on the base and surrounding islands but he hadn't been able to find much except to say the islands existed with the nearby island of St Theresa being the largest and most heavily inhabited with a population of a couple of thousand.

The base was made up of a small jetty, where the hydrofoil that was the bases main link to the surrounding islands docked, and a small airfield. The bases buildings on the surface were basic pre-fabricated pods but he'd already seen that most of the base was housed both underground and built into the actual volcano. The corridor that he currently sat in had been tunnelled out of volcanic bedrock. The walls had been covered with a plastic coating and the floor was carpeted to make footing safe, light fittings ran along the ceiling.

The door to the Admirals office opened and the Admirals secretary poked his head out. "Ah Commander James? The Admiral is on his way and he asked if you'd mind waiting here before going into the conference room."

Mike rose and followed the secretary into the office. There were two desks and two additional chairs by the wall. The walls were clad with wood to make the room more traditional but instead of a window there was a huge TV screen. At the moment the screen was set up to resemble a painting of an old ship at sea. The legend at the bottom of the picture read HMS Jervis Bay.

"Ah I see you've found my little fascination," A voice said behind Mike.

Mike turned to see Admiral Greene standing behind him "Sir?" Mike asked surprised.

"You've heard of the Jervis Bay of course?" Green asked

Mike thought for a moment "HMS Jervis Bay, wasn't she a converted merchant ship during the second world war?" he said thinking quickly.

The Admiral just nodded watching Mike's reaction. Mike thought furiously for a moment more.

"Yes, she was the lone escort of an Atlantic Convoy when a German Surface Raider attacked, was it the Scharnhorst? No, it was the Battle Cruiser Admiral Scheer. The Jervis Bay attacked allowing the convoy to scatter. She was lost but most of the convoy survived."

"Well done Commander. Yes, the Jervis Bay was a converted escort and it was the Scheer that attacked the convoy. Her Captain ordered the convoy to scatter and attacked. They knew they didn't have any chance, they barely even got into range for their own guns to fire but their sacrifice enabled twenty-seven of the convoys thirty merchant ships to get away. Her Captain, Edward Fegan was posthumously awarded the Victoria Cross. I keep that picture to remind me that sometimes a victory is not in winning a battle but in the lives saved by our actions." He finished thoughtfully

Mike watched the Admiral seemingly deep in thought. "But that's enough of an old man's musings eh? Come on the others are waiting." Greene said brightly leading Mike to an attached meeting room.

"Now Commander, come in and sit down." Admiral Greene said as they entered the room.

"Sir" Mike said taking the indicated seat. There were several chairs in the room but only two others were occupied. Along the edge of the room stood a tall unit which was covered with a sheet. In the first of the occupied chairs sat a woman wearing the four rings of a Captain on her epaulettes in the other seat a civilian looked up at Mike expectantly.

"Commander this is Captain Sheila Gregory. Sheila is Captain of the Rapier and she'll be your direct superior. And this is Professor Sahota the projects scientific lead. Captain, Professor this is Lieutenant Commander Mike James"

"Commander, a pleasure to meet you." The slight scientist said quickly "I read your thesis on Naval tactics in orbital combat. You have some fascinating ideas, young man."

"Thank you, sir," Mike replied puzzled

"Indeed." The Admiral interrupted "And that's the reason you've been sent to us."

"Sir? I'm not sure I understand." Mike said, "I wrote that thesis as part of a course on Science Fiction writing while I was at University."

Admiral Greene smiled understandingly "Professor perhaps it would be best if you explain."

"Of course, Admiral." Professor Sahota replied standing. He studied the young officer for a few moments then. "Now Commander, as you know we among several nations that have been working for many years to perfect an economical and re-usable propulsion system to launch vehicles into orbit and beyond. Rocket engines are becoming more reliable and also some agencies and companies have had limited success in re-using some engines but the amount of fuel required to launch a rocket with a large payload is still extremely expensive. Some companies are researching hybrid jet and rocket engines which reduces the amount of rocket fuel required and in theory make vessels more re-usable. There have also been experiments in producing something called a RAM SCOOP system, have you ever heard of that?"

"Yes sir, Mike replied, "It's a system which harvests hydrogen from the atmosphere isn't it?"

"Yes it can also collect hydrogen molecules in space but any craft using these engines still have the same problem of expending vast amounts of fuel to reach the required speed be it escape velocity or sufficient speed for the RAM SCOOP to be able to capture hydrogen."

Mike nodded "Yes I understand that sir. That's been the main sticking point which has slowed space exploration since the middle of the last century."

"Now imagine the difference it would make if the vehicle in question, instead of having to accelerate from zero to the required speed was already travelling at a velocity which not only enabled a RAM SCOOP to work but also was sufficient to escape the Earth's gravity as it left the surface."

"That'd mean you reduce your fuel payload, drastically cutting the cost of putting vehicles into space. You could probably increase the size of the vehicle as well." Mike replied thoughtfully "But how can you possibly accelerate from zero to escape velocity instantly?" he asked

"Well you can't obviously but that's not the trick." The professor replied. "Here let me show you." He said walking over to the unit in the corner.

He then proceeded to remove the sheet. What Mike had taken to be a unit was, in fact, a small table with a tall scaffolding tower on the edge that went all the way to the floor where it ended in ramp pointing to the ceiling. On the floor, there was a small tube leading up to looked like a compressed air pump sitting on the table.

"Now Commander, what is the greatest obstacle a rocket or aircraft has to overcome in order to fly?"

"Well, gravity obviously." Mike answered.

"Yes, the field that envelopes any large body that tries to pull anything towards it. Now imagine what would happen if instead of fighting gravity, we used it to boost our vessel."

"Like a slingshot manoeuvre? But surely you need to be in orbit to do that?" Mike asked

"Similar yes, now let me show you what I mean." He said gesturing to the table.

"Now this tube on the floor represents a traditional rocket launch pad while the pump represents the fuel needed to propel the vehicle." He told Mike pumping the handle six times, he continued "Now the pressure I've just added is the fuel. When I press this switch, it will transfer the air pressure or fuel and propel the vehicle." The professor pressed the switch and a small model rocket shot up out of the tube some six feet into the air.

Going into full lecture mode the Professor continued "As we have already said, the rocket had to fight gravity which cost, in the end, all of the motive force provided by the fuel. Now suppose instead of fighting the Earth's gravity we could harness it and add it to the rocket's fuel." He then disconnected the pump from the tube on the floor and connected it to a hose that went into the scaffold tower.

"In this tower is a sledge on which is a rocket identical to the one we just launched."

Mike saw that the scaffolding tower was covered in clear plastic so he could see the model on its sledge.

The professor pumped the handle of the compressed air pump six times again. "Now see the difference." He finished pressing the launch button.

As Mike watched the tiny rocket shot along then down through the tower where it shot out of the bottom. However, this time instead of rising just a few feet, the rocket crashed into the ceiling.

Picking up the broken rocket Mike said "So instead of starting at zero mph at ground level, we start at the top of the tower, or Volcano? So when we reach the launch point at ground level we are already travelling at escape velocity?"

"Precisely." The professor beamed.

The demonstration over the Professor led Mike back to his seat explaining "The vessel we are building is designed to be in three sections. Each will launch separately from, as you've already guessed, the top of the mountain here, down through the centre of the extinct volcano and combine in orbit to form a single craft."

"Well what do you think of the Professors new toy?" the Admiral asked as Mike sat.

"Very impressive sir, a real breakthrough but I still don't see what you need me for," Mike replied cautiously.

The Admiral looked thoughtfully at Captain Gregory who nodded grimacing. "What I'm about to tell you Commander is known to only a very few people at the moment. A few world leaders, some scientists and the officers of a couple of other installations like ours around the world.

Not even all of the base or naval personnel at this station know the full details yet."

"I understand sir," Mike said sitting a little straighter.

The Admiral pressed a few buttons on his keyboard and the large screen on the wall came to life "This footage was sent back by the Voyager 2 probe outside the orbit of Uranus three weeks ago." The Admiral said.

Mike watched the grainy footage. At the bottom of the screen the Planet Neptune took up most of the picture but Mike's eyes were drawn to first one, then several objects coming around from the other side of the planet. These objects appeared to be orbiting the gas giant but any thought that they were natural was dashed as one, seeming to notice the probe altered course and approached.

"The vessels you can see are about a thousand Kilometres away from the probe at this stage." The Professor announced. Mike nodded watching in amazement as the object approaching the probe slowly grew in size.

"The alien vessel actually took about 5 hours to reach the probe so we'll just skip forward to the last part." The Admiral said fast-forwarding the film.

On the screen now was what was unmistakably an enormous spaceship. The vessel looked like a long ovoid structure widening in the middle. Along the hull of the ship various shapes stuck out. Mike saw several bulb-like shapes, long spikes, dishes and shapes he couldn't even begin to recognise.

"We estimate that the vessel is approximately a mile long and about a quarter of a mile wide at the centre. Professor Sahota said

Mike continued to watch as three much smaller craft detached from the giant spaceship and approached the Voyager probe. The smaller vessel was of a different design to the larger ship. Instead of being ovoid it was wide at the front narrowing as it went back. There were four fins each at 90 degrees to each other. It reminded Mike of Basking shark with its wide mouth open to feed. The three smaller craft seemed to halt in front of the probe and study it for a few moments when suddenly a bright light erupted from the middle ship and the recording ended abruptly.

Admiral Greene shut the screen down saying. "As far as we can tell the Aliens whoever they are made no attempt at communication before the destroyed the probe. The United States Space Command at Cheyanne Mountain have taken over NASA's space telescopes and are monitoring the Alien ships. So far, they have managed to count at least twenty-four of these large vessels. They have now all left orbit of Neptune and are headed into our system towards the Earth."

Mike nodded his understanding "How long till they get here sir?"

Well, they seem to be following a course along the plane of the solar system heading towards Saturn and its moons. If they continue along that course and keep their current speed, two, maybe three years if they stop to explore the Saturnian and Jovian mini-systems fully before heading into the inner system."

"You said other bases like this one. I'm assuming then a defence is going to be mounted. What other assets will be deployed?"

"Well we have the ship that we are building here, we're going to name her the HMS Rapier. We've also begun construction, with several Commonwealth allies, of a second base in Antarctica where any breakthroughs and discoveries will be duplicated. The Americans are putting their old shuttle fleet back into operation. The Russians are converting two of their medium-sized missile submarines into spaceships. They intend to strap several of their largest Vostok Rocket Boosters onto them and blast them into orbit that way. The Chinese have committed a number of small space capsules which they have said are configured as fighter assault craft and pretty much the whole world's nuclear arsenal is being sent into orbit and placed as mine constellations. The Europeans are assisting with that as well as providing several capsules which will be used as control stations."

Mike frowned thoughtfully. "Do you think it will be enough sir?"

"No, no I don't think it will be anywhere near enough." Greene replied "Quite honestly Commander even if we have the full three years, we don't have the technology or resources to build a proper defence. It will take at least two years to get the Rapier and all the other ships I just mentioned into space. On top of that, a whole range of new weapon systems will need to be developed. And that's where your unique skills are going to be needed. Professor Sahota here was very impressed with some of your ideas on weapons and tactics. I want you to work with both the professor on new weapons and Captain Gregory on tactics."

"Yes sir, I understand. I'll certainly do everything I can."

"We need you to Commander, I'm not overstating when I say the whole world needs you too."

After the Admiral dismissed them Mike followed Captain Gregory back to her office, Professor Sahota had said he was due at a meeting with his team but wanted to catch up with Mike later in the afternoon.

Shutting the door Gregory gestured for Mike to sit. "Well Commander, what are your thoughts on what you've just heard?"

"It's certainly a lot to take in, Ma'am, to be honest. It will take a great deal of work but if what Professor Sahota told us is accurate, we've got a couple of years so." He replied

Gregory nodded slowly then studied Mike for a few seconds before "I've been looking at your record Commander. I can see you're certainly not a pious man but are you a religious man?"

Surprised by the question Mike replied slowly "Well I was raised a Christian and when duty allows, I attend services when I'm at sea or at a base."

The captain rose from her seat and began pacing. "I am, I believe you must be if you are to serve God, King, and Country. I'll be honest with you Commander when I was first assigned to the Rapier project, I believed it was God's way of returning Brittan to the greatness of history and restoring our nation to her rightful place in the world. But now, now I see it is also a test to see if we are worthy of that place and of that greatness. Are you worthy of that mission Commander?"

"I won't pretend to know God's will or intentions Ma'am I leave that to the chaplains but I'm an officer in his Majesties Navy and I will do my utmost to defend and serve my country," Mike answered honestly.

"I suppose that is all I can ask of you Commander," Gregory replied sitting again. "I've called a meeting for 14:00 hours in the conference room for all of the ship's officers. I'll introduce you to them then. In the meantime, you'd best get your things sorted and arrange your meeting with Professor Sahota."

Feeling that he'd just failed some sort of test Mike rose from his seat. "I'll see you at 14:00 then Ma'am."

Chapter 2

Mike's thoughts came back to the present as Duffin called that all the personnel were assembled. He went below decks where the sailors and construction workers who were all going on leave stood expectantly.

"Stand easy." He began "Right Admiral Greene just wanted me to remind you all before you go on leave that as far as the rest of the world knows we are building a base for anti-pirate operations. If anyone asks you if you know anything about the increase in space shots and satellite launches the official story is that Earth's orbit has become so cluttered with old satellite's and equipment that 'Road Sweeper' satellites are being sent up to clear the debris and new navigation satellites are being sent up to replace the old ones being cleared."

Mike studied the faces looking at him and continued. "We all know the truth; we all know what's coming but telling the world now will only cause panic and divert resources away from the defensive efforts when we need them most. For some of us, this may well be our last leave for quite some time. Make the most of it and enjoy yourselves but remember your cover stories. PO's and supervisors, I'm relying on you to look after your people alright?"

There was a murmur of agreement with a few "Yes sirs" in reply when a thud and a clang which meant the launch had docked reverberated through the room.

"Alright everyone we've docked. Remember what I just said and go and have a good time." He finished dismissing them all. The assembled sailors and construction workers quickly filed out of the compartment. Duffin stood next to Mike watching them leave.

"You know anyone who has any idea about satellites won't believe any of that bilge! And sooner or later some amateur stargazer is going to see the alien fleet and they won't be able to stop them from getting the news out in time" he said quietly

Mike looked at his friend sighing "I know but that's the story we've been given and we've got to stick to it."

The last of the sailors left the cabin Mike turned to Duffin saying "Come on I want to get booked into the hotel before all the rooms go."

"The hotel? I thought we'd nip into O'Shea's for a wee nip first."

"I know your 'wee nips'! No there are some sailors from the American sentry group coming in today as well. So, we'll book into the hotel first then go to O'Shea's." Mike finished grabbing Duffin's overnight bag and tossing it to his friend. Picking up his own he headed onto the deck his friend's guffaws following on behind.

As the two officers disembarked from the launch, they were completely unaware that they were being watched. A slim redheaded woman sat at a table outside one of the two café's that served the small harbour wearing a wide-brimmed sun hat and dark glasses. She looked down, to all intents and purposes studying the tall drink in her hand but she had been watching the launch intently as it docked. She'd watched as the sailors and construction workers disembarked but had decided not to follow them instead waiting a few more minutes just in case the officer she had seen on the deck also came ashore. Her patience was rewarded as the two officers emerged. She decided to wait a few more minutes to see which way they went before following.

Her name was Samantha Selkie, Sam to her friends. Of all the names and identities, she had worn in her life that had been her first and was still her favourite. It was also the reason her Uncle had chosen her for this mission. It had been her name when she had lived in England as a child. Her Uncle had reasoned that she still had a good understanding of the British. Her mother probably had a better understanding but Uncle had said that a sailor or better yet an officer might open up more to an attractive young woman than her mother.

She thought back to the morning four days ago when she had been summoned to Uncle's study. Uncle was the head of the clan and leader of the council of elders. Uncle had been the clan head for several years now inheriting the position from Sam's father after he had been killed by the Cabal. She knocked on the study door and poked her head in "You wanted to see me, Uncle?"

"Samantha yes come in and sit down."

She sat in the indicated chair and waited expectantly.

"There was a meeting of elders last night" he began

"I thought there must have been, my mother came back quite late."

"Yes of course. Did she happen to discuss anything said at the meeting with you?"

"No, I haven't seen her this morning, I had to go out to the plantation early this and she was gone by the time I got back. She just left me a message saying you wanted to see me and would explain everything."

"Yes, she's gone to the caverns to review them." Her Uncle explained. He paused for a moment then continued "Have you been following the news recently?"

"Only in general, I've not seen anything that I thought might be about us. Have I missed something?"

"No, not specifically but the council is concerned about several apparently unrelated items. Firstly, the British have been building a new naval base on an extinct volcanic island a short distance from here. Then there seems to be a very unusual lack of hostility between the power blocks and finally a massive increase in space launches recently. The news outlets have noticed some but our contacts around the world report that the number of launches is actually in the hundreds, not the dozens reported. The goodwill between the former enemies and satellite launches on their own are strange enough but coupled with a new British military base guarded by an American carrier group effectively in our back yard has the council worried."

Sam frowned "I see. What do you need me to do Uncle?"

"You grew up in England, you still speak English fluently and with an English accent. From what we have heard sailors and workers from the base have been coming to Port Theresa on liberty. We want you to go to the Port and see if you can find out anything that might give us some idea of what is actually going on."

Hearing the stories she's heard linked in that way brought a tang of fear to her heart. Taking a calming breath Sam asked, "When do I leave?"

"As soon as possible I'm afraid. I'd like to wait for your mother to return but this is too important to delay."

Rising quickly, she said, "I'll pack now and go straight away." As she headed back to the suite she shared with her mother she quickly composed a note in case she never returned.

Her thoughts returned to the present, the two officers had left the quay and were walking up towards the centre of the town. Sam made a quick decision; she would change quickly before following them. She would need to get closer to hear what they were saying and did not want them to recognise her. Quickly walking into the back of the café. She nodded to Miguel, who owned the café, He and his sister Monique would look after her stuff, their family had worked for the plantation for years and could be trusted. She changed in the bathroom, then as Miguel held the door open for her, she went out into the alley behind the café to follow her prey.

Mike followed his friend as he led him down a series of alley's "Are you sure this is a shortcut Engines?" he asked as they turned yet another corner.

"Course, I'm sure, it's not far now." He replied looking around uncertainly.

"This doesn't look like where the Hotel is supposed to be."

"That's cos this is the shortcut to where the Hotel is." Engines replied

"I thought you wanted to get to O'Shea's for that drink," Mike said looking around the alley they were in when a sudden crash and angry shout made him look up.

What looked like a big red dog was running along the rooftops away from them as a woman who had clearly been about to put her washing out on her balcony threw stones after it. Her basket of washing and a couple of broken pots spilt over the edge of the balcony testament to what had caused the crash.

"It's this way!" Duffin exclaimed triumphantly, ignoring the commotion.

Mike followed his friend down one last alleyway onto the town's main road where sure enough the hotel sat in front of them.

"Told you I'd get you here." Duffin crowed as they walked up the steps to the hotel entrance.

"Yeah, but next time you think you've got a shortcut I think I'll just go the long way; it'll be quicker." Mike laughed looking to cross the road but as he looked to the left a small shop caught his eye, "Hang on a second what's that?"

Duffin looked over, "It's just the small shop where you can pick up bits of tat for souvenirs," he replied.

"Yes I know but look what they have in the window!" Mike said excitedly walking over to the shop.

Duffin joined him and hanging in pride a place was a long sword. "Looks nice, but I bet it's just fake tat."

"I'm not so sure, come on," Mike said going into the shop

As if they'd rehearsed the move Duffin walked over to the shopkeeper and distracted him while Mike went to look at the sword. Just as he suspected the sword was a Rapier, picking the card up with the description he read "British long Rapier sword circa 1650. Thought to be the property of the English fencing master and Sea Hawk pirate Joseph Swetnam. Price Nine Hundred Pounds"

Seeing Mike reading the card the shopkeeper skilfully bypassed Duffin and came over to Mike "Ah I see sir has an eye for the beauty of an exceptional piece of craftsmanship. And a valuable piece of antique history."

Mike turned still holding the card "It's certainly a nice piece but I'm not sure it's that much of an antique."

"Ah but sir, this was the prized possession of the great Joseph Swetnam himself."

"I'm afraid I doubt that, for a start, this says circa 1650, that's a bit late for Swetnam by about sixty years. Plus, he was a courtier of Charles the 1st and never a sea hawk or pirate for that matter."

The shopkeeper opened his mouth to protest but Mike continued. "But it is a pretty piece, I'll give you a hundred and fifty for it."

"Sir, surely you are having a joke at old Andre's expense! For such a prize I could not go lower than Eight Hundred."

Mike's lip curled at the edge as he smiled to himself, he knew he had the shopkeeper now and continued to haggle. Ten minutes later he and Duffin left the shop, the wrapped sword clutched tightly in his hand.

"Four Hundred pounds for that, you're a madman! He's probably got a dozen of them out the back" Duffin complained

Mike looked aside at his friend "No I doubt it, I do know a bit about swords you know. This isn't 1600 and nothing to do with anyone like Swetnam but it is an antique, probably late eighteenth or early nineteenth century. I reckon it's worth a lot more than I paid. Maybe even double."

"Yeah, I'm not so sure," Duffin replied doubtfully

"You'll see when we get back to base, I'll get the prof to have a look and you'll eat your words!" Mike said laughing, "I think this is going to be a good leave." He finished but as he reached the hotel entrance a shiver running up his spine made him pause. Glancing back, he just caught the site of a large red dog disappearing around the corner.

Chapter 3

Mike had been on the base for four months when Admiral Greene called all the base's officers to the main briefing room. Mike had been going over the weekly reports submitted by the various department heads when the summons popped up on his screen. He had just closed his terminal down when Duffin pocked his head through the open door.

"Did you just get called to the briefing room?"

"Yes, and it sounds urgent, we'd best get moving," Mike replied grabbing his saucer cap.

As they headed down the corridor Duffin asked "Any idea what's happened? Is it about...?" he asked gesturing up towards the ceiling. Duffin and the rest of the project's officers had been briefed about the alien's a couple of weeks before but like many of the officers, the sheer enormity of the prospect of alien invasion was still sinking in.

"I don't know but I think we'll soon find out," Mike replied as they reached the briefing room. They both took seats in the front row as the rest of the base's officers quickly filed in. Captain Gregory and Professor Sahota were already seated along with a man Mike didn't recognise. The Admiral watched while the last officer closed the briefing door behind them. Greene waited a few moments while the latecomers sat, then standing, began to address them.

"Right, I'm not going to beat about the bush. As you all know some five months ago, we detected an alien fleet around Uranus. Since then the various space agencies have been trying to track them using various telescopes and observatories. We've just had it confirmed that our American friends at NASA." He said nodding towards the stranger "Have found them. Mr Johansson here is the civilian advisor to the American escort group which is patrolling this area. Mr Johansson?" Greene invited.

Mike watched as the American rose to join the Admiral at the podium. By 'Civilian Advisor' Mike took the Admiral to mean CIA. It wasn't unusual for US forces, especially units with Special Forces attached to have an intelligence officer with them.

"Thank you, Admiral." Johansson began switching the screen on. "Now as your Admiral has just said NASA and our air force space command have been searching for these unknown extra-terrestrial vessels since the Voyager probe was lost around Uranus. Now the solar system is a big place and it's taken a while, but we've found them, or at least a part of their fleet in orbit around Europa."

On the screen, a blurry image of several of the alien motherships appeared in orbit over Europa. They watched as what appeared to be a squadron of the smaller ships detached and headed down toward the surface of the moon.

"What are they doing?" Lieutenant Singh one of the Rapier's pilots asked

"We can't really tell, the scientists at NASA assume they might have stopped to mine the ice for water."

"That would make sense, they might need water for any number of reasons, anything from basic cleanliness and drinking water to reaction mass for their engines." Mike agreed.

"But that looks like a combat formation." Singh insisted.

"That might just be their normal formation," Gregory replied

"We have thought Europa a prime candidate for life for many years." Professor Sahota mused.

The assembled officers watched in silent thought as the smaller ships as they flew down to the moon.

After the presentation finished Mike noticed Gregory excusing herself and leaving. As she passed him, Mike caught a look of abject horror on her face. He went to follow but Professor Sahota and the Admiral intercepted him.

"Well Commander, what do you think about Lieutenant Singh's idea about the alien's combat formation?"

Mike thought for a moment then "Well Raj is a fighter pilot so if he says it's a combat formation, I'd take his word for it."

Greene frowned "So it does point to them being aggressive."

"It does but we had assumed that anyway and it's actually good news."

"I'm not quite clear on how the confirmation that a potential Alien invasion fleet is hostile is good news Commander," Johansson demanded joining them.

"Well sir we've been working on the basis that they are aggressive as they destroyed the Voyager probe unprovoked, so the potential confirmation doesn't alter anything. But the fact they are using, what to us are, obvious combat tactics may well mean that they probably aren't that different from us in how they think. It means we will have a better chance of understanding what they will do, how they will attack and we can come up with better tactics and defences to fight them."

"And you think you can come up with tactics to counter them?" the American asked

"Yes sir, I'm confident we can counter anything they can come up with, the issue is whether we will have sufficient assets to be able to meet them," Mike replied.

The Admiral exchanged a knowing look with Johansson "You leave the assets to us, Commander, you just keep working on your tactics and weapons." The CIA man finished.

"Yes, which reminds me, Commander," Sahota interjected, "Dr Cummins believes she may have a solution to the overheating issue."

"Really?" Mike replied, "Admiral, Mr Johansson if you'd excuse us?"

Greene dismissed them taking the CIA man aside as Mike and Sahota left for the laboratories. It wasn't until much later Mike remembered the expression on Captain Gregory's face as she left the briefing room.

Mike looked at himself in the mirror, he'd seen that same look on Gregory's face just before he had left the base earlier that morning. Her mood had been going down-hill for some time now but he couldn't fault her performance. He was torn inside, as a fellow officer he quite liked the Captain, she was efficient, a good officer but he could see her focus slipping almost daily. He didn't want to be the one to be the cause of any black marks on her record, which if he said anything to the Admiral would almost certainly happen but something would have to be done and soon. He wondered if anyone else had noticed anything. Professor Sahota had known Gregory longer than Mike had, surely, he would have noticed if anything were amiss. He resolved to speak to the diminutive scientist when he got back to the base.

He finished getting himself ready and went down to the lobby where Duffin was already waiting for him.

"About bloody time, the pub's been open nearly an hour already!"

"Well, what are you waiting for? Come on," Mike quipped as they headed down the street to the pub. O'Shea's already seemed to be full of off-duty sailors and staff from both the base and the US carrier group which was acting as a guard detail. As their eyes adapted to the darker bar Duffin nudged Mike and pointed over to a table where two American officers sat talking with a couple of women, a blond and a redhead. Mike recognised the Americans as Nathan Jameson and Kerry Lightningblood, two of the USS John F Kennedy's fighter pilots. Jameson waved at them and pointed at two of the four spare chairs at his table.

"You go on over and I'll get the round in. find out what everyone's drinking" Mike told Duffin.

"I'll check what their having and text you," Duffin promised.

Mike went to the bar and waved the bartender over. His phone quickly buzzed with Duffin's promised list of drinks. getting the drinks Mike weaved his way through the crowded bar.

"Here you go," Mike said as he reached the table.

"Hey, Mike." Kerry Lightningblood greeted taking some of the bottles and handing them out.

The two women smiled their thanks while Jameson took a long swallow and said: "Man I needed that!"

"Well, that's what you get for being in a 'dry' Navy!" Mike joked

"Aye, banning beer aboard ship, tis barbaric," Duffin agreed

The two American pilots laughed

"Aren't you allowed to drink on your ships?" the Blond woman asked

"The US Navy is what the call dry, no alcohol aboard, but the Royal Navy does allow it. Isn't that right?" The redhead asked.

"You're English?" Mike asked noting her accent.

"I was born in England and lived there till I was twelve," She replied.

"Hey my bad, we should've introduced you," Jameson apologised "This is Miss Samantha Selkie and her friend Monique Nairne. Lieutenant Commander James and Lieutenant Duffin"

Mike took Sam's extended hand as Jameson introduced her but froze as he said her name. Seeing the look on Mike's face she frowned slightly.

"Samantha, Sam?" Mike gasped incredulously

"I'm sorry, do we know each other?"

"Yes, well I think we used to, I'm Mike James."

Sam looked quizzically back "Mike Ja...." Then eyes widening "Mikey James Oh my God, Mikey I don't believe it," She cried flinging her arms around him.

"Err are we interrupting anything?" Duffin asked loudly.

Sam let Mike go and smiled sheepishly

"We grew up together." Mike explained "Till we were about twelve when you left," He finished.

Sam smiled sadly back at him, memories of those frantic hours when her father had come home and told them the cabal had found them. How Mike's father had driven them hidden in his van to the small fishing village along the coast where they had finally escaped came sharply to her mind. Studying Mike's face, she wondered how much of that story he knew and how much had been hidden from him.

Aloud she said: "We had to move because of my father's work," remembering the story she always used to explain her movements.

Mike nodded, "Yes I remember my parents telling me that," he replied.

"So, what brings you to St Theresa?" Monique asked jolting Sam from her thoughts and reminding her of her mission.

"We have a couple of days leave so we thought we'd come over here."

"I think Monique meant why are two of the world's best Navy's suddenly taking an interest in our little region of islands," Sam interjected.

Duffin looked across at Mike before answering, "Well as I'm sure you've heard there's been a sharp increase in Piracy around the world so we're building a base for anti-pirate patrols to protect these islands."

"And that needs a full US Navy battle group to protect it?" Sam asked the Americans

"We're hardly a full battle group, just the JFK, and our escorts. No, we're just part of the normal Pacific patrol. We've only stopped over as a courtesy visit to our allies." Lightningblood replied evenly.

"So, what about the reports we've heard about Rocket engines being heard coming from your island?" Sam asked "Are they anything to do with all the space rockets being launched? Are they part of your Anti-Pirate thing?"

Mike laughed, "Firstly we haven't been launching any spy satellites or anything like that and the engines people have heard have just been from the planes launching from and landing on the JFK. Secondly, satellites aren't much good anyway when you're looking for pirate ships. Contrary to popular belief they can't see into a small ship and spot pirates."

Sam exchanged a look with Monique but laughed along with Mike.

"But enough about what we're doing here, what about you and Monique, Sam? What do you do in this paradise?" Mike quipped.

"Huh it's hardly paradise," she replied chuckling "But it is a bit nicer than a soggy British summer," She finished. As the conversation flowed back and forth, she watched Mike thoughtfully. His family had helped her and her parents in the past but she didn't know how much about her family they had known or what they had told Mike. She decided to hold back in trying to get more information from him until she was able to speak to her mother.

Sam and Monique spent the rest of the evening in O'Shea's. The American pilots left having to return to their ship after a few hours. At the end of the evening, Mike insisted on walking them back home.

"So, do you live here in town?" Mike asked.

"No, I live on my Uncle Jeremiah's plantation in the mountains, I'm just staying with Monique and her brother at their café," Sam replied.

"Your Uncle? Didn't I meet him once?"

"Yes, he came to visit us when I was ten."

"I thought I remembered him. What about your mum and dad? How are they?

"Mum's fine, she's back at the plantation." she explained, "But we lost my father several years ago."

Mike thought back to his childhood remembering Sam's father, as tall as he was broad, dark-haired with a full beard. In his mind, he was always laughing. "I'm sorry to hear that. I always liked your dad."

"It was hard at the time but we went to live with my Uncle and we've gotten on with our lives," she replied.

"Yes, on your plantation," Mike said relieved to move the conversation on. "Are there caves near your plantation?" he asked

Mike's question hit Sam like a brick wall "Caves?" She asked quickly

"Yeah, caves, I seem to remember you loved exploring the caves in the hills when we were kids. Is everything ok?"

"Oh, yes, sorry I don't know what I was thinking." She replied "There are a few in the hills. We sometimes use them for storage. In fact, you should come up to the plantation to see them. I know mum would love to see you."

Now it was Mike's turn to pause. "I'd like that, perhaps next time I'm on leave."

"How about tomorrow? You said you had a couple of days leave. I have a car and you'd both be welcome."

Mike looked at Duffin who just shrugged.

"We'd have to be back in time to catch the launch back to base but, yeah why not. Thanks, Sam."

"Good, well this is us." She told him as they reached the Café "Umm" she began but Mike quickly replied.

"Well, in that case, we'll bid you both a good night. We've got to get back to the hotel and check-in with the base but we'll see you both again in the morning?"

"We'll be ready," Sam agreed

Sam followed Monique into the café as Mike and Duffin walked back to the hotel

"Why are you taking them to the plantation Sam? Monique asked "Is that not dangerous?"

"He was my friend and his family helped mine when we had to leave Britain."

"But that was a long time ago and he is in the military now. He works for the government and the Cabal have links with governments." Monique warned

Sam looked at Monique considering "He hasn't changed, I can tell, but you're right. I will contact my mother at the plantation. She will know what to do for the best." She conceded picking up her phone.

Chapter 4

But the plans Sam made were to prove for nothing as her phone rang early the next morning.

"Hello?" she said groggily

"Sam? It's Mike, I'm sorry but we're not going to be able to meet with you today. Somethings come up and Sean and I have been called back to the base."

"Oh Mike, hi," she replied coming fully awake. "Oh, I'm sorry to hear that I was really looking forward to seeing you today. Umm, when are you leaving? Do you have time to meet up first?" she asked desperately thinking of a way to try and get more of the information she needed."

"No, I'm really sorry Sam, there's a car waiting outside to take us to the airfield. They've sent a plane to pick us up."

"A plane? That sounds serious. Is there anything I should know?"

There was a pause on the line then Mike continued "No nothing for you to worry about now, but you remember I asked you about any caves near your plantation."

"Yes?"

"Tell your Uncle it would be a good idea to make sure they are provisioned, just in case."

"Mike you're scaring me," Sam replied truthfully.

"It's probably nothing but just in case yeah? Look I've got to go but I'll be in touch if I can. Take care, Sam." He finished quickly ending the call.

Sam looked at her phone in shock at Mike's abrupt end to the call, then with a quick decision she quickly dressed and calling Monique she grabbed her bags and headed to her car.

Mike looked down at his phone thinking about what he'd just told Sam. Technically he'd not disobeyed any orders but he wasn't sure the Admiral would agree if he heard about it. But those caves could save a lot of lives if they were prepared properly.

"Mike, the cars here," Duffin called from the landing.

Mike quickly looked around then grabbing his bag joined Duffin. "Did you manage to get hold of anyone to recall the crew?"

"Aye Chief PO Isaacs was staying here as well. I told her to round everyone up and get them back to the launch."

Mike nodded approvingly Chief Petty Officer Joanne Isaacs was the Rapiers senior NCO and as solid a crew member as he could ask for. She'd get everyone back even if she had to drag them out of a cell first. Though he fervently hoped that wouldn't be needed!

Two hours and a hurried flight later Mike and Duffin landed at Damocles base and had been rushed through to see Admiral Greene. Mike could tell from the looks on the faces of the base staff something bad had definitely happened.

"Gentlemen, please sit," Greene told them as he entered the office. Taking his own seat, he looked across at the two younger men grimly. "I'm sorry I had to call you back from your leave but as I'm sure you've already guessed there have been some developments. Professor Sahota and Mr Johansson are waiting in the conference room to brief us but I wanted to see you both first." He paused for a moment to brace himself before continuing. "I am extremely sorry to have to inform you that Captain Gregory was found dead in her quarters last night."

"Jesus!" Duffin exclaimed

"Was it an accident sir?" Mike asked quietly

Greene looked hard at Mike for a second "No, it wasn't an accident. We found her note." Seeing Mike's expression, the Admiral continued "Don't blame yourself, Mike, you're not the only one who had noticed she wasn't right. I've been trying to get her to talk about what's been bothering her for a few weeks now." He finished miserably.

"What did her note say, sir?" Duffin asked

"She said this was God's punishment. That we had failed to live up to his plan for us that she had failed to drive the project forward. She said we would fight when we shouldn't and she could not bring herself to fight Gods will."

"I remember she asked me about my beliefs when I first arrived." Mike volunteered. "She told me she thought this was Gods way of returning Brittan back to being the major power in the world."

"She always was a bit obsessed. I even tried to get the chaplain, to talk to her." Greene agreed. "Anyway, what's done is done. Now we've got to decide what to do next." He finished pulling them all out of their musings.

"Mike, this makes you the Rapier's senior officer. I'd like you to take over as her Captain. Now I can request Captain Reese be sent up from Redemption base but he's not as familiar as you with the ship and it would be a rush to get him here plus I'd rather not bring someone new in at this late stage."

Surprised by the Admiral's offer Mike had to take a moment to think, "Thank you, sir, I mean yes I don't know that I could ever fully replace Captain Gregory but yes I sir I can take over."

"Good man," then turning to Duffin "That will make you second in command Sean, do you think you can handle that as well as being the chief engineer?"

"Aye sir, I'll not let you down." Duffin agreed quickly.

"Good that's one thing off my mind. Now we'd best get into the briefing room. I've been told there have been some very serious developments." He said leading them out of his office.

In the briefing room, most of the Rapiers officers and crew who hadn't gone to St Theresa were waiting along with Professor Sahota, several of his team and Mr Johansson. Duffin went to sit with his engineers but Mike followed Greene to the front where he sat in Gregory's old seat.

Instead of taking his seat Greene stood to address the assembled crew. Giving them a long searching look he began "By now you've all heard the news about Captain Gregory. Losing your Captain, especially in this way and at a time like this, is a hard thing to deal with. But deal with it we must and quickly. If any of you feel you need to talk to anyone to help you come to terms with Captain Gregory's death Father Gibbons and Dr McQueen are both available at any hour. My door is also open as well." He paused for a second before continuing. "Now, Mr Johansson here has received some new and from what I've heard so far disturbing intelligence. He will brief us all about that in a moment. However, before that, we do need to quickly cover what Captain Gregory's death means to us and what adjustments must be made.

Commander James here has agreed to take over as Captain of the Rapier. You all already know him so you will not have to get used to a new Captain. Lieutenant Duffin will step up to become the first officer as well as retaining his post as chief engineer. Those are the only changes I intend to make for now," he finished handing the stage to the American intelligence officer.

Johansson moved to the lectern and keyed on the screen. "Good morning everyone," he began. On the screen images from the previous briefing appeared showing the alien vessels around Europa.

"As you may recall NASA, along with several other space administrations have been using every available asset to try and track the movements of the Alien fleet. Two months ago, we detected these ships around the moon Europa. There was some speculation around what they were doing but the fact they were still so far away was encouraging. Since then we have tracked three more groups of the Alien ships," The screen changed to an illustration of the Jovian and Saturnine moon systems.

"We now have confirmed sightings at Europa, Titan, Ganymede but most importantly," he said changing the screen again. "Mars."

There was a shocked intake of breath as the screen now showed film images of the Alien craft, four motherships and several of the smaller warships in orbit of the red planet. The warships seemed to be holding the same formation as had been observed around Europa but from two of the mother ships, a stream of small objects appeared to be being fired at the surface.

"These images were sent by the Mars Orbiter, the satellite that NASA has around Mars. So far, the aliens don't appear to have seen it but we've no way of knowing how long that will last," Johansson told them.

"But why are they firing at the planet?" one of the sailors asked

They all watched as the mother ships kept firing at the surface of Mars.

Frowning Greene said "Mars is a dead world, there's nothing there. Could they be firing on one of our probes or landers?"

"What about that picture from a few years ago that had those figures on?" another rating asked

"We've always believed Mars to be uninhabited," Professor Sahota mused "Unless there's information NASA has been withholding?" he asked

Johansson looked uncomfortable as he replied, "NASA has no proof there's any life on Mars, but there have been some anomalous data, strange shapes on pictures, system failures."

"And over half the probes sent lost," Mike added, "most in the same areas if I'm not mistaken."

"Some areas seemed more problematic than others so we stopped sending probes to those areas."

"Areas like Olympus Mons, the face and three pyramids and the Vales Marineris the only place on the planet where liquid water has possibly been observed." Sahota finished dryly

"Look whether there is anything there or not isn't relevant at the moment. The issue is they are a lot closer than we ever imagined." Johansson said exasperatedly

Mike nodded slowly "But if there is anyone there let's hope they keep them busy for as long as possible."

With that, the briefing ended and Greene dismissed the crew but asked his key officers and staff to remain. Stewards re-arranged the room and served coffee. When everyone was seated Greene began.

"Well regardless of how long they stay at Mars, the fact they are this close has blown our timescales to bits. So how close are we to being able to launch?"

Mike paused for a moment while he gathered his thoughts, "Well sir all three sections have test-launched successfully, and all our standard defensive weapon systems have been installed. We're just waiting on the latest upgrades for our offensive systems and Ram-scoop drive."

Greene looked down at Duffin. "Lieutenant?"

"Well everything's working as per spec but we won't know how effective the drive is till we can get up to ram-scoop speeds. But even if we can't get the Ram-scoop to work the drive is operational with onboard fuel reserves"

Greene nodded "Professor, how are we with the main weapons?"

The diminutive scientist looked up from his notes. "Well on that front we finally have some good news. Firstly, Dr Cummins and her team have solved the overheating problem on the Small Hadron Accelerator Gun or Particle Cannon as Commander James prefers to call it."

The Rapiers primary weapon was based on a miniaturised version of the old Large Hadron Accelerator at CERN in Switzerland and accelerated particles to a fraction of the speed of light. The resulting particle beam had proved to be a very powerful weapon. There were a few smiles around the table as they recalled the overuse the weapon's acronym had received.

"Also, Redemption base has managed to extend the range of the Sonic Disrupter Cannon."

Based on an entertainment system where music tracks could only be heard if you stood in a light beam, the Sonic Cannon contained high-frequency sound waves in a laser which caused any solid matter to vibrate and shatter when the correct frequency was found.

Sitting forward at the Professors revelation Greene asked: "How long to install these upgrades?"

Sahota quickly conferred with his team "Redemption are sending the plans for the enhancements to the disrupters today, we should be able to make and install the new components within a few days. The same for the Particle cannon. Then we'll just need a few days for final testing."

"So, we should be able to launch the Rapier within a fortnight? What about your crew Commander?" Green asked.

"We're fully trained sir and I think in the circumstances giving the crew something to focus on would be a good thing. What about the Claymore and Excalibur at Redemption?"

Greene nodded "Unfortunately they are still at least a month or two behind us. What about the allies Mr Johansson?"

The CIA agent checked his tablet, "The satellite mine constellations have about sixty-five per cent in position. Our shuttles are working on the next section already we should be up to seventy-five per cent by the time you can launch. The Russian ships are effectively two medium attack subs strapped to several Soyuz rockets. They'll be ready. Europe has several command capsules ready for launch. That won't be enough but with the ISS and our shuttles to take up the slack we should be ok. The Chinese will have two squadrons of their orbital combat pods ready within three weeks."

Greene listened intently while Johansson listed the readiness of the other assets. "Well, ladies and gentlemen we have a great deal of work to do and not a great deal of time."

Chapter 5

Mike stood at the bottom of the massive hangar section at the base of the extinct volcano that formed the base. Around him, engineers and ground staff busily manned their stations or hurried around on last-minute tasks while the Rapiers crew began to assemble.

The Rapier currently in its three component sections sat on the cradles which would raise them up to the launch ramp at the very top of the hollowed-out Mountain. His eyes expertly flowed over each part, first the Command section where the main Bridge was located. This section held six of the Rapier's ten auto-cannon, the latest and most advanced antiballistic defensive weapons which could fire a hundred ball-bearing sized bullets every second, shredding any incoming missiles to pieces. The Command section would launch first using its advanced defensive ability to cover the other sections. Next came the Heavy Weapons section. This section held the Particle Cannon or S.H.A.G gun as most of the crew called it, the two forward and one aft Sonic Disruptors plus the last two auto-cannon and the Ram-Scoop collector which ran down through the centre of the ship along with the Particle Cannon. Last came the main engineering and drive section. The Command Section had two hybrid jet/rocket engines to boost it into orbit while the Weapons section had four. The Drive section contained the main engines and wouldn't need anything else. In his mind's eye, Mike put the three sections together. The Command section riding the Heavy Weapons section just forward of mid-point with the Dive section with main engines enveloping its rear.

"She's pretty incredible don't you think?" "Greene asked coming up to Mike's side.

Mike looked to his side, "She's a beauty." He replied admiring her lines.

"She's that as well." The Admiral agreed, "I wish I was going with you, Mike." He finished.

This time Mike turned and looked directly at the Admiral, "I know, the Doc's would never allow it with my heart." He said knowing what was on the younger man's mind.

"You'll be with us in spirit sir," Mike replied softly.

Greene smiled squeezing Mike's arm, "Oh enough of an old man's fantasies. Let's get this done."

"Sir," Mike said as they turned to face the assembled crew.

"Attention!" Mike called out.

As one, the officers and crew snapped to attention. Admiral Greene stepped up to the podium "At ease everyone," he began before pausing for a moment. "Before you board your sections I just wanted to say a few words, but first I believe Commander James, you were able to find a little something on St Theresa on your last leave."

"Yes sir," Mike replied brightly as he retrieved the long package from behind the podium and handed it to the Admiral.

Greene took the package and undoing the string unwrapped the paper to show the sword Mike had brought. "A rapier for the Rapier!" handing it back to Mike, Greene continued "I believe it would be appropriate to hang this in the Rapiers wardroom as ships mascot." The crew and base staff who had stopped working all clapped as Mike took the sword. Then turning back to the crew Greene spoke again, "Today you will all be making history as you take the world's first truly operational multipurpose spacecraft into orbit and beyond. Now we know what you are going to do up there is not what we originally intended the Rapier for but we are all sailors in his Majesty's Navy and we knew when we signed on what that might mean.

Today when you launch, alongside our allies, it will be as a shield to protect the entire planet Earth. It may seem like we are entering dark days, that the odds you face are overwhelming, impossible even but these are not the first dark days the Royal Navy has endured. Decades ago, during the Second World War when the days were at their very darkest, it was the Royal Navy that kept our supply lines, in the form of convoys of unarmed merchant ships, open. That protected our islands from the aggression of our enemies. One ship in particular, responsible for protecting a convoys faced impossible odds. The HMS Jervis Bay could have retreated, they knew they were outgunned, but they chose to stand, chose to hold the enemy at bay and because of their action most of the ships in their care survived. Indeed, one of them was able to double back and rescue the surviving crew of the Jervis Bay.

Today you are descendants of all those brave sailors who have gone before. Today you are not responsible for the protection of a convoy of ships but responsible for the protection of the whole human race. And like those who went before, all of us will stand, be it in space or here on the Earth, we will say NO! You will not hurt our people; you will not harm our world. Remember those who have stood before, REMEMBER THE JERVIS BAY!" he finished with a roar.

Mike led the cheers from the crew and assembled base staff as the admiral finished. He let them cheer for a few more minutes before calling them back to order.

"I believe I speak for the whole ship's company when I say thank you for your confidence, sir, with your permission?"

"Of course, Captain."

Mike turned to his crew "Chief Petty Officer." He said.

"Sir." Chief Petty Officer Joanne Isaacs said as she moved to the front. "CREW OF THE RAPIER ATTENTION!" she paused for a moment before "TO YOUR DUTIES, DISMISS!"

Are you sure you can handle command and piloting the Command section into orbit? I can still assign you one of the supply sledge pilots."

"It's only till we've docked all the sections together then Raj can come up and take over. Besides assigning one of the sledge pilots would leave us short-handed on the supply runs and I think we'll need those more before the end of this."

Greene nodded, "I thought that's what you'd say, if you're sure I won't hold you up any longer. Good luck Captain," he finished.

"Thank you, sir, we won't let you down."

Leaving the Admiral, Mike boarded the Command section and made his way through the narrow corridor to the wardroom where he hung the sword above the picture of the HMS Jervis Bay that Greene had given him. It was the same picture which had hung in the Admiral's office. That done he made his way up to the second deck where the Bridge was located. He emerged onto the bridge to a hive of activity. The small bridge was cramped. At the front were two consoles where the helmsman and navigator were stationed. In the middle slightly behind was the Captain's chair. Around the edge were several consoles dedicated to communications, tracking and LIDAR each responsible for a ninety-degree ark around the ship. Each console then feeding information down to the Combat Direction Centre which then prioritised each target and assigned defensive fire.

At the back of the bridge were three consoles which dealt with the ship's status and then connected to damage control in the engineering section.

Mike sat at the Helm station and began the pre-launch checks; he was soon joined by second Lieutenant Patricia Kelly the Rapier's Navigator. Before long each duty station was manned.

"All sections report readiness," He ordered and patiently recorded each section as they reported in.

"Signals connect me Damocles control please," He ordered.

"You're on sir." Petty officer Jeremy Rogers told him

"Damocles control this is Rapier Command. We are ready to launch. Over," he transmitted.

"Roger Rapier Command. Please stand by while we confirm the Weapons and engineering sections ready." Admiral Greene's voice replied.

Mike waited a few minutes before Greene's voice came back, "Rapier Command This is Damocles control. All Rapier elements report ready. Stand by to ascend to launch platform." The Admiral announced. A few moments later Mike felt his craft begin to rise as it was lifted to the launch platform at the top of the mountain. Mike looked out through the small windows that lined the front of the bridge at the launch ramp.

"Just like the rollercoasters at Disneyland," Kelly said next to him.

Mike grinned chuckling. "Just a ride in the park." Then switching to the ship's intercom, he said. "Okay people let's do this. Raise heat shields," he ordered. In front of him, the heat shields slowly covered the windows as they slid over the hull. "Secure for launch and confirm." He watched the lights on his panel come on as each compartment signalled its readiness. He knew the same scene would be played out in the other sections as each reached the top of the mountain.

"Damocles Control this is Rapier Command. We are secured and ready for launch. Over."

"Rapier Command, Roger. All indicators are green. Confirm ready for Launch Sled ignition. Over"

"Damocles Control, confirm all-ready."

"Roger Rapier Command. Launch sledge ignition in Thirty that's three zero seconds."

Mike watched the countdown on his console as it slowly decreased. At twenty seconds he felt the vibration as the engines of the launch sledge which the Command section sat on began to come alive. Mike pressed the commands to bring the command sections own engines online so they would be ready to take over when they separated from the sledge. Ten seconds, gripping the helm controls, he felt the whole ship seem to hold its breath 5 seconds, 4, 3, 2, 1! With a roar, the launch sledge's engines sprang into full life. Mike felt himself being pushed back into his seat as the Command Module surged forward then over the edge of the ramp. He felt the G-force pushing him even further into the padding of his seat as the ship sped down through the bottom of the mountain then starting to arc back up towards the sky.

As the Rapier's Command section leapt out of the launch tube an indicator flashed on Mike's board "Firing engines now!" he cried as he punched the control to activate crafts engines. "Separation in fifteen seconds...... Ten, Nine," he counted down.

In Damocles' control room, Commander Rachel Sinclair the flight control officer looked up from her board. Next to her Greene watched as the sledge separated from the Rapier's Command section as it thrust toward space. "Godspeed Mike." He quietly said to himself.

"Admiral," she said gaining his attention. "The Second Rapier section has reached the top of the launch ramp.

"Very good Commander, carry on I've got to report to the joint chiefs. Notify me when all three sections are in orbit."

"Aye aye sir," She replied as he left.

Chapter 6

Mike held grimly onto the controls as the Command section fought its way through the Earth's atmosphere. Slowly the oppressive G forces began to ease until almost instantly they were gone. Looking around the bridge he saw the rest of the crew slowly relax.

"Well done everyone, secure from launch stations, Signals. Make to Damocles control we have achieved orbit, lower the heat shields. Let's see where we are." He ordered.

A series of aye aye sirs answered him but his eyes were on the bridge windows as the screens covering them began to fall. As they came down Mike quickly checked the tactical screen on his console to make sure there were no other vessels nearby, but the nearest ships were two of the resurrected American shuttles out at the mine constellations over a hundred kilometres away. Mike relaxed slightly but a gasp from Kelly made him look up at the windows.

Before them, the crescent of the Earth filled the sky, they were orbiting over the day side of the planet, white clouds merging with a brilliant blue sky with the continents and seas below.

"It's beautiful," Patricia Kelly said in awe

Mike glanced over at her and she smiled embarrassedly "It is" he replied softly "And precious, and it's our job to protect it."

"Sir," Petty officer Rogers interrupted "Damocles control reports the weapons section is already on its way and the drive section is about to launch."

"Thanks, Jez, ok people, keep an eye out for them, we want to keep a reasonable distance till we're all up." He ordered turning back to the board.

Less than an hour later all three sections were in orbit, Mike gently guided the command section down to dock with the main weapons section, like the rest of the crew Mike had carried out the docking numerous times in simulation and now had a near-perfect score but this was the first time anyone had carried out the operation in real life.

On the helm panel, Mike studied the small screen which currently showed a split view. On the bottom section, a graphic showed the two sections lining up as the docking heads 'pinged' each other to line them up correctly. These now were in perfect alignment. On the top section, cameras showed real-time images as the docking clamps slowly closed on their counterparts on the weapons section. Sensors counted down the distance separating them, slowly inch by inch Mike brought the Command section down until with a barely audible clunk the two sections finally docked.

Mike relaxed at his console "Well done Mi.. Captain, that was smooth" Kelly congratulated him.

Mike grinned back at her almost slip, "Just like the simulators back at base Pat," Then turning his head he called "Signals, put me through to the Drive section."

"You're through sir," Rogers replied.

"Ok Raj, you're on. See if you can dock as smoothly as that." Mike said looking around at the appreciative grins of his bridge crew.

"You just sit there in your comfy command chair 'Captain' sir, you won't even know you've been mated!" the reply came.

Mike grinned as a series of chuckles answered Singh's reply.

"Just take it easy, we'll see you in a few minutes. Out." Mike finished.

If anything, Lieutenant Singh's docking was even smoother than Mike's. There was no sensation at all as the drive section docked. It was only the docking sensors that gave any indication the manoeuvre had completed. But as all the lights on the docking panel turned green Mike nodded in satisfaction and ordered.

"Docking complete, open all internal hatches, secure from docking stations. Signal's, send to Damocles control all docking successfully completed we are at full readiness."

Mike was still receiving confirmations when Raj Singh and Engines Duffy pulled themselves through the hatch onto the Bridge. They were quickly joined by Dr Ellen Rand, the Rapier's doctor, who had come up from the sickbay in the centre of the weapon section. Mike unbuckled himself from the Helm and floated out of the seat, grabbing a handhold he gently turned himself to face the three officers.

Duffin grinned, "Takes a minute or two to get used to moving in this zero gravity doesn't it?"

Mike grinned back self-consciously, "It's the first time I've been out of that chair since we launched." He admitted.

Raj Singh snorted a laugh "Well if you're finished with that chair," he said

"All yours Raj, far be it for me to keep a maestro from his seat."

Singh pulled himself into the Helm seat and grinned a hello to Kelly as he set about changing the helm console to his preferences. Mike turned to the others

"So, Engines, any issues with the drive section coming up?"

"No, a couple of things shook a bit loose but the crew has already put them right. Everything is showing green across the board."

"Good, I want to get us shaken down as quickly as possible. There's no knowing when things are going to heat up."

"Aye, well if we're going to kick right off, I'd best get back down to my engines and see their ready."

"Right," Mike said dismissing his friend as he dove back through the hatch. "How about you Doc, any problems with the weapon's section on the way up?"

Although she wasn't in the command chain Rand, was the senior officer in the weapons section of the ship.

"No, no, problems at all Captain, everything went according to plan."

"Good, any injuries amongst the crew?"

"Nothing to mention, a couple of bumps when people unbuckled in zero gravity for the first time but everyone is fine."

"Excellent, well I'll let you get back to sickbay, as I said, I want to get underway as quickly as possible and with the drive on we'll get some feeling of gravity back so you'll probably get one or two more bumps to keep you busy." Mike joked.

"I'll get my ointment jar out ready," Rand replied with a smile as she turned and pulled herself elegantly through the hatch.

Wishing he'd managed to learn how to move so gracefully in zero gravity, Mike pulled himself to the Captain's seat and buckled himself in. Then livening up his own console he rechecked all system readiness indicators, a green flash on the drive sector told him that Duffin had reached the engine room and was ready.

"Ok people, let's show the world what the Navy's first purpose-built space warship can do. Pat, I want you to set a least time course around the moon. Raj, I want to start off slow, ten per cent power, then speed up in stages."

Kelly and Singh acknowledged his order as Mike keyed in the all-hands channel on his board. "Attention Rapier, this is the Captain. We are about to get underway on our first shake-down cruise. We are going to make a least time pass around the moon where we will be able to test weapons on some selected targets then return to orbit. Be aware there will be a return of the sensation of gravity while we are under power. Captain out." He finished

"Course for the moon set and programmed in sir," Kelly reported.

"Thank you, Pat, Signals put me through to Rampart control on the ISS."

"You're through sir," Rogers replied

"Rampart control this is Commander Mike James, Officer Commanding HMS Rapier, please be advised we are going to commence our shakedown with a cruise to lunar orbit. Please stand the mine constellations down to allow our transit."

"HMS Rapier, this is Rampart control, please stand by for Colonel Kaminsky." The ISS communications officer replied. A few moments later a new voice came on.

"Commander, this is Colonel Brett Kaminsky. I just wanted to say you guys did a pretty neat job of putting your ship together. She looks mighty fine out there."

Mike smiled to himself "Thank you, sir, we're very proud of her."

"So you should be. Ok, the sky is clear, we're standing the constellations down for your transit out. Good luck and Godspeed Commander. Rampart control out."

"Thank you Rampart control," Mike finished then looking back to Singh and Kelly, "Right, let's do this. Mr Singh all ahead ten per cent power."

"All ahead ten per cent aye," Singh replied

As the Rapier's engines eased to life and the ship began to move Mike settled into his seat and watched as the crescent of the Earth in the Bridge's windows began to dip out of sight.

"We're at ten per cent now, sir" Singh announced.

"Engines?" he asked over the com

"Aye, all good here." Duffin reply

"Ok, let's be a little more adventurous. Take us up to twenty-five per cent."

"Aye aye sir," Singh replied

Mike tried to feel some difference as the Rapier increased speed but through the windows, the scene remained the same and there was no discernible vibration.

"Twenty-five per cent and stable," Singh said.

"Engines still fine. Go to fifty?" Duffin asked.

"Take us to fifty per cent," Mike ordered. Again, there was no change to be felt as Singh reported the increase complete.

Mike nodded satisfied. "Well, I read before we launched that the record for a journey to the moon is currently held by the New Horizons probe, at 8 hours 35 minutes." He mused aloud "I do not intend to be beaten by a probe. Raj, take us to Ramscoop speed. Engines, standby to activate the scoop." He ordered.

This time there was a definite sensation as the Rapier leapt forward, through the windows Mike watched as slowly the moon grew larger.

"Ramscoop speed now Captain," Singh called out.

"Engines." Mike began but Duffin's voice came back immediately

"Ramscoop activating." He said excitedly

Mike waited for what seemed an eternity then Duffin's voice came back "Hydrogen detected! Confirm we're scooping hydrogen and fuel tanks are filling!" he finished,

Mike grinned, in the background, he could clearly hear the cheers from the engineering crew. "Well, the fuel's clearly not going to be an issue. Mr Singh, all ahead full!"

Again, the Rapier leapt forward as her engines charged up to full power, the moon clearly now getting bigger.

"ETA to Lunar orbit," Mike asked

Kelly checked her board, Mike heard her gasp, when she turned a beaming smile on her face as she said "ETA to Lunar orbit four hours forty-three minutes Captain. That's a total journey time of six hours fifty-seven minutes," She finished triumphantly.

"Excellent but let's not get ahead of ourselves, a lot can happen of five hours," he said good-humouredly.

But nothing did go wrong three and a half hours later the moon filled the sky ahead. Mike had spent the time touring the Rapier and checking in with each section as they approached the satellite. When Mike got down to the Drive section Duffin told him

"Everything's working just fine. In fact, we've had to shut the Ramscoop collectors down for a while because our fuel tanks were full."

"Outstanding, well if the tanks are full how about we use some of it?" he asked

Duffin looked quizzically then a slow smile spread on his face. "Aye, I think we should." He agreed.

"You'd best get back to your engines, they might need a bit of TLC." He finished

Leaving Duffin to get ready Mike quickly headed back to the bridge. "At least we've got a bit of 'gravity' now so I don't have to pretend I can move like a ballerina." He thought to himself as he made his way back to the Command section.

Back on the Bridge Mike took his seat. Singh who'd had the bridge in Mike's absence transferred the Command systems back to Mike's console.

"Everything ok Raj?" Mike asked

"Yes sir, she's handling like a dream."

"Good, well let's see how she handles now," Mike announced activating the ship's intercom. The all-hands alert sounded and Mike said quickly

"We're nearly at the moon and so far, everything has gone fine. You've all done a great job, but we're not here to cruise to the moon and back, it's time to see what this ship can really do. All hands action stations! Brace for manoeuvring." He ordered. "Raj, evasive pattern alpha one now!" he finished

Grinning wolfishly Singh crouched down over console "Evasive alpha one aye." He replied and suddenly the deck pitched over to the side as the Rapier swerved over and down.

"Hard aport!" Mike ordered and again the ship swung around hard, "Vector positive ninety degrees" he instructed and the deck tilted almost horizontal as the ship climbed straight up. "Level up face one eighty degrees." He cried holding onto his seat.

Singh brought the Rapier level punching the thrusters to spin the ship one hundred and eighty degrees so the bridge pointed back towards the Earth.

"Bring us back to our previous course, cruising speed," Mike said

"Aye aye sir," Singh replied. The ship swung back towards the moon.

"Guns, load the autocannon with dummy rounds and standby to release target drones." He called

Sub Lieutenant Christine Archibald the Rapier's weapons officer looked up from her console

"Uh, yes sir, umm" she replied quickly typing commands into her keyboard

"Is there a problem Lieutenant?" Mike asked turning to look at her.

"Uh no sir, no problems exactly, just two of the drones seems to have gotten stuck. I'm trying to free them now."

Mike sighed inwardly, Archibald was the newest member of his crew, she'd only just qualified as an officer and this was her first posting.

"Leave those ones for now, just launch the other six."

"uh yes sir is there any course" she trailed off seeing Mike's face

"Random course then bring them back to attack us. I take it our defensive weapons will be alright to engage them?"

"Oh yes sir, I'm pretty sure all our defensive guns are ok." She replied, sending the remaining drones out.

"You're pretty sure?"

"Um yes sir, I mean."

"Lieutenant, run a diagnostic on all weapons. You've got time while the drones head out on the first part of their run."

Archibald, flushing at Mike's mild rebuke, busied herself running her diagnostics. He pretended not to hear her swearing quietly as her first readings came in but he did raise an eyebrow as he heard her quietly but urgently saying "I don't care what it takes, those drones will be in attack range in less than ten minutes! Clear the fucking jam!"

Seven minutes later a rating at the central LIDAR station called out, "Incoming targets sir, four minutes to engagement range."

"Raj, let's open the range a bit, evasive pattern beta three." He ordered

"Beta three aye," Singh replied

"Lieutenant Archibald, weapons status?"

"All guns now showing green, number four autocannon showed a blockage but all clear now sir."

Mike nodded his understanding but let his look linger on the young Lieutenant a few moments longer. Secretly he was impressed that she hadn't tried to hide the jammed weapon which was a good thing because Mike would have chewed her out completely if she had. Though a chewing out might still happen if the guns didn't perform.

"Sir, incoming targets will enter engagement range in two minutes." The Lidar tech announced.

"Understood, Guns, open fire when targets are in range."

"Aye aye sir," Archibald replied

A few moments later Mike felt the vibration as the autocannons opened up on the approaching drones. Mike switched his screen to the tactical feed where the Rapier's computer turned the data from the ships Lidar and optical sensors into a real-time view of the 'battle' between the drones and Rapier's defences. As he watched three of the drones recorded terminal hits which meant they would have been destroyed and another two partial damaging hits. The 'destroyed' drones broke off to reform for another attack while the remainder continued in.

"Helm, Evasive pattern Beta." Mike ordered and watched as the 'Rapier on his screen dodged down and to port shaking off the remaining drones, two more took terminal hits and broke off while the last drone lost contact. Mike let the mock battle go on for another few minutes with the drones attacking again and again while the Rapier evaded and the hit rate from the autocannon slowly improved before he called a halt.

"Ok, cease-fire and disengage, Helm, resume course to the moon optimal velocity, I still want that record! Guns recover the drones." Then opening the all hands channel, he continued. "All hands, this is the Captain. Combat exercise is finished, repeat combat exercise finished. Well done everyone. All section heads to report to the wardroom in 30 minutes where we will review the exercise. Captain out." He finished.

Mike handed over the bridge to Patricia Kelly and went down to the officer's mess. Although technically a department head Mike knew Kelly would have nothing to add to the debrief and was senior enough to be left in command. Besides any thoughts she had, she gave to Raj Singh her partner on the helm.

Mike was sitting at the wardrooms only table, checking the status updates, when Raj, Duffin, Rand, Archibald, Lieutenant Suresh Chand the Rapier's logistics officer, and lastly Chief Petty Officer Joanne Isaacs arrived.

"I've been reviewing the action log from the combat exercise," he told them when they'd all sat down. "On the whole, I'm very pleased but there are a couple of areas I want to touch on. Firstly, though how did you all feel it went?" he asked

Duffin answered first "Well from my perspective the engines were fine. We shut the Ramscoop down while we manoeuvred but it came back up no problem."

"What about you Raj, did the engines perform ok?"

"Aye sir, she handled better than I expected, not an F38 but she was fast and responsive."

"No problems with any of the pre-programmed moves?"

"No none" Raj confirmed

"Lieutenant Archibald?" Mike asked

The young lieutenant frowned down at her hands, then looked Mike square in the face, "For most of the exercise our guns performed well but I'm afraid to say the obstruction in number four autocannon returned and the gun jammed at the end of the exercise, Sir."

Mike nodded but made no comment, "Dr Rand?"

The South African Doctor looked around the assembled officers before saying, "We had a few casualties, again mainly bumps and bruises but I've had to admit able seaman Holloway with a fractured collarbone and cracked ribs." She finished.

"How was he injured?" Mike asked tightly.

"There was some kit hadn't been stowed properly, it came loose during the manoeuvre's and caught Terry uh Seaman Holloway, Sir." PO Isaacs explained.

"And these other bumps and bruises, were they caused by equipment not stowed properly?"

"Some," Rand admitted, "Others were caused by the crew's unfamiliarity with working in zero gravity and the violence of the manoeuvres."

"None of us is familiar working in this environment Doctor but we aren't all clumsy idiots." He snapped. "Need I remind you all," he continued voice rising "That this is a warship of the Royal Navy and that very soon we will be going into battle against an enemy whose capabilities we know absolutely nothing." He paused for a moment then continuing in a lower voice "Jammed guns, equipment not stowed and secured properly, Crewmen being clumsy and not taking enough care are not acceptable ladies and gentlemen. Am I making myself clear?"

He was answered by a series of nods and yes sirs

"Very good, we will be at the moon in a little over two and a half hours. Christine," he said switching to her first name, "I intend to test our main weapons there before we return to the Earth. I suggest you use the time to make sure they are one hundred per cent operational."

"Yes, sir." She replied

"The rest of you make sure everything in your departments is stowed and secured properly and make sure EVERYONE takes more care moving around especially when we're manoeuvring. I do not want any more unnecessary injuries, dismiss." He finished.

As the officers rose Mike signalled for Duffin and Dr Rand to stay behind. When they were on their own Mike turned to Rand "How is Holloway doing? Will we have to evacuate him?"

The Doctor thought a moment then shaking her head she said "No I wouldn't recommend evacuation straight away Captain, the stress of re-entry at this stage would do far more harm. I'd rather let him heal a bit first. He's comfortable enough and I'll make sure he's strapped down securely during any violent manoeuvres."

"Fair enough, thank you Doc, and when it's just us, Mike is fine." He told her "but it might be worth thinking about how we evacuate wounded back to the Earth safely. We might not have any options but to put them through re-entry later."

"I will sir, Mike," she corrected herself "is there anything else?"

"No, thanks Doc, I'll let you get back to your patients."

After the doctor left Mike looked over at Duffin.

"You were a bit hard on them mate, it wasn't that bad," He said

Mike shrugged "You're right, apart from Holloway things went much better than I thought they would, but it gave me an excuse to shout at them and there's nothing like a Captain shouting at you to give you an incentive to tighten things up. Besides, I meant what I said, when we get into a fight, tightening things up now could just mean the difference between us staying alive and being destroyed." He finished.

Chapter 7

After Duffin left to return to the engine room Mike finished up his report and was back on the bridge in time for the Rapier's arrival into lunar orbit. "Time?" he asked

Patricia Kelly looked around beaming "Seven hours forty-seven minutes, Captain."

"Outstanding," Mike answered keying the all hands channel. "All hands, this is the Captain. I thought you'd like to know including our weapons and manoeuvring tests our total transit time from the Earth to Lunar orbit was seven hours forty-seven minutes. The record is ours! Well done everyone." He paused for a moment as cheers echoed through the ship, it wasn't strictly speaking naval discipline but under the circumstances, he wasn't going to take the crew's moment away from them. He waited for a few breaths more before continuing, "We will make two orbits of the moon testing our main weapons on the second pass." He finished, the turning to Christine Archibald he said "Guns, we'll be passing over the Montes Apenninus Mountain range, I want you to pick a few targets for the Particle cannon and disruptors. Pass them to Helm and Navigation to plot for the second orbit. Raj, Pat, I want a fast-evasive course as we pass. I want to test the weapons but I also want to test our accuracy firing on the move." He looked at his three officers, in turn, to make sure they understood what he wanted. Satisfied he sat back and waited for the second orbit.

"Course plotted and locked, Captain," Kelly announced as they came around for the second orbit

"Tracking targets, sir," Archibald added quickly

"Execute!" Mike ordered.

Above the moon, the Rapier suddenly dived towards the surface swerving round towards the towering mountains of the Montes Apenninus. As the range fell Mike watched the tactical readout on his console. Through the windows of the bridge, the mountains grew ever larger but as Singh veered to Port the particle cannon stabbed out at a mountain peak blasting the top to rubble. Moments later the disruptor's tore out, shaking giant boulders to powder. The mountains flashed past but each of the weapons fired three more times gouging vast craters out of the rock as the warship soared over and past the mountain range. As the last mountain passed beneath them Raj finally lifted the Rapier's nose back out to space.

Mike checked his readouts "Four direct hits and three partial hits with only one clear miss. Not bad for our first try. Well done everyone." He said to the bridge in general but as he looked directly at Archibald he continued "well done indeed."

Then noticing Lieutenant Hobbs, the Night watch officer, with her relief crew, standing at the hatch he said: "Now I think that is an excellent point to end what's been a very long day."

Taking Mike's cue Hobbs came forward saying "Relieving you sir, any orders?"

Standing Mike realised just how tired he actually felt. "Thanks, Sonja, no I think we've had enough excitement for now. Just set a standard orbit around the moon, run a few light exercises tracking drones but nothing too severe. I've got a few bits I need to do but I'll be in my cabin if you need me." He said as he left the bridge with the rest of the watch.

When Mike got back to his cabin Duffin was waiting for him with Jessop his steward. Jessop was holding two meal packs. Mike frowned at the two of them "I didn't" he began but Duffin cut him off

"No, you didn't and probably wouldn't have if Jess here hadn't told me you've not stopped to get anything to eat today. So, with the Captain's permission, I thought we'd eat together and go over the launch and exercises."

Mike stared at the two resolute faces then chuckling he said: "Ok I give in."

Mike sat the small table Jessop had already set up, Duffin sat opposite while Jessop quickly set out the meal packs.

"Thanks, Jess," Mike said as the steward opened his tray. The aroma of the food drew a rumble from Mike's stomach which elicited a raised eyebrow from Duffin as he opened his own meal pack.

With both, the officer's meal's ready Jessop retreated to the small utility room he used when looking after Mike saying "If you need me for anything sir just call."

As Jessop left Mike asked, "So, be honest how did you think it went today?"

Chewing his first bite Duffin thought about his answer. "Well, as your chief engineer I think it went well. The Ramscoop and engines performed fine, better than we thought they would. As your first officer, again ok. There are a couple of points we can improve on but on the whole, I thought we did alright."

Mike chewed as he listened to Duffin's opinion nodding slightly. "Yes, I agree we did okay but is okay good enough?"

"It's our first day up here don't forget, and they did much better on the main weapons test. Plus, we've got time. It'll take the aliens or whatever you want to call them months to get here from Mars."

"We don't know that for sure engines. Yes, it would take us months but we still really don't know their capabilities. That's what worries me."

Duffin stared at his plate for a moment taking in Mike's concerns before sighing "Aye, we don't know squat about the bastards really, all we can do is give it our best."

"And that's what I want. I know I can't do anything about what the aliens have got or what they do, but I can control what we can do and how good we are at doing it."

"When the time comes, they'll do their best. They're a good crew and we've got time."

"I know they are and I'll try not to ride them too hard. I just hope we have enough time."

After they finished their meals Duffin left Mike to finish up and get some sleep but Mike's fears were soon realised as four short hours later Mike was roused from his sleep by the insistent buzz of his intercom.

"James here." He answered groggily

"Captain? It's Hobbs, sorry to disturb you but we've just had an urgent communication from Rampart Control asking to speak to you."

Fully awake now Mike sat on the edge of his bunk, "That's okay Sonja, I'll be right up. Can you put a call through to Lieutenant Duffin? Ask him to join me on the bridge."

"Yes sir, Bridge out."

Mike quickly dressed and headed up to the Bridge, Hobbs had already vacated his chair and was sat at the signals console. Mike nodded a greeting as he sat, "Send a message to Rampart Control," he began but Hobbs interrupted him saying.

"I've got Colonel Kaminsky holding sir."

Mike looked over surprised "Okay, put the Colonel through."

"You're through to the Captain, Colonel," Hobbs said keying the signal to Mike's console.

"Colonel?" Mike asked

"Commander James, I'm sorry to have disturbed your rest period but there have been some developments. How soon can the Rapier get back to Earth orbit?"

While the Colonel had been talking Duffin had arrived and stood next to Mike listening. Mike looked a question up at his friend who nodded once.

"We can be back in around seven hours," he replied.

"Seven? Ok, that will have to do but make all possible speed Commander."

"What's happened?" Mike asked

"I'll give you a full briefing when you get back Commander, just get here as quickly as you can."

Mike looked at Duffin who had been using a different intercom channel from the signals console. Duffin gave Mike a thumbs up as he turned to head down to the drive section.

"We're on our way Colonel. Rapier out." He finished signing off. Turning to the Petty Officer at the navigator's station Mike said "Chang, plot us a least time course back to Earth orbit. Lieutenant Kelly's course that brought us here should still be in your console. Use that to backtrack."

"Aye aye, sir," Chang replied.

As the Navigator programmed the return course Hobbs moved into the vacant Helm position and began conferring with him.

"Sir." A voice said behind him.

Mike looked up to find Jessop standing there holding a tray with some drinking bulbs.

"Your Chai tea sir."

"Shouldn't you be asleep?" he asked taking the bulb.

"A good steward is never asleep while his Captain is awake sir." He deadpanned.

"Well thanks, Jess, but make sure you get some rest."

"Of course, sir." He replied taking the tray of drinks round to the rest of the bridge crew.

"Sir," Hobbs interrupted him, "If we do a couple of fast orbits, we can use a slingshot effect to boost us on our way back"

"Ok do it."

"Aye sir, course set and locked in," she replied.

Just then Mike's intercom buzzed and Duffin's voice came on. "Captain, engineering here. We're all set whenever you're ready."

"Roger engineer." Mike replied, "Ok Sonja, take us home." He finished.

Chapter 8

A little under seven hours later the Rapier began to slow for her approach to the space station which was once known as the ISS but was now home to the Earth orbital defences. On Mike's tactical screen the area around the planet was very different from the previous day when the Rapier had left on her brief shakedown cruise. On Mike's now 'crowded' screen along with a third American shuttle that had joined the two already in orbit, there were three more ships around the station. One looked like a cylinder with four smaller pods attached, Mike identified it as a fighter tender designed by the Chinese People's Liberation Army. The central cylinder was basically a small habitat module hosting four small one-man armed capsules which were the actual fighters. Once deployed the fighter's extended long gossamer-like solar sails for power and propulsion which resembled the flowing forked tail of the Swallow giving the small craft their name. But it was the twin laser projectors, an advancement of the Silent Hunter anti-missile system, which made them deadly. The second and far larger was a long black cylinder tapered at the back and flattened along the top, the vessel had obviously started life as a Russian Borei IV class submarine. Mike could see where the conning tower had been removed, as had the planes at the rear. Two small stubby 'wings' had been added but their purpose was to house auto-cannon turrets, similar to those on the Rapier but larger. But it was the third vessel that caught Mike's attention, He knew about the Chinese and Russian ships but the small craft already docked at the station was completely unexpected. It looked very much like one of the small commercial space planes that carried tourists into orbit. What surprised Mike was that the space plane had made it as far as the station.

"Captain, signal from Rampart Control."

"Go ahead," Mike replied

"Colonel Kaminski requests you join him and the other senior officers aboard the ISS at your earliest convenience."

Mike checked his monitor, Like the Russian ship, the Rapier was too large to hard dock with the station. He would have to transfer across. "Acknowledge and tell them we'll insert into a holding pattern in approximately twenty minutes. I'll shuttle across then." He told Rogers. "Then can you tell engineering to prepare the Gig for launch."

"Aye aye, sir," Rogers said as he set about his tasks.

Twenty minutes later Mike was down in the drive section with Duffin "Engines, is the Gig ready?" he asked

"Aye course it is." His friend replied leading him to an airlock hatch.

Mike followed him through into the small cramped 'hangar' which was really nothing more than a big airlock chamber, the Gig sat on its launch ramp. The Gig itself was little more than a pressurised box the size of a small mini car. In the front instead of an engine compartment, there was a pilot's saddle and a docking port designed to match the airlocks on not only the ISS but also the Russian and Chinese vessels. A Vacuum suited rating stood next to the Gig; he would sit in the pilot's position to guide the Gig to its destination. There was a second airlock at the side of the docking ring for him to use. There were no engines but instead pairs of tubes protruded from all six sides. These were the 'manoeuvring thrusters' that fired compressed gas. It was these 'thrusters' which were the gig's only method of propulsion.

"As it's her first launch I thought we'd best suit up just in case," Duffin announced.

He was already in his combat suit. Unlike the full vacuum suit worn by the pilot, which itself was almost like a small self-contained spaceship, the combat suit was more like a deep-sea diving suit, far lighter and more flexible the combat suite had an outer and inner surface weave which had been developed from a synthesised material derived from wood, thin and light it was four times stronger than Kevlar, Between the two layers thin pipes looped round carrying a liquid which cooled or warmed the wearer depending on the environment. Each suit came with a backpack with a small battery pack for the environmental system and a re-breather attached to the helmet. The helmet could be attached to the combat suits belt when not needed.

"I got Jess to bring yours down earlier." He said handing Mike a small kit bag.

Mike quickly put his suit on and the two officers boarded the Gig and strapped in. Mike nodded to Duffin who keyed the radio "Ready when you are 'Manny'," he said to Seaman Boyce the Gig's pilot.

"Roger!" the reply came, looking out the Gig's windows Mike watched as the lighting slowly seemed to become flat as the atmosphere was drawn out of the hangar. On the wall, the signal lights turned red and with a slight jolt the floor began to tilt and the clamps holding the Gig in place released as the hangar opened to space. With a puff from the thrusters, Boyce guided the small ship down and out towards the space station.

In the Gig, Mike could not resist looking back towards the Rapier behind them. He knew she was in a holding orbit around the station but she appeared to hang silently in the space behind them. The weapons section long and darker in colour, sharp and sleek like a sword held ready to thrust. Mounted on top slightly to the rear the command section sat proud, like a knight on his charger and at the rear solid but exuding power the drive section. On all three sections, he could make out the hybrid jet/rocket engines retracted against the hull. Both the command and drive were mottled a dark and light pattern for camouflage.

"Ah sure, she is a sight, isn't she?" Duffin said quietly

Mike looked up, embarrassed, to be caught but smiled at the look on his friend's face. "She is." He agreed.

"Excuse me, Captain, we'll be docking in about seven minutes." Boyce's voice came through the intercom.

"Thanks, Manny," Mike replied turning back to look ahead, through the forward windows the station loomed ever larger as they approached. The space station had been developed considerably in the months since the Alien armada had been spotted. It now had more than double the number of components and docking ports than when it was the International Space Station or ISS. Mike could also make out several auto-cannon and interceptor missile batteries. He could clearly see the docking port they were heading for. Looking up he saw the space plane he'd seen earlier.

"Who do you think that is? Do you think that's why we were called back?" Duffin asked seeing Mike looking up.

"No idea. But I'm sure we'll find out soon enough."

Fifteen minutes later Mike and Duffin floated through the airlock where a crewman helped them through into the corridor proper.

"Commander James?" a voice called.

Mike thanked the crewman then looking up saw an older fit-looking man with a greying buzz cut and moustache and silver Eagles of a USAF Colonel on his jumpsuit. "Colonel," he replied pushing himself gently forward.

"Welcome to Citadel Control Commander." Kaminski greeted him reaching for his hand as Mike anchored himself.

"Thank you, sir," Mike said taking the Colonel's hand. "This is Lieutenant Sean Duffin. My chief engineer and first officer." He finished.

"Lieutenant," Kaminski said shaking Duffin's hand. "If you'll come this way Commander Zhang of the Chines Swallows and Commodore Aleshco of the Russian Federation defence forces, are already here."

Mike and Duffin followed the Colonel through the heart of Citadel Control, technicians moved purposefully on their various tasks while others sat at weapons, communication and control consoles. Mike paused for a second to look at one of the screens. On it was a close view of the lunar surface where the Rapier had tested her main weapons.

Seeing Mike pause Kaminski stopped as well.

"We monitored your shakedown cruise from here," he told Mike, "that was a pretty impressive show you put on."

"Thank you, sir, if I'd known we were being watched I'd have put in more of an effort." Mike joked

"Let's save all the effort for the aliens when they get here." Kaminski finished moving off toward the conference room.

Mike followed the Colonel through the entry hatch of the conference room. Five of the seats around the small conference table were already occupied. The first by a tall willowy Chinese Woman, her silky black hair pulled into a tight bun. The other chairs were occupied by four men. In the second seat next to the woman sat a slim but muscular Chinese man, in the next a solid heavy-set young man with jet black hair and next to him a slim blond man who watched Mike intently. Lastly sat a tall slim dark-haired man who nodded to Mike. Kaminski moved to the head of the table indicating Mike and Duffin to the two remaining seats.

"This is Commander Mike James of the British ship HMS Rapier and his executive officer, Lieutenant Sean Duffin. Commander, this is Commander Zhang Mi of the Chinese People's Liberation Army, Commander of the Chinees Swallow squadrons, and Captain Shin Lei her second in command. This is Commodore Victor Aleshco of the Russian Federation Navy." He said indicating the Blond man who had watched Mike intently. "Commodore Aleshco commands the two Russian ships being deployed, with Commander Alexander Timoshenko, and lastly this is Major Raoul Lafayette of the European Space Agency, my executive officer," Kaminski said.

Mike took in the seated officers, "Commander Zhang, gentlemen, pleased to meet you" Mike said

"Commander, I must congratulate you on a very pretty little ship. Almost as pretty as Commander Zhang's little capsules, they do put my poor Yuri

Gagarin to shame." The blond Russian said brightly. "But unfortunately, we are not here for a beauty pageant." He finished darkly.

Mike felt Duffin tense beside him so he put a warning hand on his friend's thigh. Aloud he said smiling "Why, thank you, Commodore, we are very proud of her and she may surprise you when it comes down to business. But I shouldn't worry about your ships looks. As I believe has been often said 'U tya sho zhopa sho rozha: vse prigozhe.'"

There was a moment's silence where Timoshenko's eyes widened in shock before Aleshco seemed to explode with laughter. Shin and Lafayette looked round in bemusement at the Commodore's reaction while Zhang raised an amused eyebrow. She studied Mike with renewed interest.

"What did you say to him?" Duffin asked quietly while the Russian guffawed loudly

"I told him 'his arse was the same as his face, all beautiful." Mike quietly replied

"Very good Captain, very good. Yes, I see you may surprise us yet." Aleshco said still chuckling

"I'm sure we'll all surprise each other as time passes," Kaminski said interrupting. "But I'm afraid it's not just us who are bringing them."

Mike looked up with the others at the Colonel's tone. Kaminski gave him an amused wink before continuing. "Combined Space Agency tracking picked these puppies up ten hours ago."

He switched on the wall monitor and a starscape filled the screen, in the distance, they could just make out six small objects. The camera seemed to zoom in on them and the shapes resolved into the forms of six of the Alien's smaller attack ships. "We believe these six are scout ships coming to have a look at us while their main group is tied up in Mars orbit."

"How far out are they Colonel?" Commander Zhang asked

"At their current rate of approach, they'll reach our outer defence constellations in a little over a week. What we need to decide is what we're going to do about them."

"Sir, Constellation 5 will intercept them well short of the range they can pose a problem." Major Lafayette answered confidently

"True, but 5's not fully commissioned yet, we've still got Enterprise and Columbia out laying the final layers of mines," Kaminski said

"We'd need to pull them back soon anyway if they're to be safe and we can control the mines from here," Lafayette replied.

"With respect Colonel, we can't leave them to the mines, we'll have to go out and meet them." Mike interrupted.

"An aggressive stance from the Royal Navy? You ARE full of surprises Captain. I like it." Aleshco agreed.

"Why do you say we can't leave them to the constellations Commander? They are our main form of defence and we only have a handful of ships." Kaminski asked ignoring the Russian's remark.

"That's just the point, sir, the constellations are our main defence but if we use them now the enemy will surely see them and when they attack, they will have had time to come up with some tactics to counter them."

"I agree, Colonel, Commander James's reasons are sound. We should intercept them before the constellations" Zhang said.

"You most certainly will not intercept them! Or use that obscenity of a minefield!" a cultured voice interrupted them loudly.

Mike looked over at the source of the disturbance. At the entrance hatch ignoring a crewman who was trying to stop him from entering a tall aristocratic black man glared angrily at them. Mike immediately recognised the intruder as Professor Joshua M'Benga. M'Benga had been in the news recently as an outspoken member of the executive council of the International Peace Foundation. It had been reported that he was one of the main contenders to replace Dr Ali Ben Saul as General Secretary of the United Nations.

"Professor, this is a confidential meeting. I informed you I would meet with you at thirteen hundred. Now I must ask you to leave." Kaminski replied hotly.

But M'Benga ignored the Colonel, instead, he pushed himself elegantly into the room. He looked at the charts and consoles finishing at the screen. Then turning to the assembled officers, he said scornfully.

"Nuclear minefields, warships, cannons and missiles. I expected no less from the American's and European's but I expected more from the Chinese." He finished looking directly at Commander Zhang.

Zhang returned his gaze serenely but it was Kaminsky who answered.

"Professor, I respect your principles and your right to be here but this is a confidential planning meeting to discuss how we are going to defend the Earth from the Alien threat."

"Threat?!" M'Benga replied, at last addressing Kaminski, "What threat? We are standing on the brink of history! Out there is proof we are not alone. Intelligent beings from another world are coming to us and instead of reaching out with the hand of peace you are preparing for war! We know nothing about these people and you just want to fight them." He finished angrily.

"But Professor, while I appreciate and respect your wish for peace," Commander Zhan replied "We have seen only aggression from these aliens, the destruction of our spacecraft, bombardment attacks on both Europa and Mars"

"Commander you look at things with a military eye and see aggression, I see them reacting to attempts to spy on them, they did not know what those robotic crafts were, they just sneaked up on them and made no attempt to communicate, These people just reacted to protect their privacy. As for Europa and Mars, 'attacking' lifeless world's commander, really?"

"We are now not so certain they are lifeless, professor." She replied.

"Fantasy to support a military response." He scoffed. "Fantasy and supposition but neither matter. I have here a direct order from the General Secretary of the United Nations herself that no military action is to be taken until I have had a chance to speak to these aliens and begin negotiations." He finished triumphantly.

"Professor. You can't be serious!" Kaminski exclaimed

"Yobanyi Karas!!!" Aleshco swore.

Mike sat dumbstruck, he looked across at the Commodore, he couldn't quite agree that the professor was a moron but he agreed with the sentiment.

"No action Colonel!" M'Benga repeated. "You have your orders." He looked at each of the officers in turn then pushing off from the wall glided out of the compartment.

"No action! No action he says who does that jumped up Svolochi think he is!" Aleshco stormed floating up from the table.

"Commodore please, calm down. I don't like it either but he is the UN's designated representative." Kaminski said controlling his own anger.

"Excuse me Colonel, gentlemen," Zhang interrupted gently "but if I understand correctly the professor's order forbids any action before he has attempted to negotiate only."

"Commander Zhang's right," Mike said. "There's nothing in his orders which say we shouldn't have a contingency plan."

"Yes," Aleshco agreed, returning to the table "we should plan our responses now and be ready."

Kaminsky looked doubtfully back "There is no way he will allow us to have a full combat response or anything that looks threatening ready when he meets them."

"We won't have to." Mike replied, "As I said before we should keep the mines as a surprise and it still makes sense to pull the shuttles back, but there's nothing in his orders that state we can't give him an escort or honour guard."

Zhang nodded while Aleshco slapping the table with one hand while holding himself steady with the other said: "Da, yes, I knew I liked you Tovarisch"

"Ok, I like the idea but which ships should form this honour guard?" Kaminski asked lowering himself into his own seat.

"All of them!" Aleshco replied quickly "Yuri Gagarin and Captain James's Rapier are already here as is the Commander's first wing. The Georgi Zhukov will be ready to launch soon and can be with us in time. How soon can more of your fighters be ready Commander?"

But before she could answer Kaminski replied: "No M'Benga will never agree to us having our whole fleet there."

"Aye, I can see he'll not allow that, but what if we insisted on each nation being represented?" Duffin interjected.

Zhang nodded "I agree that is after all only reasonable."

"So, my Yuri Gagarin for Russia, Rapier for Britain Commander Zhang's first wing for the people's republic but what about you Americans?" he asked Kaminski

"The shuttle Enterprise was outfitted with mini-guns when we refitted her for space. They're purely defensive but she's the best we've got in the time." The Colonel replied

"But that only gives you two warships and four fighters, you'll be badly outnumbered." Major Lafayette pointed out

"Enterprise won't have to actually engage the enemy." Mike said, "As for Zhukov and Commander Zhang's other wings we can hold them back and then bring them forward once any fighting starts."

"We could load some mines in Enterprise's cargo bay and launch them from there then when they are a safe distance away, fire them at the enemy." Lafayette offered.

Kaminski nodded "Sounds like the beginnings of a plan." He said as they began to flesh out what they needed to do.

Chapter 9

The week that followed the planning session sped by, without being able to openly train and practice the tactics they had discussed Mike and the other commanders had to rely on computer simulations. But as Mike reflected all the crews and pilots were professionals and intimately familiar with their equipment, they were as ready as they could be. Settling into his command chair Mike checked the tactical display on his console. Icons for the six alien scouts were drawing closer, but highlighted were the five Earth ships. Out at the front, in the position they had identified as 'Border 1' was Professor M'Benga's spaceplane. Two days ago, he'd started sending his 'friendship package' packed with basic scientific and linguistic data to 'aid understanding' as he put it. Now M'Benga had been broadcasting his message declaring the Earth's desire for peace and inviting the aliens to open negotiations for over an hour now. As yet the Aliens had not responded in any way. Rapier was above and to the port of M'Benga with the shuttle Enterprise above and to starboard. Slightly behind and below the Rapier was Commodore Aleshco's Yuri Gagarin while Commander Zhan's first Swallow wing, still docked to their command module, held a similar position with the Enterprise. Mike rubbed his hands together nervously and resisted the urge to order yet another all systems check; his crew had been running them regularly for the past two days and everything had checked out fine.

"Captain, the alien's ships have stopped!" the sensor tech called out.

Mike instinctively looked out of the Bridge's windows but in reality, the alien ships were still too far away to see with the naked eye, kicking himself mentally he looked back to his tactical screen where the alien's had halted. "Thanks, Kathy, can you see if they are doing anything at all?"

Leading Seaman Kathy Bates scanned her console "I'm not sure sir, they're doing something, Jerry, can you check this waveband on your comms equipment?"

PO Rogers on communications linked his console with Bates sensors "That could be a communications signal. It's no channel or bandwidth we use but look at that modulation there, and again here." He said

"Can you tap into it?" Mike asked

Rogers grimaced "Not with what we've got set up at the moment. If I had more time and lab maybe, but not right now."

Mike thought for a moment "I can't give you a lab but keep linking with Kathy's sensors and have a play. Something might pop out."

"Aye aye sir," Rogers replied indicating for Bates to share her data, but instead of linking more closely she said:

"There's something else Captain," Mike looked back at her

"Go on."

"Well I've been checking all the sensor data we had on the aliens and where they've stopped is about the same distance from the space plane as they were when they attacked both the Voyager probe and the Mars orbiter. I think that might be the limit of their sensors."

"You mean you think they stopped because they saw M'Benga but they haven't seen us yet?"

"I think so, sir."

"Damn that could make all the difference, well done Kathy. Jeremy, quickly I want you to send Kathy's theory to all commands, including what we think about their comms as well. The other ships might have different equipment which may be able to hack into them."

In the passenger section of his heavily modified spaceplane, Professor Joshua M'Benga sat strapped into his padded launch seat. The space plane had been a luxury tourist craft before it had been donated to the Peace Institute and still had most of its amenities. Though half of the passenger seats had been removed to accommodate the new computer terminal dedicated to linguistics, recording and the new state of the art communications station. He tapped nervously on the padded arm of his chair trying to hide his anxiety from his assistants. It had been three hours now since the alien spacecraft had stopped and the waiting was testing his nerve to the extreme. At long last after so many years campaigning and manoeuvring he had steadily risen through the ranks of first the United Nations, then the International Peace Foundation. When he had learned that intelligent beings from outside of the solar system had been detected he knew his time had come. He'd not been surprised that the Americans and Europeans had decided these visitors would be a threat, after all, anything that challenged their superiority over the developing world would be considered a threat but he recognised it for what it truly was. A new beginning, with his success in brokering a peace agreement with these visitors there would be no obstacle to his becoming General Secretary and with his leadership and the friendship of these visitors the United Nations would lead the world into a new era where all of the worlds, no, the whole solar systems resources would be shared equally rather than hoarded by the more advanced and developed nations.

But this infernal waiting for the visitors to respond to his transmissions was infuriating. Oh, he knew intellectually it would take the visitors, no matter how advanced, time to learn Earths languages, to even decode and translate the source material he had sent but he was impatient. He smiled to himself at the thought, his impatience had always been something he strove to contain, but it had also been the driving force behind his rise to success. Well, he'd controlled it before he would control it again.

"Professor, something is happening!" one of his assistants almost shouted

"What is it Damone'" M'Benga asked shaken from his thoughts.

"One of the alien vessels is moving."

M'Benga leaned forward to look at the sensor screen, surely enough the visitors leading spacecraft was slowly moving forward.

The alien scouts hadn't moved for over an hour so Mike had taken the time to go down to the wardroom to get a coffee and stretch his legs, he knew he could have gotten Jess to bring him a drink but as he made his way down he made sure to visit as many compartments on his way as he could, stopping to chat with crew members to show he wasn't concerned but making sure all was ready. He'd finally managed to get himself a bulb of coffee when the intercom buzzed.

"Captain to the Bridge, Captain please report to the Bridge." Duffin's Irish brogue came.

Mike quickly grabbed the wardroom's com handset and keyed the Bridge and got put through to Duffin

"Engines? What's happening?" He demanded

"Captain? One of them alien ships has started moving."

"Just one?"

"Aye, just the one at the moment, the others are just sittin there watching while the first one approaches the professor's plane."

"How long before they reach Professor M'Benga?"

"They're moving slow at the moment take em about forty, fifty minutes."

"Right I'm on my way up, but bring us to action stations now, we can't count on them staying slow." He said darting out of the wardroom

"Any change?" Mike asked as he came onto the bridge

"No, just the one coming forward, keeping the same speed," Duffin replied vacating the command seat.

Mike nodded his thanks as he sat.

"Captain, we're receiving a signal from Professor M'Benga, he wants to speak to you," Rogers announced.

Mike frowned at Duffin who just shrugged. "Put him on," Mike said

"Commander James? This is Professor M'Benga."

"Professor? We're tracking one of the alien vessel's approaching your position. Do you need any assistance?"

There was a pause for a few moments then M'Benga's voice returned "Thank you, Captain, but no, I think having a warship approach would not help the appearance I am hoping to give. On the contrary, I wanted to ask how confident you are about your earlier transmission regarding the visitor's detection equipment."

Mike thought for a moment before replying "As confident as we can be on the observations of the Alien's actions."

"In that case I want you and all of the other warships to pull back and keep out of the visitor's detection range."

"Are you sure that's wise professor?" Mike asked, "If anything goes wrong, we may be too far away to assist."

"Don't worry Commander, nothing will go wrong. Now please do as I say and withdraw. Please inform all other craft to do the same. M'Benga out." He finished abruptly

Mike stared at the now silent intercom.

"It might not be such a bad idea, Mike," Duffin said quietly "At least we'll keep the element of surprise."

Mike looked at Duffin in surprise

"I don't mean I like the idea of leavin them but we'll not be too far away, an I'll have the engines primed to go to full power so we can get back quick but if the aliens don't know we're here..."

"Ok, I don't like it either but you're right, let's make the best of it. Raj, start pulling us back. Jeremy, relay Professor M'Benga's order to all commands with my intention to be ready to return with all speed should anything go wrong." Turning to Duffin he finished, "You'd best get back to the drive section and get things ready."

"Aye I'm on my way," Duffin replied as he headed off the bridge.

Mike turned back to his tactical display and nervously chewed his lip as the image of the alien craft advanced on the lone defenceless spaceplane.

In the passenger compartment of the Spaceplane, M'Benga watched in satisfaction as all four warships started to pull back.

"Professor? Are you sure that was the right thing to do?" his assistant asked nervously from the console.

M'Benga studied his young assistant carefully "Are you afraid Damone'?" he asked

"It is somewhat daunting, being out here on our own. I mean no disrespect professor but what if the al err visitors are not as peaceful or reasonable as you hope?" he replied nervously

"Are they peaceful and reasonable? Those are human emotions and reactions Damone'. Is Tiger peaceful? Is it reasonable? Of course not! Those are human emotions, human feelings and a Tiger is not human, neither are these visitors but like with a Tiger, if we work at trying to find a way to understand them, respect them, we can find a peaceful way to live with them." M'Benga smiled indulgently "There is no shame in being afraid Damone', we stand on the threshold of history today. As"

"PROFESSOR!!" the pilot cried suddenly yanking on the controls.

M'Benga ducked into his seat as his assistant was thrown from his station. Sparing the fallen Damone' a quick glance he clawed his way forward to the cockpit "Pilot what the" but the words died on his lips as through the cockpit windows the alien craft swooped on them like an eagle, its weapons spitting death.

Chapter 10

Mike swore as on his screen the Alien ship attacked "Raj, reverse course, all ahead full." Mike ordered quickly "Jeremy send in clear, all channels, warn them off! Guns"

"Captain!" Bates interrupted

Mike looked back as the space plane banked sharply, its rocket engines at full thrust as the pilot desperately tried to evade the alien's fire.

"Goddammit!" Colonel Brett Kaminsky silently cursed as the Alien suddenly accelerated at the helpless space plane, "Hussain, clear me a channel!"

"Colonel, look the Rapier" Carl Samuels, his pilot called

Kaminsky watched as the Rapier quickly reversed course heading full thrust towards the Alien ship.

Quickly keying his helmet microphone "All units go, go, go!" he shouted. Turning to his own pilot he ordered "Samuels, take us in behind the task force, we need to be ready in case we need to recover any survivors." He finished watching as the battle began to unfold

"Commodore, the Rapier is already moving to intercept the enemy and the American Colonel is signalling," Timoshenko said at Aleshco's side as the watched the small holographic tank.

"Calm yourself, Sasha," Aleshco said as on the tank the four Chinese swallow fighters launched from their host module. "Our young English Commander is impetuous and his ship seems the swiftest. We will let him draw first blood and watch how he performs. There will be plenty of time and opportunity for us to build our own fame and glory." Studying the holo tank he indicated a new position, "I think this is where we will best make our presence known." He said sending his new course to his own helm.

"Captain the Chinese fighters have launched and are inbound, ETA to combat zone twenty minutes." Kathy Bates reported crisply

"Right, what about the Russians?"

"The Yuri Gagarin's moving, manoeuvring wide. I'd say they're positioning for a missile strike, sir." Lieutenant Archibald answered from tactical

"Sir, the remaining enemy ships have started moving, coming in fast. ETA fifteen minutes."

"Acknowledged," Mike replied grimly watching his monitor. On the screen, the space plane was still desperately trying to evade the larger alien craft. "Guns, how long to weapons range?"

"Seven minutes, sir"

"Jeremy, send to the plane tell them to keep dodging." But the order died on his lips as on his screen the space plane's port wing disappeared in a flash of debris as one of the Aliens rounds sent the small craft spinning.

"Raj"

"We're at full power already sir."

As the space plane veered away from the visitor's ship, M'Benga had managed to strap himself back into his seat. "Damone', quickly strap yourself down!" he ordered but his assistant just gripped his terminal tighter, eyes wide with terror.

"I cannot Professor, if I let go, I will fall."

"Damone' you must." He began when a massive impact sent everything spinning. M'Benga ducked as his assistant flew past him. He gripped the arms of his seat and desperately held on as slowly plane steadied itself. On his own console, the words 'Auto-pilot engaged' glowed silently.

Already smoke from burnt-out components was beginning to pollute the air, coughing he unbuckled himself and scrambled over to his fallen assistant "Damone'" he began but the crumpled body, its head turned in such an unnatural position he knew his assistant would answer no more. Turning he pulled himself towards the cockpit but stopped as he saw the emergency door was locked shut, the indicator reading only vacuum on the other side.

"Sir I've got the Professor" Rogers called

"Put him on speaker" Mike ordered "Professor, we're five minutes out hold on."

"'Cough Cough', Commander James? 'Cough' I'm sorry, so sorry, I was wrong."

"Don't worry about that now, we're-."

"It's too late Commander, do not endanger yourselves. 'Cough'. The others are all dead, Damone' the pilots, all gone. 'Cough', they have paid the price for my dreams as must I." there was a pause for a moment "Air is leaking, getting hard to breath, 'cough, cough'….. MY GOD, I see them, Commander, they are so close I can see them. Their ship, it's so shiny, not Black at all but myriad of shades, 'cough'. How can they build so beautifully?"

"Professor.."

"They are turning, Commander, they are turning to face me."

On his screen, Mike watched in horror as the alien ship lazily turned to bear on the crippled space plane, like spider studying a fly, trapped and helpless.

M'Benga's voice came again, weaker than before "Commander I…" when a brilliant flash visible through the Rapiers windows silenced the professor forever.

On the Rapiers Bridge, the crew stared in horror as the Alien's blasted the defenceless plane out of existence.

"Bastards!" a voice behind Mike cursed as a cold fury gripped his heart.

"Sir, I think they've seen us!" Bates called from the scanner console.

Glancing at his own screen he saw the Alien vessel turn to face them. Swallowing his own anger Mike looked around his crew he keyed the all hands channel.

"This is the Captain. That flash you just saw was the space plane carrying Professor Joshua M'Benga and his peace mission. The Alien ship he was attempting to negotiate with has just murdered the professor and his entire crew." He paused to let the full meaning of his words sink in. "The Alien vessel is now turning its attention to us. I intend to show them that not all ships and worlds in this system are defenceless. All hands, Battle stations!" shutting down the all hands channel he asked, "Time to intercept?"

"Weapons range in two minutes Captain," Archibald replied

Switching his display to full tactical Mike counted own in his head "Deploy Battle Ensign."

On the hull of the command section, a red cross on white with the Union Flag in the top corner blazed to life. The Battle flag of the Royal navy rose in challenge.

On Mike's screen confirmations shone and the countdown dropped to zero. "Open Fire!"

Commodore Viktor Aleshco watched intently as the Rapier and the Alien vessel drew closer together.

"Why does Commander James charge so blindly at the Enemy? Surely he sees they are far larger than his ship?" Timoshenko asked

"Watch carefully Sasha, so far all these Aliens have seen of us has been unarmed probes and the spaceplane. Commander James is not showing what he can really do to draw the Alien closer, letting their arrogance become his advantage."

As if on cue, the Rapier's particle cannons opened fire, streams of charged particles accelerated to a small percentage of light speed tore into the Alien vessel. Finally realising their danger, the Alien ship tried to break away turning their heavily armoured sides to the barrage. The Alien's had built their ships to fight against the powerful ballistic rounds that they launched against ship and planet alike and their armour was designed to survive the impact of these heavy rounds but the particles fired by the Rapier carried the explosive equivalent of half a ton of dynamite and each stream contained over a hundred of these particles.

The windows on the Rapiers Bridge dimmed as the hull plating on the Alien ship exploded, there was a brief cheer as debris flew from the gaping wound but Mike quickly slapped it down "Belay that they're not finished yet. Raj, stay on him. Guns, can you get frequency range for the disruptors?"

"If Lieutenant Singh can just get us a bit closer" Archibald replied

"SIR ENEMY RETURNING FIRE!"

"Guns"

"On it sir."

Mike gripped the arms of his chair tensely as the vibration from the autocannon on full rippled through the ship. Tracer fire streaked past the windows followed by three small explosions as the enemy's rounds disintegrated.

The Alien ship banked again but Singh kicked hard on the manoeuvring thrusters swinging the Rapier inside the Aliens turn. Seeing her opportunity Archibald stabbed the controls of the Particle cannon raking the Alien's underside, explosions tore the stricken ship gutting it completely but before Mike could order Archibald to finish the job Bates called out

"Incoming hostiles, Range ten miles and closing, they're firing."

"Raj, evasive pattern delta two."

"Sir, the enemy ships are splitting into two formations, I'd say they're going to try and pincer us" Bates reported.

Mike expanded the view on his terminal, sure enough, the aliens had split into two groups, three and two. "Raj, bring us onto a heading 3372 by 9245"

The Rapier swung up and away from the larger group of ships but the pair in the second group bore down on them.

"Time to intercept?" Mike asked,

"Four minutes sir, Enemy ships firing!"

"Recommend evasive bravo one sir" Patricia Kelly offered as Mike stayed silent

"Negative hold your course, Guns, defensive fire as targets come into range."

"Yes sir," Archibald replied keying the Autocannons automatic fire setting.

"Sir, Gagarin's launching!"

Mike checked his screen as a small missile icon separated from the Russian flagship

"Launching from that range? There's no way they'll score a hit" Archibald said appalled.

"Mind your guns Lieutenant, Commodore Aleshco knows what he's doing," Mike ordered

Suddenly there was an eye-searing flash which darkened a whole section of the Rapiers windows. "What the fuck!?" someone shouted but moments later Bates called

"Sir, look, the outer of the three enemy ships"

Mike looked where Bates indicated and instead of three alien ships, there were two making evasive courses away from a steadily expanding band of debris.

Mike replayed the action on his screen, "Bloody hell, the mad bastards have strapped an Orion Drive to their missiles!"

"A what drive?" Rogers asked

But it was Archibald who replied "The Orion drive was a theoretical drive they came up with in the 1950s for space flight. Basically, you drop a nuclear warhead behind you, detonate it then ride the shockwave."

"Sir, enemy ships are closing!" Kelly called out, as the vibration of the autocannon increased.

Commander Zhang Mi pulsed each of her fighters, in turn, she could see on her Heads-Up Display (HUD) that each craft was in its set position but she was too cautious not too make sure they were all at peak performance. "Deploy wing sails'" she ordered. Around and behind the fine gossamer solar sails that gave her craft their name flowed swallow like. She registered with satisfaction the power increase as the sails gathered the solar energy that would feed her laser projectors.

"Commander, the British ship is under fire,"

"Commander James is screening us, hold course and observe radio silence" Zhang ordered.

The Rapier shook as one of the Alien's rounds exploded just off the starboard beam. Mike shook himself checking his screen again, "Raj, keep your course, steady…… Now, Negative port 90 degrees!" he ordered

The Rapier dived straight down veering to port, the two Alien ships went to follow but as the Rapier dived the four Swallow fighters of Commander Zhang's first combat wing flashed past, their laser projectors slashing into the Alien's exposed top hulls.

"Raj, bring us back around, Guns, let them have it when you get a target but watch out for those Chinese fighters!" Mike ordered

But as the Rapier came about the Alien's appeared to have had enough, harried by the four fighters and with the prospect of facing both the Rapier and Gagarin the Alien ships turned to retreat.

"Keep at them," Mike ordered as the Rapier's main weapons lashed out again.

"Sir, I've got a disruptor frequency lock!" Archibald called.

"Well done, guns, capture the optimum frequency but hold fire for now."

"Sir, signal from Colonel Kaminsky. All ships follow to border one but cease-fire unless they attempt to return."

"What? but they killed the professor and all his crew! We can finish them now, send their main fleet a real message!" Singh replied outraged.

"As you were lieutenant, we've got our orders," Mike replied bitterly as on his screen the Chinese fighters also dropped back and the mauled remnants of the Alien's probe accelerated away.

Chapter 11

Samantha Selkie paced nervously in her room, since her return from Port Theresa she'd been increasingly uneasy. She'd returned to the plantation immediately after Mike and his friend had gone back to their base. The council hadn't been happy with what she had been able to find out from the British and American officers. No one had voiced it but Sam felt they thought that meeting Mike had distracted her from her mission. She had passed on what Mike had said about the caves but several councillors, Old Pegra, in particular, had said that may be a ruse, so when the cabal and their government friends came, they would find the clan trapped and unable to escape.

The council had ordered her to return to Port Theresa immediately and find the American officers she had met that night but when she arrived at the port, Monique had told her that all of the sailors both the British and Americans had left the island. She had stayed with Monique and her brother for another two days speaking with the locals who ran the bars and restaurants, even the brothels which entertained the sailors to see if they could get any clues or information, but nothing had been forthcoming.

She had returned to find the council had done nothing, fear of being watched and acting 'out of the ordinary' had paralysed them so now they just waited.

Sam stopped pacing and stood in front of her mirror looking at her reflection. "We can't just do nothing," she told herself. Finally making up her mind she left her rooms, she'd find Uncle and make him see sense and the council could go to hell!

Mike floated weightlessly in the command hub of Citadel Control, around him duty personnel monitored the Alien fleet and space around the Earth. Mike noted that the Georgi Zhukov and the Chinese second Swallow wing had taken up their position at 'Border 1'. Like the Rapier, the Yuri Gagarin was already in orbit around the station while the first Swallow wing, now all docked on their host module was on final approach.

"Commander James?"

Mike turned around slowly, making sure to keep hold of the hull, Colonel Kaminsky stood in his office doorway "Come on in Commander." The Colonel said.

Mike pushed off from the wall and glided towards the Colonel's office. Kaminski moved gracefully aside as Mike entered gently catching him as passed.

"Take a seat, Mike." He said nudging Mike towards the seats opposite his desk. "Still not used to freefall?" the Colonel asked taking his own seat.

"We don't get that much opportunity to practice, sir, while the Rapier is under power, which is most of the time, we have some semblance of gravity."

"Must be nice to always have some gravity, took me a couple of weeks to stop feeling sick," Kaminsky replied studying Mike.

"Look, sir, I know what you're going to say."

"Do you Commander?"

"You think I endangered the Rapier by taking her into the combat zone without waiting for support."

Kaminsky nodded slowly "Go on."

"With respect sir, I didn't rush in recklessly regardless of how things looked. The Rapier is our fastest ship. I knew the Gagarin and Swallow squadron would be following but Professor M'Benga's ship was under direct attack and if there was any chance of saving them, any chance at all there was no time for a coordinated response."

"And yet you still didn't manage to save them and you put your command into a position where five enemy ships were almost in a position to surround you in a pincer movement."

Mike went to reply but Kaminsky held up a silencing hand "I know you deliberately led the smaller group into the path of Commander Zhang and screened her fighters till the last minute but you are extremely fortunate that Commodore Aleshco's missile was as effective as it was, for God's sake you didn't even know he had the Orion missiles."

Kaminsky took a calming breath before continuing. "Now I have spoken to your Admiral Green at Damocles base. I'm aware you were forced to take command of the Rapier after Captain Gregory's unfortunate death and I wanted to discuss with him whether this step has been too much for you."

Mike gripped his seat waiting for the Colonel's judgement as Kaminsky paused. "However, Admiral Green believes, and I agree with him, that under the circumstances your actions were justified and you are still the best candidate to command the Rapier. But we still only have three actual warships against God knows how many alien ships. If your actions endanger your command or you act in any way recklessly, I will seek to replace you. Is that clear Commander?"

"Yes sir, I understand."

"Good, you're a good officer Mike and you've got good instincts, you just need to temper them with a little bit of caution. Now consider yourself chewed out; Commander Zhang's just arrived so let's get this after-action briefing done." He finished leading Mike out of his office.

Sam strode down the corridor to her uncle's office, the door was closed but she could see the light inside was on, grasping the handle she thrust the door open "Uncle I'm…" she began but as she walked in, she saw her Uncle wasn't alone. Sitting at opposite ends of the office where Sam's mother and Pegra.

"Ah Samantha, I was just going to call for you, do come in." her Uncle Jeremiah said gesturing her to the couch that ran along the far wall of his office.

"Uh, yes thank you, Uncle," she said taking the offered seat. Pegra glared at her eyes narrow, she looked to her mother who just looked placidly back with an amused air.

"Now Samantha, Pegra, your mother and I were just discussing your reports from Port Theresa. As you may have heard the council is at an impasse which is why I asked your mother and Pegra to join me today. I'm sure it won't surprise you to learn they are the respective leaders of the two opposing factions on the council."

Sam smiled slightly at the description.

"But I want to hear your thoughts, not just the facts as you so eloquently stated in your report but your feelings as well."

"Her feelings?" Pegra interrupted "I'm sorry Uncle," she said looking again at Sam "but her feelings are precisely the issue. Turning to Sam Pegra continued "It is clear from your report that your feelings for this Commander James have compromised your objectivity. He is a government officer and the Cabal have infiltrated the government so deeply we cannot trust any of their officers or officials."

Sam bridled at the older woman's condescending tone but it was her mother who answered.

"May I remind you Pegra, Samantha is a daughter of the line of Lycaon" she snapped "Unlike some others, Samantha has seen the evil and ruthlessness of the Cabal in the flesh. But she has also seen the generosity and kindness of humanity. Of all of us, she is the best judge of those she met."

"Thank you for the reminder Sheena," Jeremiah interrupted gently, "Pegra, you have made your thoughts known but I want to hear Samantha's thoughts myself. Then I, not you or Sheena nor the council, will decide what we will do. Now Samantha please carry on."

Sam composed herself for a moment "As you know Uncle, I went to Port Theresa to try and obtain any information I could about the British naval base and the American naval task force. I did speak to several sailors and officers from both forces before I met Mike, as did my friend Monique, her brother. Everyone we spoke to gave the same explanation, the base was being set up for anti-pirate operations, but the stories were too consistent. Something is definitely going on Uncle but I honestly don't think it is anything to do with us. As my mother pointed out I have seen how the Cabal operates, how they infiltrate an area with their hunters over a period of months. How they settle in, become part of the community but this is nothing like that.

I won't say Mike was being honest with me, clearly, he wasn't but the last time I spoke to him, when he said we should stock the caves, there was a genuine concern in his voice. Something is coming, I don't know what but last night there were several strange flashes in the sky. The media are saying it was meteorites colliding but all of the world's governments have suspended independent space telescopes and instructed amateur's not to use their own telescopes as these meteor explosions could cause eye damage. There's just too many co-incidences Uncle and I'll be honest I'm scared." She finished

Jeremiah sat silently, contemplating what Sam had said for several minutes then "Pegra, I want you to begin organising the supply of the caverns. Sheena, we will need to hide the entrances to our deepest caves as best we can. You are best at that, also get word to our friends in the town, tell them if anything happens, they have my permission to hide within our lands."

When Mike and Kaminsky arrived at the Conference room Commander Zhang was already seated along with her deputy and the Russians and Major Lafayette.

"Commander Zhang, Gentlemen, thank you for coming so promptly." Kaminsky began immediately as Mike took his seat nodding a greeting to the assembled officers.

"I've asked you here so we can review the recent action, see what we can learn about the enemy and apply anything we learn to future tactics."

"Surely we are not yet all here?" Commander Zahn asked looking at Mike, "where is your lieutenant Duffin?"

"As well as being my first officer, Lieutenant Duffin is also my chief engineer. We took some minor damage during the combat and he's overseeing repairs. Also, our gig is quite small and we had a wounded crewman who we needed to transfer in order for him to be returned to Earth so with the crewman and my Doctor there was no room." Mike explained.

"How much damage?" Kaminsky asked

"Just some scoring and hull impacts from where enemy shells were destroyed by our auto-cannon fire. We weren't holed and none of our systems has been compromised but my command crew felt that if we could recover some of the shrapnel it could be returned to Earth for analysis."

"Let us have anything you recover and I'll make sure it's returned on either the next shuttle to return to Earth or one of the re-supply sledges. Commodore, I've had notification from your command centre at Korolyov, they will be sending a resupply mission for your ships to build a missile cache."

Aleshco nodded his understanding and spoke quietly to his executive officer.

"So down to business," Kaminski said, keying a command the briefing rooms monitor came to life. On it was a computer representation of the battle.

They watched in silence as the first alien ship approached then attacked Professor M'Benga's spaceplane. Mike felt a pang of guilt as he watched the Rapier charge the alien vessel completely unsupported but the guilt turned to pride as his ship's weapons tore into the alien vessel. As the battle progressed Mike found himself studying the alien's actions and manoeuvres, how and when they reacted.

As the recording finished Kaminski shut the display down. "So, any thoughts?" he asked

"Well, I think the first thing we have learned is our British friend has no fear of taking the fight to the enemy," Aleshco said drily.

Mike glanced across at the Russian with a feeling of lead in his stomach, the reprimand from Kaminski still fresh in his mind.

"Oh, I do not mean that negatively Captain, quite the opposite. We Russian's appreciate the spirit that drives a soldier against overwhelming, some might say, impossible odds. During the great patriotic war, hundreds of young peasants would charge the fascist's lines with just one rifle between ten, when a soldier with the rifle fell another would pick it up and continue the charge. Sometimes we must take great risks to achieve victory"

Mike nodded slightly, acknowledging the Russians support.

"Thank you for that insight Commodore but I'm more interested in what we learned about the alien's" Kaminski replied testily

"I was watching when they responded to our actions, I think Kathy Bates, my sensor operator, is right about their sensor range being so short." Mike offered.

"I agree," Zhang said. "Also, their sensitivity is less efficient. Commander James was able to screen my squadron's approach very effectively and the second group of vessels gave no indication of being aware of Commodore Aleshco's ship being anywhere near them."

"That is true, even after we destroyed one of them, they seemed to be more intent on scattering than counter-attacking like they were reacting to the missile, not the ship that fired it," Aleshco added

"Ok, that's good, what else?" Kaminski asked

"They're fast but not much faster than Commander James' Rapier. They are manoeuvrable as well when they feel threatened but their attacks against the space plane and also when they chased after the Rapier was almost clumsy." Zhang offered.

"What about weapons?

"When they fired at us it was exclusively heavy projectile rounds." Mike said, "Our auto-cannon were able to take care of them relatively easily but if one were to hit, I'd say it would be devastating."

"No other weapons? Commander Zhang, Mike, you came into the closest combat with them are you sure you didn't see or encounter anything else?"

"As we closed there was some sporadic light fire, similar to machine-gun fire but as I say it was light," Zhang replied.

"And the projectiles they fired at us seemed to be single or volley shots, no missiles, no energy weapons, nothing. In fact, the more I think on it I'd say if it wasn't for the fact, they clearly have an interstellar capability I'd say they were no more advanced than us, perhaps not even as advanced as us." Mike added thoughtfully

Kaminski nodded in agreement, "Ok, what about our own performance? On the whole, I'd say we fared pretty well but does anyone have any thoughts?"

"I believe all of our craft performed as broadly expected, though the Orion drive missiles were somewhat a surprise," Zhang observed

"You can say that again!" Mike agreed. "You must be mad keeping those things inside your ship."

"HA!" Aleshco laughed, "Maybe a little my friend but it was effective no?"

"Yes, it certainly was, it made short work of that scout. And if we're right about their detection equipment you can fire them from outside their detection envelope."

"And that could be very important." Kaminski interrupted "But it also means you can't fire from inside one of the mine constellations, the detonation of the warhead that powers your missile would destroy any of our own mines near it."

"That is a minor point Colonel, Aleshco replied confidently "We considered the mines when we decided to incorporate the Orion missiles. My ships can position themselves above or below the plane of the constellations to fire on the enemy."

"Hmm, but that could leave you exposed, still you will have the advantage of being outside their detection range I suppose." Kaminski mused

"Exactly! So, while their ships seem as fast as our own, their weapons appear to be somewhat primitive. While both our ships and weapons have proved to be extremely effective." Aleshco put in proudly. "They are no match for us as they will soon learn if they continue to attack."

"I agree Colonel, with my Swallows and Commander James, HMS Rapier, positioned within the mine constellations and Commodore Aleshco's vessels sniping from range. I am confident we can at the very least hold the enemy until more assets become available." Zhang added.

"Ha well said Commander," Aleshco said beaming.

"Ok," Kaminski said, "is there anything else? No? well if any of you think of anything else please let me know. I'll forward our conclusions to space command, thank you for your input." He finished ending the briefing.

As they began to leave Aleshco noticed Mike's thoughtful frown. "Why so concerned my English friend, I thought it was we Russians who were supposed to be brooding and surly."

"I was just thinking of another battle where we had the enemy completely outmatched technologically. A place called Isandlwana in South Africa."

"I have never heard of it, what happened?"

"Our entire force was wiped out!"

Chapter 12

During the weeks following what would later become known as the first battle of the Solar system, events began to unfold at speed. On the Earth, a total blackout had been imposed on any amateur telescopes. The cover story which had been spread was that a large unstable asteroid field was passing the Earth which if any exploded could cause a danger to unprotected eyes. The explosions from the first engagement had gone a long way to prove this.

Only observatories linked to or controlled by the world's governments scanned the skies feeding their data to monitoring stations. It was the job of these stations to search for all of the Alien ships scattered around the Solar system and plot their movements. The result of these plots whilst not unexpected was now ominously clear. The Aliens ships were on the move, and they were all heading towards the Earth.

For Mike, those few weeks were a mass of training exercises and coordination meetings. At the first co-ordination session, Colonel Kaminski had divided the area covered by the mine constellations into five sectors and assigned the fighter groups and warships each to support one of the sectors.

The Rapier has been assigned to the central sector facing the most obvious route of approach for the alien fleet with the two Russian ships either side and the Chinese fighters out on the flank.

Mike sat back tiredly as he shut his terminal down. He'd just finished what seemed like the hundredth co-ordination review with Oberleutnant Hans

Goering, the German commander of watchtower two, the primary control module for Mike's sector.

"Tea Captain?"

Mike almost jumped at Jessop's enquiry

"Sorry, sir didn't mean to surprise you." The steward said but Mike could see the glint of amusement in Jessop's eye.

"That's ok, Jess, didn't hear you come in," Mike replied with a rue smile. "And yes, a cuppa would be wonderful." He finished taking the plastic drinking bulb from the tray.

"Doctor Rand and Commander Duffin are waiting to see you as well sir," Jessop said as Mike took his first sip.

"Oh good, send them in please Jess, can you get them some drinks, and get one for yourself."

"Sir," Jessop replied letting Duffin and Rand in as he left.

"Doc, Engines, take a seat," Mike said waving his officers towards the two, fold-down seats attached to the bulkhead. He took another sip to compose his thoughts while Duffin un-dogged the seats and Jessop reappeared with the drinks.

"Thanks, Jess, don't disappear just yet," Mike said as Jessup handed Rand and Duffin their drinks. Turning to his officers he began, "Firstly, thank you both for coming so promptly. Now I just wanted to get an idea of how we're doing before things kick-off. Now, Jess, I wanted you here because I'm sure you hear things the officers don't. How are the crew? What's moral really like?"

Jessop's eyes widened in surprise but quickly recovering he replied "Well sir I'd be lying if I said everything was perfect. The guys are worried, naturally, after all, we're going into a fight and a big one. But they're all professionals and this is pretty much what we signed up for. And they trust you not to get them killed."

"Thanks, Jess, that's good to know. Well, I've kept you long enough, off you go before you get too contaminated by officer contact." Mike said jokingly,

"Don't worry sir, I've had my inoculations." The Steward deadpanned as he left.

Mike chuckled as Jessop closed the hatch after him. "Well Doc, do you agree?" he asked looking at Rand

The South African Doctor looked at the hatch the Steward had just left by for a couple of heartbeats before turning to Mike. "On the whole yes, I'd say Jessop was right. The crews moral is reasonably good, there are one or two crew members I'm watching a bit more carefully than others but that's normal."

"That's fair enough, if you haven't already, have a quiet word with their watch commanders, I know," he said quickly at the Doctors expression, "you don't have to go into details, but we can't afford anyone losing it in the middle of any action. I just want to make sure we give them all the support they need, ok?"

"All right, I'll talk to the individuals first and give their watch commanders as much information as I can." She reluctantly agreed.

"Thanks, doc. Engines, how about the ship. Any concerns?"

"Ahh no, she's as sound as the first day she came together. The few holes the alien shrapnel put in us have been filled and reinforced and the engines are purring like a kitten. When them alien Gobshite's try anything, we'll be ready for em."

Mike nodded, "Well let's make sure we keep her that way. God knows how much notice they'll give us"

But Mike's words were barely out of his mouth when they were interrupted by an urgent call beep from the intercom.

"Sorry to disturb you sir, but we've got an urgent signal from Rampart control. The Colonel has requested all unit commanders attend an immediate virtual briefing." Rogers' voice said.

Mike leant forward pressing the send key said. "Understood Jerry. Connect me through please."

Duffin and Rand both went to leave but Mike waved them back to their seats. "I want you to stay and listen in, I may need your opinions afterwards." He told them quickly while he waited for Rogers to connect him.

A few moments later the screen on Mike's desk flared to life with Colonel Kaminski's face in the middle and the commanders of the other ships and watchtowers spread around the edges. Noting that all the commanders were now present Kaminski said "It's started! Fifteen minutes ago, we detected the leading motherships begin advancing toward Border 1. Based on what we believe to be their maximum detection range they should see the outer mine constellations in another ten to fifteen minutes."

"Colonel!" a voice shouted behind Kaminski. The Colonel looked across towards Rampart Controls main monitor and Mike saw his face pale.

Turning back Kaminski quickly said, "I patching this through to you all, it's what our forward telescopes are seeing."

On Mike's screen, the conference portion shrank into the top right-hand corner. On the main part of the screen, they saw the leading nine motherships seeming to haemorrhage their smaller craft.

"My God there are dozens of them!" Rand gasped.

"No, more like hundreds," Mike said as the larger warships, in turn, launched what appeared to be smaller attack craft.

On the screen, the Alien fleet formed up into a formation with the scouts supported by the attack craft in the lead followed by the larger warships with the Motherships bringing up the rear.

"Time to the forward constellations ten minutes," Kaminski announced. "Looks like your estimate of their detection range was a little off Mike." He added

"Not necessarily, Colonel," Commander Zhang interjected from her command pod. "My own specialist has just theorised the equipment on the mothercraft would need to be more powerful in order to travel at interstellar speeds."

Kaminski nodded, "Yes that would make sense, we should have considered that earlier."

"Maybe, though at this stage it probably wouldn't have made much difference." Mike offered

"Probably not but I don't like the thought we've underestimated them." The Colonel replied.

"Sir, Watchtower two control, the enemy fleet is about to enter my engagement envelope, do you wish me to switch to manual override?" Oberleutnant Goering interrupted hastily.

"Negative Hans, let the mines go on auto. We don't want to tip them off that you're out there just yet." Kaminski ordered.

"Sir, with your permission I and my officers are going to relocate to the bridge," Mike said quickly

"Yes, you'd better but remember Mike do not engage the enemy unless it looks like the mines are not holding them!" Kaminski reminded.

"Sir" Mike said shutting down his terminal. "You two had best get to your stations. There's no knowing how this is going to pan out." Mike finished herding everyone out of his ready room.

Mike walked quickly the few feet from his ready room to the bridge, "Action stations, yellow alert!" Mike ordered as he entered. He quickly sat in his command seat saying, "Jerry, transfer the Colonel's feed to the main screen please."

On the bridge's main screen, the feed from the Rampart control appeared. On the bridge, everyone seemed to hold their collective breath as on the screen the alien vanguard closed with the mines.

Over a thousand kilometres away a small satellite hung in its geostationary orbit. The satellite had only the most rudimentary of computer intelligence, it did not need much computing power after all. Surrounded by thousands of its fellows it sat patiently in the centre of its own 'spider's web' of radio pulses. Searching as it had been programmed to, waiting for any prey, which did not match up to the parameters which would mark it as a friend, to enter its web.

Now, at the very edges of the satellite's awareness, something was gently touching the strands of its radio web. Just as it had been programmed to, the satellite turned so the focusing lenses faced the prey and waited.

The touch of the prey on the satellite's web was firmer now, a clear target formed. Still, the satellite waited for the notification the target was friendly. No notification came so slowly the satellite extended the focusing lens. Ten, twenty, fifty meters. Just far enough to survive the first few milliseconds. The satellite waited a few more seconds, moving slightly so the prey was squarely in its sights. The satellites tiny computer confirmed its readings matched the required parameters and carried out its last task.

The hundred kiloton warhead contained within the satellite detonated! The directed nuclear blast hit the focusing lens turning it into a directed x-ray laser. Less than a minute later, the first alien scout craft ceased to exist.

The bridge crew of the rapier saw the scout along with three of its consorts die within moments of each other.

"YES!" a voice behind Mike cried in triumph.

"Belay that" Mike snapped. On the screen, he watched as the alien fleet reacted. The scouts fell back while the smaller attack craft fanned out. As they watched three of the mother ships moved forward slowly. "What are they doing?" Mike wondered aloud.

"They're using the better detection range of their motherships to see where the attack is coming from," Bates replied.

Sure enough when the mother ships reached their detection range they held position while the rest of their fleet arranged themselves around them.

"Captain, signal from Rampart control. All ships to go to combat readiness, all watchtowers switch constellations to manual control." Rogers called from communications.

"Clever," Mike said quietly, then "Ok people, you heard the Colonel. Battle stations. Deploy battle ensign. Jerry, acknowledge the Colonel's order then go to radio silence."

Mike sat back studying the main screen as a series of acknowledgements to his orders came back. After what seemed an age but was less than an hour later the entire alien formation started to advance.

"Time to range?" Mike asked

"Enemy lead elements have just crossed the constellations engagement envelope. Ten minutes to our range, sir." Bates replied.

"Guns, standby. Kathy, make sure Guns and her team have a constant sensor feed." Mike ordered.

"Aye aye Sir,"

"Yes, Captain!"

The replies came but Mike barely registered them as he watched the alien fleet slowly creep forward. Suddenly the alien attack ships leapt forward, weapons blazing! Mike's heart leapt as mines started exploding, tearing gashes in the constellations.

"All watchtowers, as you bare, open fire!" Kaminski's voice came calmly "All ships, you're released to independent action." He finished.

"Raj! Take us forward slowly, keep us hidden." Mike ordered as on his screen the leading rows of mines detonated blasting waves of x-ray lasers at the wheeling alien attack ships.

As Mike watched he saw that the alien attack ships were faster and more manoeuvrable than they'd previously thought. They were still dying but not as quickly as had been expected, and each miss was another mine which could not be used again. Worse the aliens had worked out the location of the mine constellations and their warships were now adding their own weight of fire to the destruction.

"Dammit! We need to hit those warships. Watchtower's 2, 4 and 5 activate hunter-killer assets." Kaminski's voice ordered.

Hans Goering studied his board intently

"Herr Oberleutnant, do you wish me to acknowledge the Colonel's order?"

"No, he will see we have received the order momentarily." He replied keying his commands in. he watched in satisfaction as his selected HK satellite groups began to move.

Kilometres away the computers that controlled some of the larger satellites received their instructions. While their smaller brethren immolated themselves, they had sat waiting. Now they had been summoned to the fray. Linking together they cast their radio detectors towards outer space. They were soon rewarded as dozens of targets lit up their boards. The computers busily sorted the data discounting the smaller, faster craft, they locked onto the larger cruisers. As one they ignited their thrusters and began slowly moving forward.

As the sky around them flashed and burned with the deaths of dozens of the earth's artificial defenders, the Rapier advanced cautiously through the layers of remaining mines. On his screen, Mike noted the squadrons of hunter-killer satellites also on the move and ordered Singh to alter course to avoid them.

"Time to weapons range?" he asked thoughtfully.

"We'll be at maximum range in fifteen minutes sir?" Archibald replied

"Kate, how long before the HK's are in range?"

"At their current speed, they'll be in range in just over ten minutes, Captain."

Mike nodded "Raj, increase speed to thirty-five per cent. Guns, I want us to be ready to engage the enemy directly after the first HKs. Don't forget people we'll only have a short window before their mother ships will be able to detect us"

Noting his officer's acknowledgements Mike studied his screen "where are the Russians?" he thought to himself.

At that moment dozens of kilometres away Commodore Victor Aleshco of the Navy of the Russian Federation stared into his Holo-Tank "See Tasha, the Colonel is sending out the hunter-killer satellites to engage the alien cruisers there." He said indicating the icons which represented both the satellites and Alien vessels. "If I am not much mistaken our English friend will also be moving forward to take advantage of any confusion those satellites cause."

Commander Alexander Timoshenko nodded thoughtfully "Yes I see Commodore, so we move to this point here with Captain Rostova there?"

"Just so Tasha, so when the Aliens react to Captain James' attack we can catch them in a crossfire."

Mike counted the time down till his ship was within the range of the Aliens weapons, "Raj, keep us in the constellation but be ready to move when the HK's fire."

"Aye, aye Captain," Singh replied instantly.

The Rapier edged slowly closer to the Alien cruisers, making sure to keep hidden when suddenly the sky around them blazed with atomic fire as the Hunter-Killer satellites struck. Invisible lances of energy lashed out striking the alien fleet. The massive cruisers bucked and reeled as armour tore and hulls burst but to Mike's dismay only a bare few seemed to suffer any disabling damage.

"Raj, Positive ninety-degree vector now, Gun's, open fire!"

Anticipating the order Singh executed the pre-set command and the Rapier surged up out of the constellation which had hidden it. As her target board finally cleared, Archibald confirming her targets stabbed the fire key and the Rapiers small Hadron Accelerator cannon flared! Streams of tiny charged particles tore into the already weakened hull of the target cruiser punching straight through the stricken vessel.

Mike watched in morbid fascination as explosive decompression tore the cruiser apart and debris, including the bodies of the alien crew he suspected, expanded like a cloud around the wreck. Nearby another cruiser exploded!

"X-ray laser must have hit a magazine or something" the clinical part of Mike's mind noted. But he didn't have time to dwell on the thought as Archibald had already switched to a new target.

"Raj, keep us moving!" he ordered, "Don't let them get a lock on us."

"Sir! The enemy mother ships are coming about." Bates suddenly called.

Mike cursed silently as the alien mother ships moved, their detection beams sweeping the space around them. Then as if pulled by some invisible string the cruisers swung towards them.

In Watchtower 2 Hans Goering grinned wolfishly as his hunter-killers struck. Around him his three crewmates cheered loudly, congratulating themselves on their kills. Seven alien cruisers hit, two of them clean kills he sent his instructions to the next hunter-killer squadron as a third cruiser exploded.

"Heir Oberleutnant, his sensor operator suddenly called, "the enemy motherships are moving!"

"Raj, evasive pattern Beta two! Kathy, have they spotted us?" Mike asked quickly, his stomach turning as Singh instantly took the Rapier into a series of fast manoeuvres.

"I think a couple might have, sir, though several seem to be looking elsewhere."

"Ok, Raj, keep us moving. Guns, if you get any opportunities to hit them, take em but try and keep your fire random so they can't track us."

"Aye Captain," Archibald replied. Singh grunted his acknowledgement concentrating on his board.

"Sir, two of them have definitely got a bead on us" Bates called

"Raj?"

"On it sir" the pilot replied

Mike watched as on his screen two of the cruisers began to move into intercept trajectories when suddenly two ships appeared on his flanks. He had just enough time to register several detonations on his screen when the nearest cruiser exploded. Seconds later the second cruiser's flank blew out and spun away as the second Orion missile clipped it.

"YES, good old Aleshco!" Mike exclaimed.

"Sir?" bates asked

"It was the Russians. They had our backs all the time." Mike explained. "Raj, take us back up. Guns, fire at will!"

The Rapier charged forward, Particle cannons blazing while the two Russian ships added their own fire. Alongside them more Hunter Killers and standard mines detonated, sending more x-ray lasers into the massed alien ships. The Chinese fighters also appeared adding their own laser fire.

As the onslaught continued more and more alien ships began to die as hits mounted. But still, the aliens attacked. The Rapiers auto cannon screaming as tracers intercepted the alien's projectiles being fired almost randomly at the Earths defenders.

As Mike watched, the Alien ships seemed to pull together ceasing fire.

"What are they doing?" Patricia Kelly asked

"I'm not sure," Mike began to reply when suddenly the Alien's let loose one final volley before they turned and fled.

"EVASIVE!" Mike shouted

Again, the rapier was forced to dive back into the constellations as the flood of projectiles pelted out. Mike watched the other ships manoeuvre violently in their attempt to avoid the enemy fire. Relieved he saw the Yuri Gagarin dive below the rain of projectiles but as he checked the Zhukov his heart seemed to stop.

"Oh no!" he gasped

On his screen he watched in horror as an alien projectile clipped the Russian ship's engines, spinning her over into the path of two more shots.

The forward section seemed to disintegrate as the first hit, but it was the second, hitting dead centre which tore the Russian vessel apart.

The first battle for the Earth was over. Later as they viewed the footage and logs the analysts concluded the Aliens had lost over 130 ships to the Earths 1. It was a tremendous victory they would say. But as the other alien fleets converged, building a force ten times stronger than the first, they could, Mike decided, afford to lose those ships.

Chapter 13

Mike watched as his officers slowly filed into the wardroom for the morning briefing. "They look tired." He thought to himself. Hell, the whole crew were exhausted! The first week after the battle had been spent rebuilding the mine constellations. The Aliens had quickly identified the shuttles as easy targets so Rapier, Gagarin and the fighters had been quickly pressed into service escorting and guarding the shuttles against raiding attack ships as they replaced the mines.

But by the end of the first week, the rest of the alien fleets had joined the first force. Two days later they attacked again. This time they came more cautiously, waves of attack ships assaulted the mines, coming in fast and retreating after a single salvo. They still took losses but slowly and inevitably they ground the Earths defences down. Already nearly two-thirds of the mines had been destroyed.

Instead of supporting the mine constellations the now General Kaminski had also changed his tactics. He's decided his fighters and two remaining warships were too valuable to risk in direct combat against the vastly superior enemy. Instead, he relied solely on the Mine Constellations with the Hunter-Killer's taking the battle to the aliens while his ships continued in the role as escorts for the shuttles during the brief spells between waves when they tried to fill the holes in the constellations.

Just as the mines were being ground down, so were the defenders. Already two watchtower stations and one of the X-37B unmanned shuttles had been lost along with three of the Chinese fighters.

As Duffin took his seat Mike looked at each of his officer's in turn. "It's not just physical, they all know we're being ground down." He thought to himself.

Mike waited a couple of moments for the officers to settle themselves then began, "Ok, you don't need me to tell you things aren't going quite as well as we hoped."

"Aye, we had noticed something of the sort!" Duffin replied

This drew a few rue smiles and chuckles. Mike nodded slightly to his friend. He knew given half a chance the engineer would find some comment to break the solemn mood.

"I'm glad you're keeping up with things Engines." He said lightly "Anyway, The General has come up with a plan." He paused for a heartbeat as the assembled officers seemed to lean in a little closer.

"At the current rate of loss, they will be through the mines within days and the mines just aren't killing enough of them to make them stop. So the General intends to 'lure' them into killing zone so we can hit them hard en-masse and hopefully hurt them badly enough that they'll back off."

"But how are we going to do that sir?" Christine Archibald asked

"Aye, so far they've been very careful, hitting the mines in layers supported by their big ships. It'd take a lot to make them change tactics like that." Duffin agreed.

The Admiral's plan is to make it look like there is a failure in the mine constellations which will force us to send all of our ships out to re-set them. Every time they've spotted a chance to hit our ships, they've jumped at it. He hopes by making us look overextended they'll attack."

"Wow, that's a pretty risky plan Captain. I mean sure they're killing the mines quicker than we'd like but there must be another way we can slow them down? At least until we can launch the other ships being built." Singh offered.

Mike sat back and sighed. "There aren't going to be any more ships coming, Raj." He studied their shocked faces before continuing "GHQ, in their infinite wisdom, has decided we don't have enough ships to make a difference at the moment. As such our orders are to hold as long as possible causing the enemy sufficient losses to allow our forces on the Earth to organise a deep enough defence to prevent the enemy from landing."

"But" Archibald began

"That's enough Lieutenant," Mike said gently cutting her off. "GHQ has more facts available to them than we do and we have our orders." Mike paused a moment before continuing "Now to all intents and purposes we're going to be escorting the shuttles as normal, but we need to be ready to respond the instant the Alien's attack. I want us at one hundred per cent readiness for when the Admiral gives the order" He finished.

He was answered by a series of Yes sirs and nods. He studied his officers intently. He could see they weren't happy but they were professionals, they would do what was necessary.

"Ok, we've got a lot of work to do and not too much time. Doc, Engines can you stay behind, the rest of you dismissed."

As the last of the officers left the wardroom, Duffin closed the door. "Jesus this is a real cluster fuck and no mistake!" he said vehemently.

"Sit down Engines," Mike said tiredly

"This is insane Mike; can't you speak to Admiral Greene?" Rand asked

"I already have. He agrees with us but Space Command in Cheyanne Mountain are afraid that we'll just prolong the inevitable if we send ships up piecemeal, Moscow and Beijing both agree with them. They've ordered Kaminski to hold as long as possible and this is the best plan he could come up with."

"So, what are you going to do?" she asked

"I've no choice but to follow my orders, but there's nothing to say we can't be prepared," Mike added quickly.

"Now you're talking," Duffin said firmly.

"Don't get too excited engines, I haven't come up with some dazzling plan to win the war but I'm not going to throw this ship and this crew away. Doc, I want you to review all of the crew's medical records, I want all wounded crew evacuated back to the Earth. Engines, we may need to separate the ship in a hurry, I want you to make sure we'll be able to. I also want you to operate the bulkhead doors personally. If we have to evacuate any of the sections I don't want anyone trapped if at all possible."

"Aye, I'll get right on it," Duffin said as he rose again

Also rising Rand checked her tablet "It'll be quicker if you can get the Admiral to send a supply sledge to us directly rather than evacuate to the space station and wait for a shuttle."

"I'll make the call now. Is there anything else either of you can think of?" he waited as they both thought for a moment. "No? Ok, well let's get as much covered now as we can." He finished opening up his own tablet.

"General, HMS Rapier confirms their supply sledge has disembarked and they are secured for manoeuvring."

"Tell them acknowledged and ask them to standby," Kaminsky replied crisply.

"Sir, enemy vessels have started moving again!" a sensor tech called out.

"Well, it's now or never sir."

Kaminsky looked across at his executive officer. "It'll work Raoul, it's got to."

Lafayette nodded slowly "Yes sir"

Kaminsky looked at Lafayette for a moment more before turning to his screen and keying his com. "Engage Operation Sucker Punch, phase one." He ordered.

On his screen aboard Watchtower two, Hans Goering watched intently as his forward mines began engaging the alien fleet. As the battle had drawn on the Alien's had evolved hit and run tactics, designed to destroy individual mines then retreat out of range. To counter this tactic the watchtower crews had programmed the mines to fire in clusters of four, scattering their x-ray lasers over a larger area hoping to catch the enemy as they fled. Both sets of tactics had proven to be relatively effective. The enemy was losing ships, but the Earth was losing mines. It was just a matter of who ran out of assets fastest.

"Herr Oberleutnant, Orders from Rampart control, Engage Sucker Punch!"

Goering glanced over at his comms officer grimly. He'd been expecting the order but actually hearing it given sent shivers down his spine.

"Ok Willie, let us hope the General knows what he's doing because we are hanging our asses out here." He replied keying the deactivation commands into his board.

"Commodore, the General has ordered the mines to be shut down." Gagarin's radio operator reported.

"So, he is going through with his plan then," Timoshenko said quietly next to Victor Aleshco.

"It would seem so Tasha, are our little charges ready?"

"Yes Commodore, Both Atlantis and Discovery have signalled their readiness. As has Captain Chang."

"Good, so now we wait to see whether the enemy will swallow the bait."

Chapter 14

In Citadel command, silence ruled as the entire command crew seemed to hold their breath while hundreds of miles away the Alien's had paused in their deadly game of hit and run as a wave seemed to pass through the mines as one by one, they shut down.

"Come on take it," Lafayette said quietly to himself as the Alien armada sat motionlessly.

"Sir, we are now at eighty per cent shutdown." A report came.

"They're not biting," Lafayette said in frustration.

"Then let's give them something a bit juicier to bite on. Go phase two!" Kaminsky ordered.

"Captain, signal from Rampart control, we're to go to phase two."

"Thanks, Jerry," Mike replied, "acknowledge the General's order then send my compliments to Endeavour, Enterprise and Commander Zhang and ask them to follow us out."

"Aye, aye sir."

"Raj, take us out all ahead fifty per cent power."

"All ahead, fifty per cent aye Captain."

"Engage battle Ensign, action stations." Mike finished

General Kaminsky watched his screen intently as first the Gagarin and her shuttles began to move closely followed by the Rapier and her charges. "Status?" he asked.

"We're at ninety-four per cent shutdown now sir," Lafayette replied quickly

On the main screen, the shuttles and escorts began to accelerate as they rushed to bring the mine constellations back on-line.

"How long before the enemy spots them?" Kaminsky mused.

"If our estimates of their capabilities are accurate, they should see them any minute now, sir." His sensor tech answered

"OH MY GOD! General the watchtowers!" Lafayette cried.

"What?" Kaminsky began to ask but as he looked amongst the blackness of the powered down mines the fully powered up watchtowers burned like tiny stars.

"Sir's enemy ships are moving!"

The whole command crew of Rampart one watched in helpless horror as the Alien Armada charged forward, swooping down on the exposed watchtowers.

"Here they come; Raj put us in front of the shuttles. Jerry, tell Commander Zhang to get ready to launch on my mark." Mike ordered "Guns, status?"

"All weapons ready and fully operational sir," Archibald replied crisply

"Captain, there's something wrong, they're not coming for us," Bates called.

"What, put your monitor on the main screen, Kathy."

On the Rapiers main view screen, the view changed from Mike's tactical display to show Bates's sensor data. The minefields now dormant faded leaving. "DAMN. They're going for the watchtowers! Jerry, send this to all commands, tells Commander Zhang we're moving to intercept and recommend she diverts to protect the watchtowers. Pat, plot an intercept course."

"On it!" Kelly replied sending her plot to Raj's helm console

"Raj, all ahead full. One hundred per cent power." Mike ordered as he keyed the all hands channel.

"All hands hear this. This is the Captain. It looks like the General's plan has hit a bit of a problem. The Alien fleet have spotted the watchtowers and are attacking them directly. We are moving to intercept in order to hold the enemy long enough to bring the mines back online. It's going to get a bit hairy but do your jobs, keep your systems online and we'll get through this. Captain out." Mike finished. Glancing around he noted with satisfaction the professional concentration of his crew as they bent to their tasks.

"HERR OBERLEUTNANT!"

"I see it Willie," Goering replied grimly as he studied the com from the British warship. "Henning, get the auto-cannons and SAM batteries activated, Willie, get our mines back on-line."

"But the General's orders were to…"

"To Hell with the General's orders, get me those mines back online now!"

"RAOUL, command override! Re-activate all the constellations!" Kaminsky ordered, "How long before they're in range?"

In the command centre, Major Lafayette pounded his keyboard as the rest of the command crew rushed around desperately trying to bring the

Earths defences back online. He'd just brought up the command override when a sensor tech cried out in fear. "CONTACT!"

Lafayette looked up to see a single alien scout had managed to sneak all the way through the Earths defences. "TAKE IT OUT!" he cried at the weapons technician manning the defence console.

As he spoke the space stations defence cannon roared to life, he watched as the scout was blasted to atoms but not before it managed to fire three rounds of its own. The whole crew held their collective breaths as the first two rounds passed harmlessly past.

"PAUL! THE OVERRIDE" Kaminsky cried urgently

Shaking himself the Major turned back to his terminal as the whole station seemed to explode as the last round struck.

"Commodore, Rampart one has been attacked!"

Both Aleshco and Timoshenko looked up from the Holo-tank at the sensor operator's words.

"What is their status?" Timoshenko demanded

"Unknown sir, the station is still there but they appear to be off-line."

"There is nothing we can do for them now." Aleshco decided. "Communications, notify the other ships."

Turning back to the Holo-tank Aleshco highlighted one of the Alien's leading formations, "we will target these vessels first, prime the Orion missiles and fire as soon as we are in range."

"Yes, Commodore," Timoshenko said hurrying over to the weapon's station.

Aleshco stared into the Holo-tank and frowned worriedly.

"Captain, message from Gagarin, Rampart one has been attacked and is out of action," Jessop reported.

"How? never mind, Kathy, are they still under attack?"

Bates studied her readouts as she scanned behind them. "I don't think so, sir. I'm reading debris from an alien scout along with a fair amount from the station but no other ships."

"Captain, range to leading enemy ships is three minutes." Kelly interrupted.

"Ok, Rampart one is going to have to take care of itself. Guns, target these ships first." He said pointing out the two leading ships. "Raj, on my mark take us into evasive pattern Delta."

"Captain, the Russian's have engaged!" Bates called.

Mike glanced at his tactical screen as three of the Gagarin's Orion missiles leapt forward on nuclear flames. Within seconds two Alien ships exploded, and a third ship spinning away as the last missile clipped its hull.

Mike grinned wolfishly "Open fire." He ordered.

The Rapiers forward particle cannons spat their lethal volleys as the small warship charged forwards. The leading alien ships span away as charged particles shredded their hulls. As if they'd only just noticed the Rapier, the following ships swung around, hurling projectiles as they came.

At Mike's command, Singh threw the Rapier into a series of evasive manoeuvres dodging the bulk of the projectiles, any that came close were blasted by auto-cannons on full fire. Suddenly the Rapier steadied herself and darted in toward the largest alien battleship.

"Forward Disruptors, FIRE!" Mike cried

A pale light leapt from the Rapier, enveloping a section of the alien hull twenty metres square. Sound waves, set to an extreme frequency sped along the light waves. As they hit the battleship's hull they began to vibrate. Suddenly the hull disintegrated, explosive decompression tore the battleship apart, scattering the alien ships nearest.

"BOZE MOI!"

Aleshco looked up at the surprised cry

"Commodore, the British ship just blew up one of the Alien's battleships!" Timoshenko gasped

"Show me."

Timoshenko toggled a command and Aleshco watched as the Rapier's disruptor flashed out and the Alien battleship exploded. "Well, well Captain James. It appears you did have some more surprises for us. They have done well, Tasha, now let us return to our own task." He said returning the tank to the current view.

"The enemy is still advancing on the watchtowers, and see, Tasha, they are destroying any of the dormant mines they can. Alter course ten degrees port negative, standby all weapons" he finished. As Timoshenko left to pass on his orders Aleshco studied the tank planning his next move.

"Herr Oberleutnant, we have incoming enemy craft across the board and I still can't raise Rampart one!"

Goering winced as watchtower four disappeared from his screen. The Italians had put up a good fight but without any of their mines active, they hadn't stood a chance. "Willie, what's our status?"

"Autocannon and SAM batteries are live and tracking, sir."

"What about our mines?"

"They are still cycling up, estimate five to ten minutes."

Goering checked the wave of Alien warships on his screen "Ten minutes is too long!" he said to himself. Looking up he shared a look with his second in command. "He knows that too." He thought.

"Shall I ready the escape pod, sir?"

Goering looked again at where watchtower four had been, at the other stations still there, and the planet beyond. "No Willie, not yet. We need to slow them down first." Taking a breath, he ordered "Open fire, everything we've got."

"Commander, they're hitting the Watchtowers!"

"So I see Major Kowalski, please continue on your current course." Zhang Mi replied coolly. Switching channels to include her squadron she continued "All Swallows prepare to detach in three minutes. We will engage the enemy in pairs, wing crews ensure you remain in close support of your primaries." She finished

As the two space shuttles, Endeavour and Enterprise closed on the Alien vanguard some of the lead ships altered course. In the cockpit of the Shuttle Enterprise Major, Maxine Kowalski called out.

"Ok people, here they come. Ricky engage the auto-cannon. "Commander Zhang? I'm opening the cargo bay doors now."

"Very good Major, we are ready." Zhang's voice came back

Nestled tightly in the cargo bay of the shuttle Enterprise Commander Zhang Mi sat in the cockpit of her tiny Swallow Fighter. Two other fighters sat next to her with another three fighters in the Endeavour's cargo bay. Above her, the Enterprise's cargo bay doors slowly split open. As the gap grew Zhang's eyes widened as Alien attack ships grew visibly as they closed.

"Damn, those Goblin's are fast! Commander, hang on we're going into evasive."

Zhang watched helplessly in her cockpit as the alien ships slowly slid aside and suddenly tracer fire from the Enterprise's auto-cannon filled the sky.

Kowalski threw the Enterprise into a tight bank and turn as the Alien attack ships bore down on them. She felt the shuttle vibrate as at the weapons console Lieutenant Rick Johansson fired the shuttle's auto-cannon.

"Major, the Endeavour is following us." Matt Keenan, the Enterprise's co-pilot reported.

"Tell them to break off, see if we can split them up," Kowalski said firing her thrusters to shove the shuttle aside.

Helpless spectators, Zhan Mi, and her pilots sat watching as the two shuttles dove and weaved to evade the alien attack ships. Tracer fire and the alien's projectiles filled the space between the dodging vessels. One attack craft banked suddenly bearing on the Enterprise but flew directly into a stream of Tracer rounds. The Alien ship bucked as he rounds tore through its hull "GAN TA!" her pilots cheered as the enemy vessel span away.

"Silence, be ready." She snapped, her eyes following two more attack ships as they closed on the other space shuttle. The Endeavour tried to bank out of the way as both Alien vessels fired. Zhang Mi held her breath as the aged space shuttle pulled out of its bank trying to accelerate away but as she avoided the first ships rounds, the second vessels projectiles clipped her port side smashing her wing and sending her spinning into the sights of a third attack ship. Zhang Mi closed her eyes in silent grief as the Endeavour was torn apart, taking three of her precious little fighters with it.

Maxine Kowalski winced as the Endeavour exploded. Throwing the Enterprise into yet another hard dive she silently cursed the shuttles lack of missiles.

"Major, we must launch now, we cannot take the risk that we will be destroyed in the same way." Commander Zhang's voice called.

"If we fly level for any time, they'll nail us!" Kowalski replied

"Spin your shuttle at forty-five per cent velocity, we will use the centrifugal force to scatter so they cannot target us," Zhang replied.

She waited a moment while Kowalski considered her plan. "Okay give me sixty seconds to line us up."

"Acknowledged." She replied switching to her flight channel. "Chang, Xiou, we will launch in fifty seconds, the Major will spin the enterprise to confuse the enemy and we will use centrifugal force to aid us. When we have launched, we will be scattered. We will fight as champions of old, avenge our fallen comrades and make the aliens pay. Good fortune be with you." She finished as Kowalski's voice cried

"Launch now!"

Zhang Mi punched the launch button on her control panel "GAN TA!!" she screamed as her fighter blasted away from the shuttle.

Light danced blurrily slowly coming into focus as General Kaminsky stirred. "Major, he's coming around," a voice said. Kaminsky slowly raised his hand to touch his face but a clear obstruction stopped him. "I must be wearing a helmet" he realised.

"General?"

Kaminsky looked up into Raoul Lafayette's worried face. As the world around him started to come into focus he saw crewmen and women frantically pulling themselves around, making repairs. The main lighting was off but in the red glow of emergency lighting, he began to make out damage and scorch marks all around the command centre, and over to the side what were unmistakably three body bags. "What?" he began but memory returned in a flash. The alien attack ship, impossibly close, the missile strike and resulting explosions, the feeling of helplessness as he was blown across the command centre followed by an impact and merciful darkness.

Trying to shake himself he asked "How bad?"

"Don't move General, you're hurt," Lafayette said quickly gently pressing Kaminsky back as he tried to get up.

Laying back down Kaminsky asked again "How bad is it, Raoul?"

Lafayette paused for a moment but something in the Generals calm gaze made up his mind. "It's bad sir. That round from the attack ship took out our main transmitter and half the station before we could send the reactivation signal. We've lost half our gun and missile links too. The watchtowers have begun reactivating the mines but watchtowers four, six and seven have already been destroyed."

"What about the mobile units?"

"The Gagarin and Rapier have engaged the enemy but they're completely exposed." He paused for a moment before continuing, "The Endeavour has been destroyed along with all her fighters. The other shuttles have managed to get their fighters off but they're completely scattered."

Kaminsky's eyes closed while he took Lafayette's words in. the Major was about to call a medic over when the general asked: "How long?"

"Sir?"

"How long before they breakthrough"

"Not long, sir, hours at best."

Kaminsky nodded, "What about Coms? Can we reach anyone?"

"That round took out our entire radio suite. We're routing a laser node to link to a communications satellite now. We should be able to send and receive signals soon but it will be limited."

"Order the watchtowers to put all mines onto full auto and to evacuate. Tell James. Aleshco and Zhang to cover them. Then get the shuttles back here, we're going to evacuate."

"But General!" Lafayette exclaimed

"It's over Raoul, we've lost. I'm not going to let my people die for nothing. All we can do is slow them down and bleed them before they get to the Earth."

The major nodded, deflated. "Yes, sir,"

As Lafayette left to carry out his orders a medic came over and began checking "Don't worry sir, we'll get you back home ok and they'll be able to take care of you."

Kaminsky just nodded as he closed his eyes, grief and failure crushing in on him.

"Willie, target those attack ships coming in from 38 degrees red! Hit them with everything you've got. Henning watch your port flank." Goering cried.

Around the small station, another squadron of alien attack craft whirled and dived blasting out rounds at the watchtower and mines alike. So far Goering and his crew had managed to hold the alien's back but over half of watchtower Two's mines were gone. On his screen, Goering could see the two warships and surviving fighters desperately battling the tidal wave of alien ships. The Earth's defenders were throwing everything they had to try and slow the invaders, even the last three shuttles with their small auto-cannons were doing what they could but the overwhelming numbers were too much. As he watched another group of the Alien's attack craft broke through. Desperately he swung the targeting sensors for his SAM battery round trying to get a lock.

After what had seemed hours, Zhang Mi had finally managed to fight her way back into visual range of her two wingmen. The battle was going badly and the final outcome, in her mind, had never been in doubt but her fighters and allies were making the aliens pay dearly for their victory.

"Chang, Xiou, form up on my position," she began when Chang Lee her second in command signalled

"Commander! The Watchtower!"

Zhang looked down below her starboard sail-wing and her eyes widened in horror as five Alien ships broke through. "Cancel order, intercept those attack ships." She barked as she hauled on her control stick to bring her fighter into a steep dive.

On his console the missile lock began to pulse with partial contacts as the group of attack ships bore down on watchtower two, their guns already blazing. Goering hit the fire key and prayed his weapons lock was good enough. He watched as his missiles streaked away, three detonated almost immediately as they intercepted the alien's deadly projectiles. The last missiles would pass wide but Goering nodded with satisfaction as the Alien ships sharply manoeuvred to avoid them.

Ahead of her Zhang saw Chang and Xiou both charging the aliens on full thrust, the Alien craft had split up and were manoeuvring wildly to avoid the watchtowers missiles. Quickly designating each ship, she radioed "They are divided, if we act now, we can catch them before they re-group. I am sending you target designations. Break and attack!" she ordered

Xiou Lin had been a combat pilot in the People's Liberation Army Air Force for over ten years, he was a great pilot but as he had been told numerous times he had a reckless streak which had cost him several promotions. But it had been that recklessness, that drive to push boundaries, which had led to his appointment to the swallow squadrons and one of the highest kill rates among his comrades. On the Heads-Up Display of his helmet visor, the target Commander Zhang had selected pulsed brightly. Checking his scanner Xiou pulled on his control stick, pushed his thrusters past maximum and dived at the alien. His tiny fighter looped down and round, as he neared the Alien craft, he saw small gun turrets, their muzzles flashing as small calibre projectiles blasted away turning towards him. Grinning wolfishly Xiou muttered, "you're quick but not quick enough." To himself as he pressed the 'fire' key for his lasers.

Xiou's eyes widened as error and system failure warnings flashed across his panel. Quickly he tried to re-set his lasers before the alien's weapons could get a lock on him but more failures began to fill his screen. Looking up he saw the enemy attack craft begin to turn.

Sparing one eye to watch her pilots Zhang arced her fighter down in a tight spiral bringing her target's mid-flank directly into her sights. Her lasers flashed and the alien attack craft shattered like an egg. She pulled away sharply avoiding debris from the smashed vessel when a flashing indicator on her panel caught her eye. One of her fighters, Xiou Lin's, was experiencing a full system crash.

Searching the sky, she quickly found Xiou's fighter closing on an enemy attack ship. "Xiou, disengage and withdraw." She barked but to her horror, Xiou's fighter continued to close. "Xiou!" she called but as she watched the alien attach ship turned almost lazily as Xiou's fighter charged in. Zhang turned away as the fireball which had once been her pilot expanded across the sky.

Goering's crew cheered as in quick succession two of the Alien's had been destroyed. He hadn't realised the fighters were that close but gave a silent prayer of thanks as he concentrated on his board. Hard missile locks were beginning to appear as he busily began programming his missile solutions. He concentrated so hard that he didn't even notice the rounds that took his and his crews lives as watchtower two was blasted to dust.

"Captain! Watchtower two is gone!" Bates cried.

Mike grimaced at the announcement, he hadn't particularly liked the German commander of the station but Goering and his crew had been good at their jobs and their loss was a real blow.

"Kathy, can you take control of their mines?"

"No, sorry sir, they're going over to full auto."

"Ok, Raj, pull us back, there are no safeties on those mines now. Jerry, signal all ships and tell them to pull back as well."

"Aye sir, the Enterprise is already heading back to the ISS, there's just a couple of fighters."

"Send it to everyone anyway. Have you had anything from Rampart control?"

"No, noth, wait" Rogers replied.

Mike glanced over to his radio operator as he read something on his console.

"It's a text-only message routed via a satellite. The General is ordering a full retreat and evacuation, sir, we're to cover the watchtowers and shuttles as they evacuate."

Mike wore silently if they'd gotten the signal five minutes earlier! Mike looked around and saw the same thought on the faces of his bridge crew. "Jerry, send that signal as voice to all commands. Raj, pull us back, Pat, Watchtower five is the nearest station, plot us a course to cover them as they evacuate." He ordered as another group of alien warships tried to breakthrough.

Chapter 15

The bridge of the battleship Yuri Gagarin was a frenzy of activity. Like the eye of a storm, Victor Aleshco stood at the holo-tank observing the battle unfold around them.

"Commodore, we have received a signal from Rampart one! The Rapier is also repeating it" Timoshenko called from the Gagarin's communications station.

Aleshco looked up from the holo-tank "Yes?"

"General Kaminski has ordered all units to withdraw starting with the evacuation of the watchtowers. He has ordered us and the Rapier along with the remnants of the Chinese fighters to cover the evacuation."

Aleshco looked over to where the rapier had been operating and watched as she banked and fell back to a new position as Timoshenko re-joined him.

"The British ship is already retreating," he observed.

"Yes, but Captain James is quite clever, see how he first launched a feint making the enemy think he was attacking before falling back to cover the watchtower. Unfortunately, we are not so fast and manoeuvrable as the Rapier so we must plan our movements carefully." Aleshco paused for a moment, Tasha, we will move to here, we should be able to cover these watchtowers adequately. Order the Chinese fighters to cover us while we move." He finished staring again into the tank.

"Captain, the watchtower five crew are away!" Rogers reported.

"Ok, Raj, prepare to pull us back again, Pat.."

"CAPTAIN, CONTACTS BEARING 025 DEGREES!" Bates cried suddenly.

Mike glanced down at his monitor as two alien battleships suddenly broke through the mines heading straight for them, their weapons already hurling projectiles

"SH.. Raj, hard a-starboard, evasive Charlie three, guns!"

"On it sir," Archibald replied bringing the Rapier's auto-cannons round to bear.

As his ship veered sharply away Mike desperately searched for a way to escape the battleships as the vibration from the Rapier's auto-cannon shuddered through the hull.

"Chang! Behind you! Alter course ninety degrees negative now!" Zhang Mi ordered as the alien attack ship bore down on her last pilot. Her warning came just in time as projectiles tore through the space the fighter had occupied moments before.

The alien attack ship dived after Chang's fighter as Zhang banked sharply around bringing her flying past the Alien's engines. She thumbed her lasers as the attack ship flashed past her, she spared a glance back but looked away as the alien ship exploded.

Blinking away the afterimage Zhang checked her HUD for the next target but Chang's voice interrupted her.

"Commander, Enemy warships have broken through and are targeting HMS Rapier!"

Zhang studied her HUD "Form up on me, we will dive on them and strafe across the top hull of the nearest ship and then the second as we pass between them."

"Raj, Hard a port, Gun's all weapons fire as we pass, we probably won't hit them but if we can make them veer off," Mike ordered as two more attack ships joined the fight

Singh took them into a steep dive as the alien attack ships wheeled around herding the Rapier closer to the waiting Battleships. The Rapier suddenly veered back up, her main cannon blasting streams of charged particles at the Alien Battleships. The nearest alien ship shook as the Rapiers first volley smashed into its hull armour forcing it to evade but just as Mike thought they had found a way out a third attack ship suddenly appeared.

"GUNS! Autocannon on full now!" Mike barked as the attack ship swooped down. As projectiles flew from the attack ship the Rapiers auto cannon roared blasting them to pieces but on Mike's screen the other aliens were closing fast. Mike desperately looked for an escape when suddenly a brilliant flash filled the Rapiers Bridge as the attack craft exploded.

"Captain James, you have an opening I suggest you use it quickly" Zhang Mi's voice came over the radio.

Mike looked out as the two fighters sailed past. "Raj, you heard the lady, get us out of here." Keying his com Mike replied, "Thanks for the assist Commander I suggest you do the same."

"We are already…"

Mike winced as the two Chinese fighters suddenly disappeared from his screen.

A shocked silence filled the bridge when Rogers reported quietly, "Sir, signal from the Enterprise, all watchtowers evacuated."

"Ok, thanks, Jerry. Raj, Pat get us back to Earth orbit but keep us between the aliens and the shuttles."

The Rapier fell back slowly, Mike quickly scanned his secondary monitor for a damage report. Unbelievably they had escaped any major damage with only a handful of shrapnel impacts on the hull and minor injuries mainly resulting from the Rapiers hard evasion manoeuvres. He looked back at his main screen as the Alien fleet inexorably ground its way through the last of the mine constellations and prayed they would hold long enough for the last of the defence force to get back home.

"Sasha, what is the status of our missiles?" Aleshco demanded as the Gagarin inserted herself into Earth orbit.

"Not good Commodore, we are down to less than fifteen rounds for our missile batteries and our autocannon are on their last re-loads."

"And the Orion missiles?"

"All gone sir."

Aleshco nodded thoughtfully. "Very well, I believe we have a short time before the enemy will arrive. Lieutenant Varishkova has a re-supply pod here." He said gesturing to a point on the holo-tank. Order her forward to rendezvous with us here."

"But surely we must make re-entry while we can Commodore, the battle up here is lost. We must preserve what we can for what is to come."

Aleshco looked up in surprise at his first officer's outburst. He saw several other bridge officers looking over. The same worried question in their eyes.

"The battle up here is lost yes but see the Enterprise and several escape pods have not yet reached orbit, nor has the HMS Rapier. If we do not stand and fight, many of them will perish. I will not flee and leave our comrades to die. Is that understood." He finished forcefully.

Timoshenko looked down, embarrassed "Yes sir, I understand." He said simply.

"Your concern is valid but do not fear. We will give these Aliens such a fight their grandchildren will speak of it in hushed voices for fear of us." He said addressing the whole crew. Then smiling at his first officer he continued "But we will be very hard-pressed to do it without Varishkova's ammunition!"

Brightening Timoshenko straitened "Yes Commodore, Vassily, set course to rendezvous with the re-supply pod. Alexei, get a crew together to bring the supplies aboard." He said setting off on his task.

Aleshco watched his young first officer busily arranging the re-supply. He glanced around the bridge meeting a few glances and nodded reassuringly. Satisfied his crew were once again bent to their tasks he looked back into the holo-tank and his own fears.

The Rapier arrived back into orbit to what could only be described as semi-organised chaos and Mike didn't need his monitor to see it. Before them, the surviving shuttles and escape ships were lining themselves up for re-entry. The three surviving Chinese fighters slowly moved among them. The Chinese mother ships along with several other transport pods queued up waiting to dock with the crippled space station to evacuate its surviving crew and to Mike's intense relief holding station above them sat the Gagarin.

"Sir, signal from Commodore Aleshco asking to speak to you."

"Put him through Jerry," Mike told him. "Commodore, it's good to see you."

"It is good to see you also Captain, I fear we are going to be very busy soon. What is your status?"

"We've got some minor hull damage but nothing serious. I was about to report to the General."

"I regret to inform you, Captain, that the General succumbed to his injuries just after we arrived. Major Lafayette is busy arranging the evacuation of the station, so I have assumed command."

"Understood sir, do you have any specific order for us?"

"Admiral Greene has sent up a supply sledge, it is making its way to you now. Re-arm quickly, I believe you will need the ammunition before we can return to Earth."

Mike checked his monitor; the supply sledge was making its final approach. A query tab opened next to the sledges icon and he saw that Lieutenant Chand, his logistics officer, was already communicating with the pilot.

"Captain, enemy attack ships have broken through!" Bates called out suddenly

On his monitor red threat icons blossomed as the aliens broke through. "I see them. Commodore" he began

"We see them also, get your supplies quickly my friend. We will hold them."

"Our sledge is docking now, we'll be with you shortly sir, Udachi, good luck sir."

"And to you, I think we will need it. Udachi moy drug." Aleshco replied cutting the comm.

Mike watched anxiously as the Gagarin slowly changed course to intercept the alien force. Keying the Com to his supply channel Mike said: "Suresh, we need that ammunition aboard now!"

"On it Captain!" Chand replied

Mike was about to sign off when Dr Ellen Rand's voice spoke. "Captain, we've got some wounded here I need to evacuate. Can you wait till we've got them on the sledge?"

Mike glanced up at his monitor as the Gagarin engaged the alien warships and cursed silently. "I'm sorry Doc, Commodore Aleshco is holding the enemy alone. We need to get into the fight immediately. Can you get your wounded on the sledge while Suresh is unloading?"

In the Rapiers cramped docking bay Rand looked over at the supply officer who just nodded sharply.

"We'll do our best Captain." She replied

"We'll clear the supplies in sections and you can start loading the casualties as each section clears," Chand said quickly.

"Thank you, Suresh." Rand said then turning to her orderlies "Help them get those boxes out, the quicker we can clear space the quicker we can get the wounded aboard."

On the bridge, Mike double-checked the damage control systems and was relieved to see the Rapier's damage was still relatively minor. He'd been surprised by Rand's announcement that there were casualties that needed evacuating but now he saw that three crew had been wounded when shrapnel had penetrated a compartment in the weapons section. The compartment had been sealed and no longer posed any danger. Glancing back at his monitor he noted the line of escape pods and shuttles queueing to re-enter the atmosphere wasn't moving.

"Jerry, query Cheyenne Mountain. Ask why the shuttles and pods aren't returning Earthside."

"I've been monitoring the frequencies, sir. It seems Space Command is concerned that any returning ships will draw the alien's attention to planetside bases. Cheyenne is trying to work out the best places to tell the ships to make for."

Mike stared at his radio operator in disbelief. "You are joking, really!"

"Sorry sir but that's the gist of it."

Feeling his temper rise Mike said "Jerry punch me a signal through to Cheyenne Mountain. Not the communications centre I want to speak to whoever's in charge."

Rogers exchanged a worried look with Kathy Bates the sensor tech but just said: "aye, aye sir."

Mike took a deep breath and looked back at his monitor as the Yuri Gagarin continued to hold the alien armada. The tell-tale flashes as Orion drive missiles blasted away into the mass of alien warships, Mike couldn't see if they hit any but their very appearance caused the aliens to dive and weave. Other missiles followed and though he couldn't see it Mike new the Russian's auto-cannon was blasting away at the dozens of incoming enemy rounds. Suddenly his com beeped "Captain? Chand here, the sledge's just undocking now. They should be clear within 2 minutes."

"Good job Suresh," Mike replied as Rogers interrupted

"Sir, I've got Cheyenne Mountain base."

"Put them through Jerry."

"Captain James? This is General Joseph P Thinness, Space Command. Your communications officer said it was urgent."

"Yes General, I'm not sure if you're aware but we've got a line of shuttle and evacuation pods waiting here for permission to re-enter Earth Atmosphere. We are about to join the Gagarin in engaging the enemy's vanguard but I can't say how long we will be able to hold them for. I suggest you start telling those ships they can land as quickly as possible."

There was a moment's silence then "Well CAPTAIN! We may not be in orbit but you may be surprised to learn we're not completely blind! We can see how close the enemy is which is why we don't want to draw their attention to key military bases and assets. Now I suggest you go do your job and let us do ours!"

Mike opened his mouth to reply when suddenly a flash filled the sky. Mike looked at his monitor and his blood ran cold. He keyed a playback and watched in horror as the Gagarin was hit amidships. The Battleship staggered and two more huge projectiles smashed into her, splitting the drive section off. A third projectile hit detonating any missiles in the aft magazine completely destroying the drive section.

"What was that?" Thinness gasped.

"That General was the Yuri Gagarin along with my friend Commodore Victor Aleshco and over a hundred of his crew." Feeling his temper rising again Mike continued. "Now as you so eloquently put it, I'm going to do my job and take my ship and my crew and teach these bastards that what they have done WILL have cost. NOW I SUGGEST, GENERAL, THAT YOU GET OFF OF YOUR SOFT FUCKING ARSE AND GET THOSE SHIPS BACK TO EARTH BEFORE MORE OF THE PEOPLE WHO'VE ACTUALLY FOUGHT THESE ALIEN'S DIE!" Seeing the looks he was getting from his bridge crew Mike took another deep breath. "Rapier Out." He finished.

Glancing round he was surprised to see a few smiles among the worried faces of his bridge crew.

"Captain, the enemy are re-grouping!" Bates called

"Sir, landing instructions are starting to be received. We're being ordered to make for Redemption Base." Rogers announced.

"Kathy, how long before the Alien's get here and how long for all of the evacuation ships to get down?" Mike asked.

Bates looked up, "Not enough sir, half of them will still be in orbit even those who've made re-entry, most will still be on their way down."

Mike looked out at the raged line of shuttles and escape craft, the Chinese tenders looking small and naked with all of their fighters destroyed, just three wounded pilots all that was left of Commander Zhang's swallows. He looked up at his crew and made a decision. Switching to the all-hands channel he began.

"All hands, this is the Captain. We've been ordered to return to base but if we do then our comrades and friends in the shuttles and escape ships will be caught by the Alien fleet before they can get to safety." He paused for a second "Many years ago another ship of the Royal Navy had the same choice we face now. Escape to safety, at the cost of the defenceless ships in their charge or stand and fight against impossible odds. You all know the story, that ship chose to stand and fight and because of her sacrifice over 32 merchant ships survived. History remembers the Jervis Bay and in us, her legacy lives on. We will NOT abandon our comrades; we will NOT run and hide. History remembers the Jervis Bay and in the same breath WILL remember the Rapier. Now man your Battlestations! Helm, all ahead full! Remember the Jervis Bay, REMEMBER THE RAPIER!"

Throughout the ship cries of 'The Jervis Bay' and 'remember the Rapier' reverberated. To Mike's surprise even the bridge crew were cheering, looks of fierce determination had replaced the worried and concerned faces of before.

"Ah Captain?" a voice behind Mike said quietly. Looking round Mike saw Jessop standing, in his hands, he held the sword Mike had brought on St Theresa, its scabbard now attached to a belt.

"I know it's not very practical but under the circumstances"

"Ha, well I don't think I'll be able to wear it normally but," Mike said taking the sword, "I think it'll be just as good here." He finished hanging it on the back of his command chair.

Jessop beamed and several of the bridge crew grinned and gave Mike a thumbs up when Bates interrupted.

"Five minutes to contact Captain."

Sobering Mike sat back in the Command chair "Thanks Kate, Jess you'd better strap in. Raj, Pat, keep us moving I want to scatter them and keep them busy so the others can get to safety. Guns, I'll feed you targets but if you get any openings I don't see, take them. You've got full re-loads for the auto-cannon, use them."

"Yes Captain," Archibald replied.

On their monitors, five new targets bloomed as a wave of attack ships suddenly launched from the oncoming Battleships.

Mike swore as the new contacts bore down on them.

"Captain, the targeting drones!" Archibald called.

"Do it, program them for Kamikaze. Good thinking Guns." Mike replied.

As the attack ships bore down on the Rapier, their crews readied their weapons. They knew this particular enemy to be deadly but they were five and the lone enemy would not be able to survive their enveloping fire. The crews waited for their leader to give the attack order when suddenly eight tiny contacts erupted from the enemy cruiser.

The Drones normal fuel load could keep them in space for up to forty minutes but Archibald had programmed them to expel all their fuel in one short burst accelerating them beyond anything their designers had ever imagined. The drones were comparatively small with hardly any mass but with the combined speeds they had gained from launching from the Rapier and the speed of the incoming attack ships they hit with the kinetic energy of a small atomic bomb.

The attack ships tried to evade but Archibald had launched her drones at what equated to point-blank range. The first two attack ships disintegrated almost immediately; the third ship took a glancing hit which destroyed its port wing sending it spinning into the path of two more drones saving one of their sister ships in the process. The last two attack ships turned away, pursued by the last three drones.

Their way finally cleared the Earths last defender charged on toward the waiting Battleships, their guns as if on fire, the Rapier sailed into hell! Alien projectiles tore towards them, the Rapier's Auto-cannon roared back in defiance. Tracer rounds lit the sky, blasting the oncoming shells to pieces. Shrapnel tore at her hull but miraculously the small warship reached the range of her own main weapons.

Alien Battleships seemed to fill the space around them, the Rapier's Small Hadron Accelerator flared and charged particles smashed a Battleships armour to Ribbons. Her Sonic Disruptor silently screamed, tearing another Alien ship apart. Now amongst her enemies the Rapier weaved and bobbed all guns blazing, The Battleships began to pull back but only so their smaller attack ships could engage. But in the confusion, a gap opened.

"Captain! Target bearing negative 20 degrees!"

Mike looked and stared in disbelief. One of the Alien motherships had followed its fleet almost to Earth orbit.

"Raj put us through that hole. Guns, as soon as we're in range give them everything you've got." Mike ordered.

As if realising their mistake, the Alien ships tried to reverse course but it was too late. Singh took the Rapier in a tight dive, spinning the ship so all her guns came to bear. As one the Rapiers weapons roared. Disruptor beams tore rends into the Motherships armour while tracers and charged particles plunged through the wounds to ravage the alien ship further. The Rapier flew past a small section of the vast Mothership weapons blazing, explosions tore through the ravaged vessel, atmosphere, and debris poured out into space listing the mothership down. Singh tried to follow the list to put the Mothership between the Rapier and the following attack ships but inevitably their luck finally ran out.

The explosions within the Mother ship must have ruptured an internal water store blasting a new wound through the Alien's hull. A vast jet of steam and water vomited out into space shoving the mothership back towards the Rapier. Seeing the danger, Singh veered away right into the sites of two attack ships. Singh desperately spun the Rapier trying to dive away but it was too late. The attack ships fired volleys of projectiles, Archibald pounded her controls firing her auto-cannons but the rounds were too many, too close.

Mike held onto his seat grimly as the Rapier convulsed around him, around him his crew fought to regain control of the ship.

"DAMAGE REPORT!" he demanded

"Several hit's Captain, Command and weapons sections" Jessop replied from the damage control station.

"Captain I'" Archibald began but as Mike glanced back her Console exploded throwing the young lieutenant across the bridge. Other consoles sparked and a couple of small fires ignited. Smoke began to fill the bridge as the environmental systems struggled to compensate. Jessop grabbed his first aid kit and pulled himself over to the prone lieutenant while Rogers pulled Kathy Bates away from her sparking console. Jessop checked Archibald's pulse and looking up at Mike sadly shook his head.

"Raj, get us out of here!" Mike ordered quickly re-routing weapons control to his command terminal. "Jess, get back on damage control, I need to know exactly how bad it is."

Kelly got unsteadily to her feet, blood running down her face from a gash on her head. "I'll take damage control, sir, Jess needs to help Jerry with Kath." She said. Seeing Mike's expression, she added, "It's just a cut I'm fine."

"Still get Jess to check it," Mike said as she hurried past.

The hits on the command and weapons sections had shoved the Rapier away from the onrushing attack ships. Using quite violent bursts on the ship's thrusters Singh managed to spin the Rapier further away so when he called for full thrust the Rapier was heading in roughly the right direction, away from the Alien's and towards Earth orbit. A couple of attack ships tried to close but Mike was able to chase them off with a few well-aimed blasts of the particle cannon.

"Jess I need that damage report!" Mike urged but it wasn't Jessop who replied.

"Ye don't need any system report to know we're buggered!" Duffin said as he entered the bridge.

"Engines! glad to see you're still in one piece." Mike replied, relieved to see his friend.

Duffin paused to collect a printout from Jessop before continuing to Mike's side.

"Tis as I thought, the weapons section's like a sieve! The command section took some near hits and shrapnel damage but the weapons section took most of the damage."

Mike looked at the report and said "Ok, we'll separate as soon as we get into orbit. We'll have to leave the weapons section up here but we can set a self-destruct. That should cover us as we re-enter."

Duffin nodded "Aye that makes sense, we've also got the two escape pods. I'll get them prepped."

"Do that," Mike ordered turning he added "Jess, run a full check on the separation and escape systems. We need to be ready when we reach orbit. Engines, liaise with the Doc to get everyone out of the weapons section into either the escape pods or the drive section, it's bigger than the command section."

"Aye Cap'n I'll get straight on to it," Duffin replied heading for the exit.

Mike settled back into his seat checking for any further threats.

Making their best possible speed the Rapier limped back to a now-empty Earth orbit ahead of the alien armada. The column of shuttles and escape craft having all managed to return to the planet. Mike looked out of the Rapiers windows at the wrecked Yuri Gagarin and what was left of Rampart control and breathed a sad sigh of relief.

"Ok people we don't have much time," Mike said keying his com to link with Duffin in the drive section. "We'll do this as slowly as we can. Engines, Raj, on my order, open clamps and prepare to disengage airlocks." Mike waited for a second to make sure everyone was ready then "Open clamps, repeat open clamp."

There was a loud clunk as the clamps opened but then a warning light blazed on his monitor. "Raj?"

"Number two clamp won't open" Singh replied urgently.

Turning Mike asked sharply "Jess?"

Jessop looked up shocked "It's jammed sir, it must have been when that round hit. It must have taken some of the sensors out at the same time."

"Can we repair it?"

"If we had time but" Jessop replied

"Ok, we'll have to abandon the command section. Everyone get down to the drive section, the pods are all full. Raj, take over piloting when you get there." Thumbing his Com again Mike said "Engines, one of our clamps is jammed, I'm sending the command crew down to you. Launch the pods now and then disengage and get clear as soon as everyone is aboard your section." Mike finished.

The bridge crew all began to evacuate Singh rose to head out when he noticed Mike busily importing settings onto his monitor. He saw Jessop had also noticed. The two of them stopped by the command seat. "Cap. Mike come on we need to get moving." He said warily.

Mike looked up and smiled grimly. "The aliens are too close; the drive section will never make it on its own."

"Sir, no!" Jessop said horrified.

Raj just nodded and started to turn, "you'll need a pilot you won't be able." He began but Mike cut him off.

"NO, Raj, they'll need you to go to evasive on the way down, without drive all I'll have are manoeuvring thrusters anyway." Mike could see both men were about to argue so he continued. "Besides, I'm the Captain and it sort of goes with the job. Now both of you stop wasting time and get going. Raj, Engines will probably try and argue but tell him I said he's in command now. I'm relying on him, and both of you, to get the crew home." He finished

The rest of the bridge crew had paused sensing something wasn't right. Seeing this Raj gripped Mike's shoulder then pushing Jessop before him said. "Come on move, unless you want to stay up here, we've got to go now." He barked shepherding them out.

Mike watched them all go, Kelly, a dressing on her scalp looked back worriedly. Mike smiled "goodbye my friends." He whispered quietly as he turned back to his monitor preparing himself.

Duffin waited anxiously by the airlock door of the drive section. He'd made all his people move further in to make room for the command crew. They'd all fit but it would be pretty cosy on the way down. Rand came up next to him. "I've got everyone strapped in Sean; Isaacs is just double-checking."

"Grand, thanks Doc, we'll need to go as soon as their all in. And here they come." He finished as the first of the command section crew began to arrive.

As if from nowhere Isaacs suddenly appeared and began sorting the new arrivals as they entered. Jessop pushed past and looked up at Duffin, he looked like he was going to say something but Raj Singh gently pushed him onwards.

"Raj?" Rand asked

"It's Mike, he's not coming."

"WHAT?" Duffin demanded.

"He's routed everything through his terminal, he's going to cover us so we can get out. I tried to talk him out of it but he said we wouldn't stand a chance on our own." Gripping Duffin's arms he continued "Mike said it was down to us now, he said you were in command now and he was relying on us to get everyone home."

"We'll bloody see about that!" Duffin said as he moved to head out the airlock but Rand grabbed his arm. Duffin span around but the tears streaming down the Doctor's face stopped him.

"He's right Sean, I hate it but he's right. If you go and try and talk to him it'll just take time we don't have." She nodded to Singh who went and took over the pilot's position, readying himself.

Duffin swore vehemently looking away but didn't move. As the last of the command crew passed him, he punched the com button. "Bridge, we're fully loaded. Mike I."

"I know engines, it's been a pleasure mate it really has. Now get your arse in gear and get going. Those bastards are almost on top of us."

"Aye, aye Captain. We're disengaging now." He said with a nod to Singh.

"Good luck engines, get them home."

Duffin made to reply but as the drive section disengaged the com went silent as all links were finally cut.

Mike watched as the drive section slowly pulled away then gathering speed turned and headed back to Earth. On his monitor, Mike saw several attack ships suddenly alter course to pursue it. "Oh no, you don't!" Mike said quietly as he quickly targeted them and hit the fire key.

The alien commander watched as the last enemy ship shed its rear section, obviously abandoning the wrecked section in order to escape. The doctrine was clear any foe who had fought could not be permitted to survive so he ordered his advance phalanx to destroy them. He sat back contented, with these enemies destroyed the battle for the space around the planet was complete. The conquest of the planet below could then begin. He began to order the dispersal of his fleet to begin bombardment when suddenly the wreck opened fire!

Treachery! The aliens had not abandoned space! He watched in horror as his advance phalanx was quickly destroyed. So, the enemy still resisted. They would not resist long! He ordered his next wave to move in and destroy all vessels left in orbit, including the station.

As the last of the attack ships exploded the alien armada seemed to go berserk. Three ships broke off and began to blast the empty space station, several more began targeting anything in orbit conceivably large enough to be considered manned while the rest bore down on the Rapier.

Mike keyed in his last auto-cannon and began targeting anything he could. Out of the side of his eye, he watched as the Raj took the drive section into a series of evasive manoeuvres avoiding any projectiles fired their way.

The autocannons blasted away and Mike kicked in his thrusters but there was too much fire. Mike held on grimly as projectiles started to hit. Glancing blows and smaller calibre projectiles at first but it was only a matter of time before something big hit. On his monitor, the drive section had reached the upper atmosphere and had begun re-entry. Several alien ships spotted the drive section and moved to attack but Mike swung all his guns round forcing the aliens off. But in driving those ship off he gave other aliens the opening they had been waiting for. Mike was almost thrown from his seat as four projectiles hit the weapons section taking out the particle gun and half his auto-cannon. But as Mike mourned his lost weapons, he spotted another indicator flashing. The number two clamp was now free!

Angling his thrusters, Mike swung the Rapier round putting the shattered weapons section between him and the Aliens. He was just about to separate when his radio suddenly crackled into life.

"Captain James? Is that you?" an accented voice came.

Mike starred at his com "Commodore? I thought you were dead"

"Ha, not yet my friend, My Gagarin with many of my crew, including poor Tasha are gone but I still live. Can you evacuate?"

"My command section can now separate; the clamps were jammed but that last round freed them."

"Then prepare to do so my friend. As you English would say I have one more hand to play. Dosvedanya my friend." Aleshco finished.

Mike quickly keyed in the Weapons section self-destruct and held his hand over the disengage command when suddenly through the bridge windows there were two bright flashes as small atomic warheads detonated sending Aleshco's last Orion missiles toward the enemy. Almost as quickly two battleships exploded. Mike hit his disengage and kicked in his thrusters.

The Aliens reacted quickly and five ships fired on the wrecked Gagarin.

Accelerating as fast as he dared Mike brought the command section down for re-entry when two more flashes lit the sky as the weapons section and Gagarin died together. Through his windows, Mike watched as Alien ships began to close on the Earth

As the Earth's last defender plummeted home, the Alien Armada took up their positions and began the bombardment of the planet. Battleships loosed their largest projectiles while squadrons of attack ships dived into the atmosphere, their own weapons primed.

Chapter 16

Sonic booms burst like cannon shells shaking the shattering the mid-morning quiet. Sam ducked down next to Miguel's car and looked up at the sky.

"What the hell was that?" Monique asked as she ran out of the shop. She stopped next to the car and shading her eyes looked up.

"Get your family into the car now Monique," Sam said urgently

"What is it Sam, I can't see anything."

"My eyes are better than yours now get moving!" she said gripping Monique's arms

Monique looked at Sam shocked then turning she ran into the café shouting "Miguel, Corletta, grab what you can and get in the car!"

"Miss Selkie? What is it? What do you see?" a voice called

Sam whirled around; two police officers were quickly making their way over. The older woman Sam recognised her as Sargent Laurence approached while the younger constable stopped as a message came in on his radio.

"Sargent," she greeted quickly "There's no time to explain but you've got to get everyone to shelter now."

"But why," she asked, but before Sam could reply the constable hurried up "Sargent, there's an alert just come over the radio, something about meteorites?"

Laurence glanced up then looking back at Sam her eyes widened in horror. "Oh my God, Paulo, get everyone inside, NOW!" she screamed

"Tell them to get into basements if they can or under the stairs, that's the strongest part of a building," Sam said quickly as Monique and her family arrived.

"Do it," Laurence told her constable "What about you?" she asked

"We'll be fine, we're heading for shelter in the mountains." She said heading to her own jeep.

"I understand, good luck and God go with you."

"And you Sargent." She said as she pulled away.

Sam checked in her rear mirror to make sure Miguel was following her, then glancing up again she accelerated out of town.

"Admiral, Message from Space Command, 'Enemy warships have gained orbit and have begun targeted barrage."

Admiral Greene looked up from his terminal at Commander Sinclair's announcement.

"Any news about the Rapier?"

"We know the drive section has made re-entry. They're on their way to redemption base now. The last message we had from them was that the command and weapons sections were still in orbit with Commander James aboard giving covering fire."

Greene nodded sadly.

"Admiral? What if the Commander manages to abandon ship somehow, will he be able to get to Redemption base or will he come here?" Sahota asked

"If he manages to get down there's no telling where he could turn up Professor." Greene replied "But more to the point what are you still doing here? You and your team were supposed to be on the first evacuation plane out."

"My team did leave Admiral but there is a great deal of data here, I stayed behind to make sure it was properly disposed of."

"Well make sure you're on the next one," Greene said sharply.

"As you should also be Admiral" the diminutive scientist replied ruefully

The Admiral snorted but his reply was cut off by Sinclair's

"Admiral! We're detecting multiple incoming unidentified contacts; we're presuming their hostile"

Greene quickly crossed to Sinclair's station "Inform Captain Swartz on the John F Kennedy and bring our defences to full battle stations. How far out is the next transport?"

Sinclair checked her terminal and looked up at the Admiral and Professor who had joined her. "Too far sir."

The command section of the HMS Rapier plummeted through the upper reaches of the Earth's atmosphere. Mike had pulled himself forward to the Pilot's console and now desperately struggled to keep the craft level. His hand hovered over the control which would inflate the emergency retractable wings when he was low enough but just then contacts appeared on his screen.

"Shit!" he cursed as they began to close. Just then the indicator telling him he had more atmosphere pinged "Ok you bastards try and keep up with this." He said switching his hybrid engines to jet power.

For a few minutes, Mike managed to pull ahead but slowly the attack ships began to close again. Mike checked his location on the monitor. "Too far from either the base or St Theresa." He thought to himself as he looked for somewhere to ditch. Mike extended his wings gaining more control as he increased power to the engines

Onwards and down he flew, pushing the jets to their maximum as he searched for somewhere to put down. Below him, the waves grew as the altitude fell. Alerts blossomed on his screen as the attack ships finally came into range. Mike banked and weaved as projectiles flew past. The Rapier shuddered as small calibre slugs tore into his aft section. Mike fought for control banking again trying to evade when suddenly three aircraft flashed past from ahead, missiles and cannon blasting.

"Rapier keep going, we'll take care of these guys." A voice came over the radio.

"Nathan? Good to see you mate." Mike replied.

"That you Mike? Keep going buddy, bear 3 degrees North and the JFK will be able to pick you up when you're down."

"Roger that Nathan, good luck mate," Mike said altering course. Behind him, Jameson and his two wingmen banked and wheeled, dogfighting the alien's but they were too heavily outnumbered with more alien's arriving as they fought.

Sure enough, within a couple of minutes, Mike started to make out the American carrier group on the Horizon but already more attack ships had arrived. He watched as more fighters engaged the aliens while the escorts launched missile after missile. But the battle was by no means one-sided, Mike winced as one of the Destroyers exploded as the alien's struck.

Mike's radio suddenly crackled to life as a voice said "Commander James? This is the USS John F Kennedy. We have you on our radar. I'm sending you location co-ordinates now for you to ditch. Do you have any life-rafts, over?"

"Affirmative Kennedy, I have an emergency life-raft I can get to, over."

"Ok Commander, ditch and we'll pick you up just as soon as we can. John F Kennedy out."

On Mike's screen a set of co-ordinates appeared, checking them on his against his Navigation systems he nodded to himself, three miles to the north was a bit further than he'd like but it looked like The American Commodore wanted the Rapier well clear of the battle. Under the circumstances, Mike agreed it was best.

Kicking in his thrusters Mike aimed the Rapier at the new coordinates but on his monitor, two attack ships broke away from the battle to follow him. Glancing over at Archibald's blackened station Mike quickly considered setting the coordinates into his terminal and seeing if he could get any of his auto-cannon working when one of the alien ships exploded.

Jameson's voice came over the Radio. "Keep going Mike, we got this."

On his screen, Mike saw two American Fighters whirling around the last Alien ship. Looking up he could see the crests of the waves ahead of him. He gently pulled the control stick back lifting the Rapiers bow slightly and counted down the seconds before he hit the water.

Mike gripped the arms of his chair as the Rapier hit the surface of the water, the ship bounced once then with a crash hit again. The bow dipped beneath the waves momentarily and seawater covered the bridge's windows but just as quickly she was level again. Knowing he only had minutes before the Rapier began to sink Mike quickly unbuckled himself, grabbing the sword Jess had handed to him he paused for a moment to look over at the two body bags secured against the bulkhead. There's hadn't been time to move Archibald or leading seaman Roche's bodies down to the drive section or even room to store them. Standing to attention Mike saluted the two fallen sailors. "Look after her for me guns," he said quietly before dashing out of the bridge.

He sped along the narrow corridor towards the airlock but already seawater was beginning to flood the decks. By the time He made it to the emergency lockers the water was over his ankles and heading up to his knees. Mike picked up a small life raft and a rescue kit which he dragged to the airlock, opening the door he put the raft and kit in, then splashing back to the locker and grabbed one of the small motors and solar power units which he carried back to the airlock. The water was almost waist-high when Mike got back to the airlock. He clambered through and pulled the emergency release which jettisoned the airlock door. He quickly climbed through the hatch, pulling the raft with him, as soon as he was outside, he inflated the raft, tying it loosely to the airlock handle he went back to get his other equipment. Throwing them in the life raft he cut the rope and pushed away from the sinking Rapier.

Mike managed to get away just in time, sitting in the life raft he watched, numb, as the Command section slowly slid beneath the surface. He continued to stare at the point his ship had disappeared when the low rumble of an explosion shook him from his thoughts. Looking up Mike saw a billowing cloud rising from the John F Kennedy. Quickly scrabbling around, he found the escape kit and grabbed a pair of binoculars.

"Oh no!" he gasped as over a dozen projectiles rained down from Battleships in orbit. He watched in horror as the projectiles smashed into and around the American warships. One Destroyer exploded as a projectile scored a direct hit. The other ships desperately tried to manoeuvre as the sea around them boiled as round after round plunged into the ocean. Huge waves began to crash down on the embattled warships.

"Ah Sh..." he exclaimed as, like ripples on a pond after a pebble is dropped, the waves expanded out.

Mike dived back into the shelter of his little raft, he looked at the little motor but there was no way he'd be able to outrun those waves so he just sealed the opening and held on. Seconds later his little craft was lifted and thrown as the first wave hit. He held on grimly as the turbulent waves flipped and tossed his raft as if in a tumble dryer, around him his few pieces of equipment flew about. He grabbed the sword and lashed it down afraid its sharp point would rip through the rafts skin. He managed to get it tied down and looked around for the next piece of equipment when a particularly violent wave lifted the boat before crashing it down. He grabbed the motor but as he turned the metal escape kit bounced up cracking him on the head. Unconscious, Mike flopped around like a rag doll as the life raft rode out the tempest.

Chapter 17

Mike had no idea how long he'd been unconscious but when he came to the sea was once again calm. Groggily he realised he was lying in a pool of water, fortunately, he was still wearing his combat suit which as well as being proofed to withstand a vacuum was also waterproof but the realisation there was water in his boat snapped Mike fully awake. There was at least an inch of water in the raft, a quick search revealed a couple of tears in the walls of life rafts shelter but thankfully the hull appeared to be intact. There was a small repair kit attached to the hull so repairing the tears shouldn't be a problem. Mike opened the escape kit, noting a big dent in its side, and took out a cup which he used to bail the water out. The case also contained a small first aid kit, a water canteen, satellite telephone complete with GPS tracker, a flare pistol, some desalination and water purification tablets plus a handful of ration bars. There was an empty space where the binoculars had been. Looking around Mike saw them lying in the bottom of the boat.

Picking them up Mike went back outside and scanned the horizon, there was no sign of the American task force or of any land. He was adrift in the middle of the ocean. He went back inside and as he put the binoculars back in the case, he noticed some dried blood on them. There was a small mirror on the side of the first aid kit. "No wonder I've got a massive headache," he said to himself. There was a good size cut on his scalp and dried blood matted his hair. Using the mirror, he managed to put a dressing on the cut.

Mike picked up the satellite phone and scanned the frequency bands but no one seemed to be transmitting. He checked the GPS on the phone to see where he was. The small device quickly pinpointed his position, "Ok, so I'm about three days from the base, three and a half from St Theresa." He mused. He re-set the phone to scan again but still, the airwaves were silent. He sat for a moment thinking, he could send a message himself but if the aliens were scanning for signals it would give his position away. He knew where he was and the lifeboat had both a sail and the small motor so while it would take time, he could get back to base. By now his head was really starting to pound, he looked at the small sail but decided just to use the motor for now. Picking it up he climbed back outside and set it onto the hull, steering himself onto the right course he set the motor running and climbed back inside.

Starting to feel worse, he looked at his meagre supply of medicines and rations thinking, "I've got to make this last at least till I get back to base," making his decision Mike went back out and filled his canteen with seawater and put in a purification tablet. He then took some painkillers and had a ration bar before exhaustion finally took him and he fell into a deep sleep.

Mike woke the following morning to bright sunshine, he still felt a bit unwell, "probably a concussion." He said to himself. He ate another ration bar and took some more painkillers and waited a while for them to take effect before taking stock of his situation.

Starting to feel a bit better Mike checked the GPS on the satellite phone, his luck had held during the night as the small motor had pushed him along in generally the right direction but the small unit's power supply was nearly drained. That shouldn't be too much of a problem as the life rafts small sail had a solar power patch built-in. Deciding he'd be better doing as much physical work as he could now while the painkillers were still working, he set about putting the sail up making sure to attach the solar panel at the same time. To his delight, the solar panel had several small attachments including charging points for his motor and satellite phone, a light and a small filament coil which he could use to heat water in his cup.

Raising the sail and setting his equipment up alone took much longer than he had originally thought but eventually he was set. Mike sat heavily, exhausted, he was surprised at how quickly he had tired but put it down to the concussion and the fact his body had been used to lower gravity for several weeks.

He looked longingly at the ration bars but he'd already had two and there was no telling how long he'd have to make them last. Rifling through the ration box he found some freeze-dried sweet tea. Mike normally preferred his tea unsweetened but, in this case, the sugar would help keep him going.

While he sat Mike glanced up at the sky and his heart stopped. There up above him, contrails from aircraft lined the sky. Mike quickly grabbed his binoculars and scanned the sky. There, a couple of miles away several aircraft flew in formation. Mike dialled up the magnification but as he reached for the flare pistol hope died in his chest. The aircraft were alien attack ships and some other class of craft he'd not seen before. He checked his GPS, he couldn't tell exactly where they had come from but by their course, they were headed to St Theresa. Over the next couple of days, Mike kept a wary watch on the sky but he didn't see any more aircraft or any ships but on the morning of the third day he spotted land. Dialling his binoculars up to their highest magnification he scanned the island that held Damocles base, he was on the wrong side of the island to see any of the bases surface buildings but wisps of smoke seemed to rise from several areas. As he got closer his concern mounted as he began to make out small craters in the side of the mountain and debris from rock falls. With a sense of foreboding, he suddenly realised where the alien aircraft he had seen a couple of days ago must have come from.

Mike decided to try and land his raft on this side of the island rather than sailing round to the base's main jetty. If the Alien's had indeed captured the base it would be far safer to approach on foot from this side of the island. Fortunately, there was a small beach a little further along the shoreline which he could use. Gunning the small motor Mike brought the life raft through the surf to the beach, climbing out he dragged his small craft the last few feet up onto the sand. Sinking to his knees Mike slumped against the side of the raft exhausted. As he lay catching his breath, he realised how quiet the island was. While he was based here, he had walked around the island numerous times, normally it was home to several species of birds and other small animals who gave a constant background noise of calls and movement but now all was silent.

As he sat catching his breath Mike considered his next move. He had to get into the base that was certain. Even if it had been fully evacuated there was a good chance, he would find supplies and equipment he could use, he might even find a working radio he could use to call for rescue.

The problem was the base had obviously been attacked, it may even have been taken over by the aliens. If he just walked up to the bases main entrance he risked being captured or judging by the aliens' actions in orbit more likely just being killed. So, heading for the main entrance was out of the question, even secondary entrances that led to the recreation areas and lookout posts would be risky. However, as well as the bases main entrances Mike knew there were three emergency escape tunnels that came out at several points around the island. The nearest one was just under a mile from the beach on the lower slopes of the Volcano. Making his decision, he pulled himself up and grabbed the sword and flare pistol from the raft before slowly making his way inland.

Slowly he climbed up the lower slopes of the mountain, picking his way silently through the undergrowth until he found the camouflaged hatch which covered the tunnel. The island had obviously suffered from some bombing as the area around the hatch was covered in broken foliage and debris from further up the mountain. Carefully he examined the hatch to see if it had been opened recently but after several minutes of checking he was sure the hatch hadn't been disturbed. Satisfied it was safe he set about clearing the debris off the hatch.

Opening the hatch Mike climbed into the tunnel and cautiously made his way towards the base. The bombing had clearly caused damage in the tunnel, debris littered the floor and several of the emergency light fittings were down but thankfully there was enough light to see by. Moving as quietly as he could, ears straining he listened for any sign of life. Eventually, he came to the end of the tunnel, the inner hatch was still shut so again he listened for any sign of movement on the other side. Carefully Mike turned the wheel to unlock the hatch but as it opened his stomach churned, the putrid stench of rotting flesh filled the air.

Gagging Mike shut the hatch and retreated a few steps to clearer air. Calming himself he undid his suit, stripping off the top half he revealed his shirt. Taking his knife, he cut off both sleeves, putting one in his pocket he fashioned the other into a bandana which he tied around his nose and mouth. Pulling his suit back on he looked at the hatch, dreading what he might find on the other side.

Deciding he couldn't wait for any longer Mike returned to the hatch and opened it. The scene before his was just as bad as he feared. Bullet holes scored the walls, there were blast patterns where grenades and heavier ordinance had been used. Several bodies lay scattered along the corridor. Mike didn't look too closely at them as it was clear scavengers had already visited the base. Slinging the sword onto his back, mike paused just long enough to pick up a fallen assault rifle and some spare magazines before moving on.

The fact animals had ventured into the base probably meant the aliens hadn't occupied it a small part of his mind reasoned but it wasn't something Mike was prepared to take for granted and he cautiously made his way to the control room.

The control room when he reached it was a scene of utter devastation. It was clear this was where the base crew had made their final stand.

Consoles and screens where shattered by the high calibre rounds which it seemed came from the aliens' weapons. More bodies littered the floor but thankfully none of the scavengers had made it this far into the base. Mike picked his way into the control room checking the consoles to see if any still worked when something caught his eye. Over to the side, part of the wall had come down covering a body but something about it drew Mike over. Carefully he began clearing the rubble first uncovering an arm. Mike suspicions were quickly confirmed, the material covering the arm was unlike anything he's seen, it had a soft plasticky texture but instead of being one smooth piece it was linked in plates or large scales. He kept clearing until eventually, he uncovered the creature's head. It wore a helmet that should have covered the head but the faceplate was missing, whether it had been removed or lost when the wall came down Mike couldn't tell but rolled the creature over to see it's face.

The alien's skin that Mike could see was pale, smooth and hairless, it had two eyes but they were like the multifaceted eyes of a fly, slightly larger than humans and elongated running back towards the side of the head. He couldn't tell if the alien had external ears but instead of a nose, a bony protrusion ran down the centre of its face with what may have been six nostrils, three on either side. The mouth was longer than a humans in roughly the same place but the alien had no chin as such. He couldn't tell how many arms and legs the creature had as most of it was still covered in debris but the one arm he could see looked like it was jointed with an elbow but instead of a hand, it looked like the arm ended in a large claw or pincer.

"You are one ugly fucker!" Mike said to himself as he studied the dead alien.

"Is someone there?"

Mike spun round grabbing his rifle

"Who's there?" he demanded

"Water." The voice begged weakly

Rising Mike moved quickly toward the voice, he rounded a shattered console "Rachel?"

Lying propped up against the console Commander Rachel Sinclair looked weakly up "Who?" she asked

"It's Mike, Rachel." He said kneeling next to her. Mike could hardly believe the flight control officer was still alive, Alien bullets had shattered her body.

Cradling her head, Mike gently put his canteen to her parched lips. "It's ok Rachel, I'll get you to sickbay he said. As she gratefully sucked the water down.

"No, too late." She whispered

"What happened here?" he asked

"We saw you go down, thought you were dead, The Admiral ordered us to evacuate but the alien's attacked before we could all get out."

"Did anyone get out? The Admiral?"

"The Admiral's dead, some got out, not many. Tried self-destruct but damage…." She trailed off

"Come on let's get you to sickbay," Mike said gently

But Sinclair urgently grabbed his hand, "Mike listen, they took prisoners, Professor Sahota, a few others, can't let them get our tech.." she finished weakly slumping back.

"We'll find them, let's just get you sorted first." Mike soothed but she didn't reply "Rachel?" he said before reaching for her neck but it was too late, she was gone. He just sat holding her lifeless body to numb for anything else for a time. Eventually, the sun began to sink and Mike roused himself. "If Rachel survived this long there might be others" He got up and searched the base calling out as he went but no one answered. After what seemed like hours Mike returned to the control room, Sinclair had said they tried to set the self-destruct but the console was damaged. Mike opened it up and found a bullet had severed several wires. Opening another console Mike tore out some long wires and using a tool on his utility knife he quickly repaired the self-destruct. Setting the timer for 30 minutes he made his way down to the small base jetty where he had found a small skiff. Dropping some supplies into it he cast off and set sail towards St Theresa. He was a couple of miles out when the self-destruct detonated, it was a fuel-air bomb and as it ignited it sent flames throughout the base making a funeral pyre for those who had fallen. A mighty explosion tore the night but Mike never looked back.

Chapter 18

"This is the BBC world service. Allied forces are continuing to resist the alien invasion across the globe but casualties both civilian and military continue to rise. Many of the world's major cities have been confirmed as being partially or completely destroyed by alien orbital bombardment. In America, there is still no news on the fate of the President after air-force 1 was lost from Radar during the destruction of Washington.

In Europe, Allied NATO and Russian Federation troops have successfully repelled a landing by Alien forces in Eastern Europe but other alien landings still continue to gain ground.

In Asia.."

Jeremiah turned the radio down and signalled for Sam and her mother to follow him. They had evacuated the plantation just in time moving everyone into the caverns under the mountain. They were well protected from any bombing and the clan watched for anyone approaching either by land or air from several vantage points.

"They are covering up how bad things are, aren't they?" Sam asked.

Her Uncle sighed, "Yes, these aliens have the advantage of being in orbit, no matter how many times they are defeated or held on the ground they can just drop their bombs from space."

"Why don't the world governments fight back? They must have hundreds of missiles they can fire at them." Pegra demanded as she and Marcus another council member followed them.

Jeremiah frowned at the interruption but it was Sam's mother Sheena who replied: "I don't think they can have many left, you saw the flashes in the sky before the invasion, they must have put all their nuclear missiles into space to fight the alien's there."

"You think they knew that long ago and said nothing to anyone?"

"Mike knew, he must have done, that's why he told me to get the caverns ready," Sam said

"That must be what the base was for, and all the 'satellite' launches." Sheena added "It wasn't to try and find us, it was to fight the aliens"

Jeremiah nodded "I agree, but the question before us now is what do we do?"

"Do?" Marcus demanded "what do you mean, do? We keep to ourselves and watch as we always have. This confusion is just what the Cabal has been waiting for. We must remain vigilant, protect ourselves."

"Hide ourselves away while the planet is invaded, while millions of people are slaughtered? Is that what you want?" Sam demanded in disbelief.

"They are not our people; the Cabal have hunted us for centuries. Have you forgotten what they did to your own father Samantha?" Marcus retorted.

"They are not all like the Cabal, Marcus. We have always had many friends among them, people who have put their own lives at risk defying the Cabal to protect us. And let us not forget, they may not be our people, but this is our world also." Sheena interjected. "Do you think these Aliens will treat us differently when they discover us? And they will discover us eventually." Turning to her brother-in-law she continued "Jeremiah, you ask what we should do, our land, our world is threatened. I cannot say how but we must defend it."

Jeremiah stopped and studied his advisors. Sam opened her mouth to speak but her mother put a cautioning hand on her arm. Chuckling ruefully Uncle said "As always my advisors counsel opposite points. And as always both are right."

"The council of elders." Pegra began but Jeremiah cut her off.

"This is too big for the council of elders, too big for the Clan to decide alone. I must contact the other clans." He decided. Turning towards a smaller cave a shout stopped them all

"Uncle!"

Sam looked around and Neville one of the clan's younger men came running up.

"Uncle, the aliens have attacked St Theresa, they appear to be searching for the American and British Sailors who made it there after their ships were destroyed."

"Many of our friends are with the sailors, they are helping with the wounded, we must do something Uncle!" Sam said urgently

"Very well, Samantha, you know those helping the sailors best, take Neville and three others, the lower caverns run deep into the mountain, they should be large enough to hide them. Sheena, I want you to begin setting up prides and begin patrolling the forests around the mountain. We will need as much warning as possible if the Aliens come this way. Pegra, I want you to organise parties to clear anything that might be seen from the air or give clues that we are here. Marcus, summon the council for tonight, we will meet in the judgement chamber."

"What will you be doing Uncle?" Pegra asked

"I have a number of calls to make." He finished striding away.

Sam turned to Neville, "Brad, Trevor and his sister Tina were with me earlier, they can come with us." He offered.

Sam looked at her mother who nodded. "Ok let's get them and get going she said but the rolling thunder of an explosion far off interrupted them.

They all looked to the Horizon as smoke rose into the sky from the direction of the base.

"Lieutenant, come back inside, it's not safe!" Sergeant Laurence hissed

Kerry Lightningblood ignored the local police officer as she scanned the horizon "Did you hear that explosion?" she asked

"Another explosion? I thought it was thunder, but whatever it was it's not safe to stand outside." Laurence said stepping up beside the American pilot.

"No that was definitely an explosion but it was a long way off," Kerry said as she turning to go back into the shelter but a movement in the trees caught her attention. She stopped and peered into the undergrowth.

"It must be the Alien's I got a message saying they are searching the island again. A small village on the other side of the island was hit this morning." Laurence said when she noticed the pilot had stopped. "What is it?"

"Do you have bears on this island?"

"Just get inside Lieutenant please!" Laurence urged.

Kerry followed the sergeant back into the shelter where a group of shipwrecked American sailors along with a few survivors from the British base were being cared for by the St Theresa islanders. Kerry knew there were three other small camps like this scattered around the island. There were just over forty sailors here, many of them wounded. "a couple of hundred survivors all told from over four thousand." She thought grimly

"Did you see anything out there Lootenant?"

Kerry looked over at the voice, on a makeshift bed a wounded sailor propped himself up on his remaining arm. She walked over and squatted next to him aware that other sailors nearby listened in. The sailor's uniform was scorched but she could still make out his name tag.

"Ranelli isn't it?" she asked

"Yes ma'am, Will they send anyone to pick us up, you know, with the aliens an all."

"I'm sure they'll try but it might be a while before they can. In the meantime, we'll just have to look out for ourselves with the help of these people here." She said.

"Who's that?" one of the other sailors asked.

Kerry looked over to the entrance where four strangers had appeared. Sergeant Laurence was talking to a young woman who appeared to be their leader. Kerry got up and walked over to join them, as she approached, she thought the young woman looked familiar but she couldn't quite place her.

"Lieutenant Lightningblood, this is Miss Selkie from the plantation in the mountains,"

"You're Mike James's friend, Samantha, isn't it?" Kerry said

"Lieutenant, I'm glad to see you." Sam replied, "I was just telling the Sergeant I need to speak to your senior officer."

"Well Lieutenant Commander Salah is over there but he's not regained consciousness yet so until he does that just leaves me and Sergeant

Laurence running things here. I heard there were some other officers in the other camps but they're scattered around the island."

Sam nodded "Sergeant, do you know where these other camps are?"

"Yes, we've set up a network of volunteers helping any sailors we find and hiding them."

"Good work Sergeant but I'm afraid we're going to have to move you."

"I've heard the Aliens are searching the island hunting for any survivors from the ships." Laurence replied, "We've tried to hide the camps as best we can."

"I'm sure you did the best you could but we found you easily enough and before you say it, yes we are different, but we don't know what capabilities these aliens have."

Laurence nodded unhappily.

"So, what do you suggest Miss Selkie?" Kerry asked

"There are a number of caves and caverns that run deep under the mountain, that's where my people are living at the moment. There are plenty of empty caves that we can hide you in. they're deep enough that any radar or scanning equipment these aliens have won't find you." Sam told them.

"Ok, that sounds good but how do you propose we get our people there? we've got a lot of wounded to move and with the alien's searching the island they're bound to spot us."

"We've thought about that when you're ready to move my uncle has arranged for a series of diversions which should keep the aliens busy long enough to get everyone to safety."

"It's a very generous offer Samantha but no disrespect and all but you're civilians, do you have the training for this?

"Don't worry about that Lieutenant, you wouldn't believe what Miss Selkie's people can do." Laurence put in.

Kerry looked at the two islanders uncertainly.

"I trust Miss Selkie and her people Lieutenant," Laurence said quietly.

"Ok, I don't see there's much choice. What do you need me to do?"

"I need to know the locations of your other camps. My friends will go to them and get them ready. Then we need to get everyone ready as quickly as possible so when my uncle's diversions begin, we can move."

Laurence told Sam where the other camps were and roughly how many sailors were in each one. As her friends headed off to the other camps Sam said

"Thank you, Lieutenant, I know it's a lot to take on trust but we'll do our best for your people. I need to go back and tell my uncle what we've said and help to make final preparations. When everything is ready, I'll send one of my people to you. Be ready to go when they get here."

"Okay, thank you Samantha, and it's Kerry."

Sam smiled "Stay safe Kerry and hopefully, I'll see you soon."

"God willing, good luck Samantha." Kerry finished as Samantha and her friends disappeared into the forest.

Mike slashed at the undergrowth with his sword as he made his way inland from the small cove, he had managed to beach the Skiff on. It had taken him a little over two days to reach St Theresa in the small boat and a further five hours to find somewhere secluded to come ashore. He'd reasoned that like the base, if the aliens had taken the island over, then landing at the port was out of the question. The island did boast a small tourist trade with several beaches and hotels by the sea so he'd decided to sail around the coast of the island and see if he could find a secluded bay or small beach to bring the skiff into.

That had been several hours ago and now as the sun climbed its way to midday, he decided to take a break. He'd been able to make a good mile inland before the undergrowth had become too thick for him to just walk through so he hoped if anyone found the skiff his course wouldn't be too obvious. Sitting Mike unwrapped a ration bar and began to eat. As he chewed, he dug out his satellite phone and brought up a map of St Theresa. He needed to make contact with any UN forces fighting the aliens and his best chance of doing that was through the islanders. He knew there were a few small villages and Sam had mentioned her family owned a plantation in the mountains but he didn't know their exact locations. If the aliens had occupied the island, then that probably meant they would be in the main town by the harbour but that was still his best option of making contact. Finishing his ration bar Mike checked his sat-nav once more before making off toward the distant town of St Theresa.

It was the noise of breaking branches and heavy fast movement that first alerted him trouble was coming. Crouching down in the undergrowth Mike listened to the crashing sound, it seemed to be coming from his left, not coming toward him exactly but more parallel to him. There was a clearing coming up just ahead and whoever or whatever was making the noise seemed to be heading for it. He quickly made his way toward the clearing; he was almost there when he heard the unmistakable sound of heavy calibre gunfire. Ducking behind some small trees Mike readied his assault rifle.

The crashing quickly grew louder then several large animals burst out of the trees at the edge of the clearing, at first Mike thought they were dogs, he was sure one of them, the red-furred animal looked familiar, but the larger creatures that quickly followed must be bears. Two of the larger 'bears' stopped and crouched down by the thickest trees waiting.

"Don't stop you stupid animals, keep going." Mike silently admonished.

But just then three alien soldiers charged out, seeing the bears in the open they paused, raising their weapons. It was the moment the two 'bears' had been waiting for, with a roar that momentarily froze the blood in Mike's veins they leapt on the Aliens. The first 'bear' smashed into one of the aliens, it almost looked to Mike like it picked the alien up and threw it into one of the others. The second bear just reared up and slashed the third alien with its claws. The aliens went down quickly, high pitched squeals coming from them as they fell, it was the first sound Mike had ever heard them make.

With the Aliens down the two bears turned and ran after their fellows but more aliens were following, two charged out of the forest just in front of Mike, they both stopped and opened fire, with a scream of pain one of the bears went down, his fellow stopped and ran back. More high-pitched noises came from the aliens but this noise was unmistakably laughter. They raised their weapons again taking aim. The first alien shot the bear running back in the shoulder to wing it while the second put a round in the wounded bear's other leg.

A cold rage seemed to grip Mike, M'Benga murdered as he tried to negotiate, Aleshco and Zhang Mi along with all their crews, Archibald, Admiral Greene and Rachel Sinclair with the crew of the base. Now, these Aliens laughed as they tortured helpless animals. "NO!" Mike cried through gritted teeth. Unsheathing his sword, he charged into the two aliens.

Hearing a noise behind the first alien turned to see Mike crashing out of the undergrowth. It tried to swing its gun around but Mike lunged, thrusting his Rapier through the Alien's chest. he lashed out with his foot kicking the second alien in the middle as it also turned. Pulling his sword free he thrust again slicing the second alien through the throat.

In the clearing the rest of the 'bears or dogs' whatever they were had all rushed back to their injured fellows, To Mike surprise, they seemed to have managed to pull the wounded 'bears' onto the backs of a couple of the other larger animals when more aliens emerged from the forest. Dropping his sword Mike brought his assault rifle up and opened fire. with his first burst two of the aliens went down, he was sure one was a solid hit but the second was just winged. Seeing him as the major threat the remaining aliens ignored the bears and turned their weapons on Mike.

Diving flat behind a fallen tree, Mike returned fire as best he could. He glanced over at where the bears were now running for the forest, "Keep going guys I'll cover you as long as I can." He said quietly. Quickly looking around Mike saw there were a couple of other fallen boughs, he might just be able to make his own escape that way. The aliens that had come out of the forest were all on the ground or crouching behind tree's so Mike fired off several quick bursts to keep their heads down. He was just readying himself to move when a loud yelp made him look around.

Two alien soldiers were creeping up behind him, seeing Mike turn they both rushed him. Spinning over Mike lashed out kicking one where a knee would be on a human, the alien screamed but threw itself onto his legs. Mike tried to bring his rifle up but the second alien kicked it away. He desperately reached for his sword but he cried out in pain as the alien stamped on his outstretched arm. He looked up just as the butt of the alien's weapon crashed into his head. As darkness washed over him the last thing Mike saw was the red-haired dog being shoved into the forest by two of the bears.

Chapter 19

Sam paced furiously up and down the 'council chamber'

"Sit down Samantha you are exhausting me just watching you," Pegra said

Sam turned to rebuke the older woman but the look of concern on her face stopped her

"We are all worried about uncle but pacing and stressing will not help. Calm and centre yourself."

Sighing Sam took a seat next to Pegra and looked around the table, as well as Pegra there was Marcus, another elder. On the other side of the table sat Sergeant Laurence who had become the de facto head of the islander's resistance. Next to her were Kerry and another American officer, a Commander named Rosenburg.

Sam stared at her hands clenched on the table deep in thought when she felt a gentle touch on her arm. She looked up and Pegra said gently "I know you are worried Samantha but your uncle is strong."

"I know but it's not just uncle I'm worried about."

"What is it, child?"

Sam thought for a moment, "After Uncle was shot when the aliens were chasing us, someone ambushed them. I saw him attack the two who shot uncle and Derren then he started shooting at the main group following us. It was my friend Mike; I know it was."

"He saved you all?" Pegra asked

At the sound of Mike's name Kerry looked over but before she could say anything the curtain across the entrance to the chamber opened and Sheena came in followed by Gareth, the clan's physician.

Seeing the concerned looks Sheena announced. "They are both out of surgery, Gareth can you explain?" she asked taking her own seat.

Taking his own seat tiredly Gareth took a second to compose himself. "As Sheena said they are both out of surgery. I managed to get all of the bullets out of both of them. Although he was hit more than once, Deren is young and strong, I expect him to heal quickly."

"What about Uncle?" Marcus asked impatiently.

Gareth looked across at his fellow elder "The wound to his shoulder was very deep, as I said I removed all of the bullet fragments but several large blood vessels were damaged and he lost a great deal of blood. Given time I believe he will recover but we have to remember he's not a young man anymore."

"Thank you, Gareth," Sheena said when he'd finished "so the question before us, is what do we do now?"

"Uncle is going to be laid up for some time, we need to decide on a Regent." Pegra said she paused for a moment before continuing "Sheena, it is no secret you and I have clashed many times in council, but I have always known you argue for what you believe is right and for the greater good of not only our people but for our friends and neighbours as well. I believe at this time we need a leader who can look to 'the greater picture' but will also listen to more cautious advice. I nominate Sheena to act as Regent until uncle is well enough to resume his position."

The clan elders looked at Pegra in stunned disbelief, none more so than Sheena.

"A woman leading the clan? It's unheard of!" Marcus gasped.

"Have you never heard of equality Marcus?" Pegra said evenly "Perhaps it is time the Clan joined the rest of the 21st Century."

"I agree." Gareth said, "It would be best if we showed a united front Marcus, but if you insist on a vote, I will also support Sheena."

Before Marcus could reply Sheena said, "If it is the will of the council I will stand as Regent until Uncle has recovered from his injuries when I will gladly surrender leadership back to him."

"And if Uncle cannot resume his position?" Marcus challenged

Sheena thought for a second "Then we will deal with that situation if it arises. Until then I, as an elder, sister of our chieftain and wife of his predecessor, will lead the clan.

Marcus looked mutinous but could clearly see he was outvoted so chose to keep quiet. "Good, that is resolved," Pegra said. "Now, Auntie!" Pegra said giving Sheena her new title. "With your permission, I believe Samantha has something she needs to say. I believe it may be a matter of Clan honour."

All eyes turned to Sam, Pegra gently patted her arm and nodded for her to continue.

"Mother, elders with your permission," she began before explaining about how they had been followed by the aliens after the diversion they had launched went wrong a lone individual had intervened, holding the aliens off so they could recover the two wounded men and escape. "The man who saved us was my friend Mike James, I know it was, and in keeping the alien's busy long enough for us to escape he was captured by the Aliens." She finished.

"By sacrificing himself, as has been pointed out to me before, the clan is in his debt, it is a matter of clan honour, Auntie, I submit that if we can help, we must," Pegra stated.

"Samantha, how can you be sure the aliens captured him alive?" Sheena asked

"I could see clearly, the alien hit Mike with the end of his gun if it wanted to kill him it would have just shot him."

While Sam explained what had happened Kerry whispered urgently to Commander Rosenburg.

"Can I just confirm, are you talking about Commander Mike James?" Rosenburg asked

"Yes, Mike James," Sam confirmed

"It's possible sir," Kerry offered "the last we heard Commander James ditched the Rapier a few miles north of the battlegroup before it was destroyed. If he had a life raft, he could have made it here."

"Damn, if they have got him that's bad," Rosenburg mused. "We haven't said anything about this to you before and it's not been public knowledge but we've known about these aliens for some time. A defence was mounted out in space."

"The flashes of light, they were nuclear missiles weren't they," Sheena asked.

"Mines powered by nuclear warheads but there were also several ships, one of them was a British ship, the HMS Rapier. Mike James was her Captain if they can interrogate him, it could be disastrous.

"If he's alive, how do we know they haven't killed him since he was taken, or even if it is this Commander James. We cannot risk more of our people on what-ifs." Marcus objected.

"As Pegra has said it is a matter of clan honour so we should try and help if we can," Sheena said cutting Marcus off. Then looking sadly at her daughter, she continued "However Marcus is also right, Michael could already be dead. I can't risk more lives without proof it's him and he's still alive."

"Excuse me, Sheena," Laurence interrupted "The aliens have taken a number of islanders to use as manual labourers. My people are still in contact with a few of them, we could make some enquiries, see if they've seen or heard anything."

"Thank you, Sergeant, yes please see if your people can find anything out. We'll wait for now until we hear from them. Now, we've all had a long day I suggest we take a break and reconvene in the morning." She finished rising. As the meeting disbanded Sheena noticed Marcus quickly leaving as Pegra approached her.

"I wonder if we might have some problems with Marcus." She mused quietly.

"Marcus is an old fool but we'll handle him if need be." Pegra said, "but you have other, closer, things to deal with first." She finished gesturing to Sam who still sat at the table.

Sheena squeezed Pegra's arm in silent thanks as she went to her daughter.

The first thing Mike became aware of was a heavy throbbing pain which seemed to fill his head. opening his eyes slowly he tried to look around but his vision was blurry and the pain in his head made the world seem to spin. He closed his eyes again but dizziness washed over, turning his head he was violently sick. When he thought he couldn't bring anything else up he let his head rollback. The violence of the nausea seemed to have exhausted him and darkness took him again.

Awareness returned with the muffled sound of voices, he couldn't quite make out what they were saying, confused he opened his eyes again, he still felt dizzy but after a few blinks, the blurriness of his vision cleared. He glanced around, he appeared to be sitting in a dark, stone walled room. The acrid stench of his own vomit assaulted his senses and he was almost sick again. He tried to brush the vomit away but he found his arms were tied down. He glanced down and saw he had been completely strapped to a raised seat. Slowly his memory returned the trek across the island, the fleeing herd of animals and his brief fight with the Aliens.

The voices seemed to be getting nearer, behind him Mike heard a door squeal open, he heard a click of a switch and a dim light came on, he closed his eyes and pretended to still be asleep. He sensed someone come up behind him, as they came closer, he heard them gag as the smell of sick hit them, a man from the sound of the voice. He expected to hear more but next, he felt competent fingers gently probing his head. wincing at the touch Mike opened his eyes.

Bending over to examine him was an older man, seeing Mike was awake he glanced fearfully behind Mike and shook his head microscopically. Taking this as a cue Mike remained silent. The man continued to check his head for a few moments before picking up a damp rag. He began by gently wiping Mike's head and face; Mike was surprised that when he pulled back the rag was covered in dry blood. He then wiped the sick off of Mike's side and finished by getting some more cloth and wrapping it around his head. When he finished, he gave Mike a last fearful look and left.

As the door closed Mike strained to listen but all he could hear was the sound of feet leaving. He waited a short while longer but no new sounds came to him. Opening his eyes again he looked around more carefully. His visitors had left the light on so he took the opportunity to take in more of his surroundings. The walls were made of large stone blocks but the floor was dried mud. It had the look of a storeroom. There were no windows and the blocks did look slightly damp so the room was possibly part of a basement. He remembered from the briefing material he'd read about St

Theresa that some of the older colonial buildings had had basements built for storage and as shelters from tropical storms.

Looking down he tried to move his arms to see if he had any room to try and wriggle free. He managed a small bit of movement but as he decided to try his bindings strength, he heard the door behind him open again. Before he could try and turn an alien strode around and stood in front of him, like the dead creature he'd found on the base, this one was helmetless, it's skin was still pale but had a ruddy tinge to it and he could make out a pair of what looked like iris's in the multi-faceted eyes. During the fight, Mike hadn't thought to examine the aliens in any way but now he saw that this alien was definitely 'man-shaped' with two arms and legs. It was slightly shorter than Mike with a long torso and short legs, the hands, and he could see now that they were hands and not pincers had six opposable fingers, three on each side. The alien studied him for a moment before barking an order, its voice was guttural and surprisingly quite high pitched but Mike didn't have time to try and analyse it as several other aliens seized him from the sides and behind.

He tried to struggle but the aliens quickly and expertly manhandled him out of the chair and attached his bound wrists to a chain and hook attached to the ceiling until he was standing on the balls of his feet with his arms above his head, the alien who had given the order once again standing before him.

"So that's your game is it?" Mike spat "Well good luck chum, I've been trained by experts."

The alien studied Mike for a few minutes, walking around him, then without warning struck him just under his ribcage, spinning him around. Mike cried out in surprise and outrage. Steadying himself with his feet still barely touching the floor Mike glared at his tormentor.

The alien studied Mike again, still circling him, this time when the blow came Mike managed to brace himself. "Is that the best you've got? I've seen schoolgirls with a stronger punch than that," he said still swaying "Though she was Captain of the University Rugby team." He finished with a rueful laugh.

The alien stopped in front of Mike and steadied him before raising his fist again, Mike braced himself for another punch but the alien stopped, tilting its head as it studied him. Then lowering its fist, it barked some more orders. Mike heard the door open and the rustle of chains, he turned his head to see and the third punch caught him completely by surprise.

He felt hands steadying him as he gasped for breath, by the time he could breathe normally the aliens had torn his flight suit open and were holding him steady. There were two small groups in front of him, the first was made up of what he took to be two technicians who seemed to be setting up some machine, they were uncoiling leads with suckers and clips attached which Mike really didn't like the look of but it was the other group that caught his attention. It was made up of two alien guards and one short human. The human had a chain around his neck and while his wrists were manacled the had enough chain to allow him to move his hands but it wasn't the chains that made Mike gasp. "Professor?"

Professor Sahota paused from his task and looked up "Commander.." he began but the guard next to him slapped him hard.

"Leave him alone you bastards!" Mike shouted and began to struggle even harder. One of the guards went to hit him but gripping the chain that held him to the ceiling Mike lifted his feet and in one quick motion kicked out, catching the guard in the chest. As the other guards charged in Mike lashed out with his feet catching another square in the jaw when Sahota suddenly cried out

"Commander stop, please they'll kill us both if you don't!"

Mike looked up, the alien who he thought of as the leader had the Professor on his knees, a weapon pressed firmly against the back of his neck. The alien just stared at him its threat more than apparent.

Lowering himself Mike opened his hands, palms outward in submission "ok chum, you win, just don't hurt him."

At Mike's submission the remaining aliens surged forward, one of the guards raised his rifle to hit him but the leader shouted something and the guard stopped but instead of lowering his weapon he kept it trained on Mike while the other aliens held him. Another alien, one of the technicians that had been setting up the first machine, came forward. Mike noticed this one was slightly different from the others, it had a longer body and seemed more slender except for just above its 'hips' where it bulged slightly on either side. Mike wondered if it could be a female? That is if these aliens had male and females, or possibly a different sub-species?

Ignoring him the technician began attaching the leads to his chest, side and back, he winced as clips pinched his skin when they were attached. With the last lead attached the technician double checked them all then said something to the leader. Apparently satisfied the leader let Sahota stand and then shoved him back to the unit he had been working on. Mike watched as the professor connected a piece of what was obviously alien technology to something that looked like an internet personal assistant device.

Looking directly at the leader Mike said "Ok professor, don't say anything just nod or shake your head. Are there any other survivors from the base here?"

Working slowly Sahota nodded slightly

"Ok has the UN surrendered?"

A shake

"Right, do they know what you did at the base?"

Another shake

"Good, try and keep it that way. I'm going to get out of here professor and when I do, I'll find you and the others and I'll get you out. Tell the others that, tell them to stay strong."

Seeing the professor had finished his task the alien overseeing him said something to the leader then grabbing the chain around his neck pulled him towards to door.

"Stay safe Professor," Mike called as the cell door shut. Looking back at the leader he said: "Ok chum, what game do you want to play now?"

The Alien leader once again paced around Mike, studying him. Mike braced himself but no blows followed. Instead, the leader said something to another technician who had replaced the Professor at the second piece of equipment. The technician replied and handed the leader a small device, watching Mike intently the leader spoke into it.

To his amazement, the personal assistant's synthesised voice suddenly spoke: "State your purpose." It said "so, you got the prof to build you a translator, clever," Mike replied

The leader said something to the technician who made some adjustments then the voice asked again "identify yourself."

"ok chum, here we go. Mike James, Commander, Royal Navy 5808376."

The aliens conferred briefly the "Where are the others who resist?"

"Hah, Sorry chum, I only just got to the island. I've no idea if and where there are any resistance fighters."

The alien leader stepped closer "You assisted those who resist. Where is their location."

"I told you I only just got to the island; I haven't seen anyone since I got here."

The leader said something to the first technician and liquid fire exploded through Mike's nerves. Surprised Mike screamed and his body shook as he writhed in agony then as swiftly as it came it was gone. Hanging limply, he tried desperately to suck in air.

"Lie," came the voice. "false and evasive answers will be punished. You were found when you assisted resisters. Where is their location."

Mike stared at the leader incredulously "You're mad! Those weren't resistance fighters; they were just a pack of wild animals."

The leader just gazed at Mike impassively as the fire came again.

Chapter 20

Samantha was down in the lower stores checking on what they had when Monique called her name. looking up she saw her friend waving her over.

"What is it, Monique?"

"Lieutenant Kerry sent me to get you. One of Sergeant Laurence's people has just arrived. He has some information about those taken by the aliens." She looked at the tablet in Samantha's hand "Here give me that I can finish here you'd better get going."

"Thanks," she said handing the tablet over as she quickly left.

Samantha raced through the maze of tunnels that linked the caverns that had become her people's refuge. These caverns had seemed so large but now they were beginning to get more crowded. Her people had been joined first by the survivors from the Navy ships then by refugees from some of the outlying villages that had been attacked by the Aliens. Thankfully those attacks had died down for now but who knew when the aliens would start them again? Samantha knew her mother was worried about that, there was room at the moment but they couldn't hide all the islands people and sooner or later their supplies would run out.

As she reached the level of the meeting chamber Samantha slowed her pace and her breathing, it wouldn't do to burst into the chamber panting. She reached the entrance and took a couple of calming breaths before knocking and entering.

The whole council of elders, Sheena her mother, Pegra, Marcus and Gareth were already seated. With a pang, she noted the empty seat that should have been her uncles. Also seated were Sergeant Laurence, Kerry and Commander Rosenburg, who had come to form an extended council for the settlement. Next to the Sergeant was a tired-looking man, a blanket had been draped over his shoulders and he held a cup of broth which he was sipping from. Samantha studied him quickly, his clothes were torn and grubby, his skin that she could see was scratched and bruised, whether it was from his trek through the jungle or ill-treatment she couldn't tell.

With the exception of the stranger, the whole council looked up as Samantha entered.

"Mother, council member's" she greeted "You wanted me?"

"Samantha, yes come and sit down." Her mother said gesturing to a seat next to her. As she sat Sheena continued "This is Mr Ramirez, until recently he was a captive of the Alien's in their compound at the old Governors Manor. Sergeant Laurence's people managed to help him escape and brought him here. I want you to listen to what he has to say."

All eyes turned expectantly to Ramirez who was still looking down exhaustedly into his cup. Laurence gently touched his arm and spoke quietly to him. He looked up nervously, suddenly aware that everyone's attention was on him.

"Mr Ramirez, I know you're very tired and I promise you are safe here and you will be able to rest soon but first, please we need you to tell us what you know," Sheena said gently.

Laurence patted Ramirez's arm reassuringly, looking around the table he asked: "What do you want to know?"

Sheena nodded to Rosenburg. "Firstly, Mr Ramirez I'd like to thank you for agreeing to talk to us." He began "Now what can you tell us about the aliens themselves? Do you have any idea about how many there are of them, what defences they've put in place for their base? Any idea of how many prisoners they have, civilian or military?" he asked

"The aliens? I'm sorry I can't tell you how many there are but it's lots, probably a few hundred. They look a bit like us but different. Their eyes." Ramirez shuddered.

"It's alight Jeremiah," Laurence interrupted him "We've seen them. How do they act, how did they treat you?"

"Oh, It's like to them we're nothing. At first, they just pointed and gestured, when we didn't get what they wanted, well let's say a good beating makes things clearer. They must be stronger than us cos after a few people died they started using these poles, like cattle prods. They were worse than the beatings but at least they didn't kill. Anyway, that was just at the beginning, there were some other prisoners there, American sailors and British from the base. One of them must have been a techy or something but he somehow managed to rig up a translation device using a computer and internet home device. After that they could just tell us what they wanted, didn't stop the prods but they only used them if they thought we weren't working quick or hard enough, or if they were just bored." He paused to take another sip.

"What about the other prisoners? The sailors, where are they kept? Are there any treated differently?" Samantha asked

"They've got a couple of big pens fenced in by some sort of electric razor wire, around these, they put up some walls with guns that can swing either in or out. They keep most of the sailors in one and us in the other. The only exceptions seem to be the techy and a couple of his assistants who are kept in the manor. Oh, and the new guy they brought in a few days ago. He was pretty badly beat up and they stuck him in the old food store in the basement. Mario, you know him, Sergeant, the chemist, he told me they took him down to treat the poor guy, he was in pretty bad shape to start with but after he cleaned him up Mario said he saw them taking down the tech with his translator and some equipment Mario really didn't like the look of. Like the prods but much worse."

"That's got to be Mike." Samantha said hurriedly "We've got to try and get him out of there."

"No, we must not!" Marcus interrupted. "The clan may owe him some debt but that debt cannot be paid at the cost of us all. To try and storm this base would be suicide."

"But mother, Pegra, we owe him." Samantha began but her mother raised her hand.

"Mr Ramirez, you've been there, are there any weak points or any hidden spots we could use to get into the base?" Sheena asked

Ramirez thought for a moment, "I'm sorry but I don't see how. They cleared the forest for a hundred meters all around the base, they got guns and guards all over. I managed to sneak away from a work party but even then, I wouldn't have made it if the Sergeant's people hadn't been waiting to meet me."

Sheena considered for a moment before looking sadly at her daughter. "I'm sorry Samantha but I have to agree with Marcus on this point. I can't risk the clan or any of our friends for just one man, no matter who that man is or what we owe him." She finished.

Samantha stared at her mother in shock, she tried to work her mouth and argue but her mother reached out and squeezed her hand.

"Thank you, Mr Ramirez, I think we've kept you long enough for now. It's time for you to rest and for us to think about what you've told us." Sheena finished. She glanced around the table once then at her unspoken command the council began to rise and leave.

Kerry looked around as everyone began to leave, Sheena was saying something to her daughter but Samantha just stared down at the table shaking her head. Over in the corner, she noticed two of the other members were talking quietly, the third Marcus had already left. Pegra called over to Sheena who saying a last few words to her daughter got up and went over to the other elders. Kerry watched Samantha carefully as the look of despair slowly gave way to one of determination. Quickly glancing over to where her mother was busily talking Samantha rose and walked briskly out of the room.

"Excuse me, sir, there are somethings I need to sort out," Kerry said quickly rising. Rosenburg who was talking to Laurence glanced up following Kerry's gaze he nodded

"Ok, keep me appraised if you need to Lieutenant." He replied waving her off.

Kerry quickly followed Samantha out of the door but she was already halfway down the corridor. "Hey Sam, wait up a second," Kerry called

Hearing her name Samantha looked over her shoulder, seeing Kerry hurrying behind her she paused long enough for the other woman to catch up.

"Say where are you off to in such a hurry?" Kerry asked.

"I've got to finish checking our stores." Samantha lied

"Yeah? Well, why don't I come with you and help?"

"No, I couldn't ask you to" Samantha began but Kerry interrupted her.

"Or you could just tell me what you're really planning and stop wasting both our times."

"Kerry, this is none of your concern," Samantha replied sharply.

Taking the other woman's arm Kerry led Samantha into a small room. "look, Sam, Mike is my friend too and if I let you go off half-cocked he'd never forgive me. Now I know that look, tell me what you're planning. I want to help."

Samantha looked at Kerry for a moment "you're right, Mike is the best friend I've ever had, he was closer than a brother to me and I'm not going to leave him to die in some cellar. If the council won't act, I'm going to get him, even if I have to dig him out myself."

"Ok, I get that, but have you thought how we're going to do that?"

For what seemed the first time in ages Samantha smiled savagely "I just told you, I'm going to dig him out myself."

"Where are the other creatures that resist." The translator's voice asked again.

"I told you, they aren't resisting, they're just animals, AAAHH!" Mike screamed as the fire came again. He flopped, hanging from his wrists. The alien commander had returned each day now for the past week, always asking the same questions.

As he hung the voice came again "You are all animals. You resist. Where are they."

"You need those bug eyes tested chum," Mike answered defiantly, bracing himself for the fire but this time pain didn't come. He looked up to see the Commander directly in front of him.

"I don't know where they are, I don't know where the humans on this island are. Get it through that thick skull of yours, I don't know and I wouldn't tell you if I did!"

The alien commander studied him then called one of his guards over.

"If you can't tell me where the resisters are, Tell me of this." He asked

Mike looked over the guard and his eyes widened in horror as in its hand it held the helmet from Mike's suit. Mike looked the commander in the face "Mike James, Commander, Royal Navy 5808376."

Mike started to brace himself but the guard behind punched him in the back, Mike gasped and twisted, The commander waited a moment while Mike bucked then struck him across the face. The blow caught Mike completely by surprise, blood began to fill his mouth.

"Speak of your warcraft, where are they." The commander grabbed Mike by his torn suit raising his fist. His mouth full of blood he spat it straight into the alien's face.

Letting go the commander flinched back leaving Mike once again to hang limply. Wiping his face, the alien picked up the control to the device. Mike watched, trying to brace himself as the commander made a show of placing a thumb on the button, it waited for a second longer then Mike screamed as the fire came again, but this time it didn't stop.

The sun was near to setting when Kerry made her way down to the spot where she'd agreed to meet Samantha. She carried a small backpack with water, ration bars and a small first aid kit as well as her holstered service pistol and a light assault rifle. She'd decided to get there a little early but as she cautiously entered the clearing, she heard her name being called softly. Turning she saw Samantha and two others standing just outside the clearing.

"Sam," Kerry said as she joined the others.

"Kerry, I'm glad you made it, you know my friend Monique of course and this is Neville."

Kerry nodded a greeting to her new companions "Are any of you armed at all? I've for a spare pistol and utility knife." She offered

"Thanks, Kerry but neither Neville or I need a weapon, besides if we have to shoot our way out, we've as good as failed," Samantha replied.

"I'd still rather you took something just in case." Kerry said "but if you're sure. We'd best get going."

"We're sure. Now this will be the best route to the old Governor's Mansion." Samantha said opening out a map.

Kerry watched Samantha sketch out the route "Ok, looks good but one of us should scout ahead in case there are any patrols out."

"Leave that to Neville and me." Samantha told her, then taking Kerry's arm she said: "You take the first stint, Neville."

Kerry tensed as she sensed Monique move behind her but her eyes widened in disbelief as Neville, stripping off his overalls began to change. Thick black hair sprouted all over his body, his jaw slowly extending as it formed a short muzzle his canine teeth extending to thick fangs. There was a loud click as his knees reversed and he went down onto all fours and moved off into the jungle. But it was his eyes that Kerry found most disturbing as they were the only thing that didn't change

Mike lay on the floor of his cell twitching spasmodically as the neurons in his nervous system, so abused by the alien torture device, fired randomly.

The last interrogation session had lasted for what seemed hours with the questions going backwards and forwards between local resistance and the spacecraft. The last shocks had been so severe he had blacked out. How long he'd been completely out he had no idea but when he came to, he had found he'd been cut down, he'd tried to move but the spasms had been too great and he'd been lapsing in and out of consciousness since.

Coming too again Mike tried to open his eyes, but only the left one seemed to be working. He couldn't tell if the right had been blinded or was just swollen shut. The room was pitch dark except for a slight glow around the door where light from the other side leaked through. He tried moving again, managing to move his fingers and his arm slightly but as he tried to move his head another wave of dizziness and spasms made him stop. Unable to do anything he just lay there until the spasms died down, he wasn't sure but he thought they were getting weaker and passing quicker. Taking a breath, he prepared himself to try moving again when a shuffling noise caught his attention. He paused to listen, there it came again, it seemed to be coming from behind him. He tried to move his head again but a touch on his leg made him look down. Climbing up his body was one of the biggest rats he'd ever seen, behind it Mike could just make out several more. Even to his pain addled brain, Mike knew the danger these creatures posed. Tensing he tried to knock the rodent away but all he managed to do was bring on another wave of spasms though this proved to be just enough as his shaking made the rats scatter.

As the tremors subsided Mike tried to roll but the continuous spasms had drained him leaving his muscles like jelly. Sensing his weakness, the big rat leapt back onto Mike's chest, desperately he tried to shake the rat loose, the other rodents seemed to take this as a sign and they surged forward but a low throaty growl from somewhere behind Mike made them pause. The one on his chest screeched its rage as a large shape suddenly landed next to him. The animal, whatever it was, seized the rat on Mike's chest in its jaws, the rodent squealed shrilly then there was a loud crunch as its spine snapped. Powerful claws lashed out shredding small bodies and scattering the other rats to the far reaches of the room. In the gloom, Mike recognised the auburn fur as the dog-like creature hurled the dead rat across the floor.

The creature seemed to stand protectively over him checking the floor for any more threats, Mike took a moment to look closer.

"Hello girl," he said quietly as the animal checked the area around him. As he spoke the creature seemed to glance up but otherwise ignored him as it finished checking the floor. He tried to follow the 'dog' as it moved but it disappeared behind him.

"Mike?" a voice said quietly

"Who?" he began but a figure appeared next to him. "Sam? How?"

but she shushed him as she gently probed his right eye, "Oh Mike, what did they do to you?" she muttered quietly.

"You should see the other guys." He joked but another wave of spasms wracked his body.

"Can you move at all?"

"They used an energy device, like electric shocks. I keep going into spasms but I can try."

"Don't worry, there's a small tunnel, I'll drag you."

"Sam," Mike started but Samantha had gone. He started to think he'd imagined things when he felt the animals muzzle gently touching his neck as she grabbed the back of his collar. He felt himself being pulled along the floor, he thought about trying to push himself along but the animal seemed quite strong so he just let himself go limp. The creature dragged him towards the back of the room but before they reached the back wall the animal let go of him. He let his head flop round and he could just see the animal's hind legs, but he quickly had to pull his head back and shut his eyes as dirt began to fly backwards where the 'dog' seemed to be enlarging a hole.

The dirt stopped flying so Mike opened his eyes again but before he could try and look, he felt the muzzle on his collar again and he was pulled towards the hole. He felt himself tip down and before he knew it, he was being dragged along a tunnel, the light beyond his feet disappearing quickly.

Kerry found herself sitting in a small clearing, she must have walked there in a daze she reasoned. Monique was half kneeling in front of her, she held Kerry's assault rifle and was watching her nervously.

"Lieutenant?" she whispered "are you ok now?"

Kerry looked at her rifle pointedly. Monique smiled "I thought I'd better carry it for you, you didn't look too steady on your feet." She said handing it back. "I know it can be a bit of shock, seeing them change for the first time."

"Thanks!!" Kerry said checking the weapon. "Where are the …. Others?"

"Neville is scouting around; Samantha has gone to find her friend." She said sitting.

Tightening her grip on the rifle Kerry's eyes darted around "Uh-huh." She replied.

"Samantha thought it would be best for just me to be with you when you came to," Monique told her.

"Why just you?" Kerry asked

"Because I'm not one of them, I'm like you."

"How do I know that?" Kerry asked

"Because I told you, why would I lie?"

"Well, you could be trying to trick me, to make me trust you." Kerry challenged.

"Lieutenant Kerry, they rescued you and your people, they've saved so many islanders and let you, let us live in their caves with them. They didn't have to do any of that. Why on Earth would you not trust them?" Monique asked earnestly

"Because they're… they're, what are they?"

"They're wonderful! Amazing! They're our friends. They came to our island and gave us so much. They've protected us even when others would hunt and murder them. And now they've protected you as well."

"But why, why are they helping us?"

"Because this is our world too!" a deep voice rumbled.

Kerry started and looked up as Neville stalked silently into the clearing.

"We may not be the same as you lieutenant, but Auntie is right. We must look beyond our differences, beyond the clan. These Aliens are everyone's enemy, we cannot just hide and watch anymore. You, all of the people of this world are our clan now." He finished earnestly.

Kerry just looked at him thoughtfully when there was a rustling noise and Sam stumbled into the clearing half carrying and half dragging Mike. Jumping to her feet she quickly made to help but Neville beat her to it gently taking the unconscious officer and lowering him to the ground.

"What happened to him?" Kerry demanded as Sam sat tiredly.

"They tortured him," Sam told them as Monique handed her a ration bar, "some sort of machine he said, like electric shocks but worse. Every time he tries to move his whole body seems to go into some kind of fit. I had to drag him through the tunnel then go back and seal it so they wouldn't be able to follow us."

"Damn, we're going to have to carry him all the way." Kerry said looking worriedly at the sky, "how long till it's light?" she asked

"Only two or three hours," Monique replied looking at her watch.

"I'll carry him," Neville offered "you can strap him to my back. We'll be able to move faster that way."

Sam thought for a moment "Ok but we need to go now." She agreed tiredly

Kerry watched in fascination as Neville, stripping off his overalls, began to change.

"I've only seen Samantha change a few times but it is always beautiful," Monique said quietly beside Kerry.

Kerry had to admit Monique had a point, she'd seen her fair share of werewolf movies but they bore no resemblance to the gentle creature standing before her now. The great bear-like creature turned to look at her but as she gazed into his eyes, she saw Neville looking back at her.

"Help me with Mike," Samantha called softly shaking Kerry from her thoughts

Kerry and Monique hurried over and between them, the three women lifted Mike onto Neville's back. Using Neville's overalls and some vines they securely strapped Mike down, Samantha folded some cloth and placed it under Mike's head to stop Neville's fur from getting into his face, fur that Kerry found remarkably soft.

"Are you alright with this?" Samantha asked Kerry as they finished

Kerry glanced at her "My folks are Cree, I grew up with stories about you people but I thought that was just what they were, stories." She said shaking her head. "Now I'm standing in the middle of an alien invasion, with a couple of living mythical creatures rescuing a spaceman. Huh, all we need now is a Wendigo to stroll out of the forest."

"oh, I told him to stay home, I didn't want to push things," Sam replied.

Kerry looked up sharply but at the other woman's half-smile she chuckled "You people!" she said shaking her head.

"It's almost dawn," Monique said, "Is it safe to try and get back to the mountain?"

"I was worried about that as well, but we at least need to get as far as we can," Kerry replied.

Sam looked up at the sky, "we still have an hour or so. There are some small caves not too far from here, we should be able to get there and wait till night to head back." She finished leading the way.

Chapter 21

With Neville carrying Mike, Sam led the group towards the small caves she had told them about. Kerry was surprised at how quietly they moved but unfortunately, there was no way of completely covering their tracks.

"Do you think they'll be able to track us?" she asked Sam quietly

"They will need to find where our tracks begin first. The tunnel I dug came out over two hundred meters from the tree line around their base and I made sure to cave in at least the first ten meters of it from the cell so they shouldn't be able to trace it that easily. The only problem will be what sort of tracking technology they have."

"You dug a tunnel over two hundred meters long that quickly?" Kerry asked astonished.

Sam grinned "Two hundred meters was a stretch but in our other form our women are good diggers, our natural instinct is to build a burrow to give birth in. Of course, now we normally have our kids in a hospital but the instinct is still there."

"your other form, man I'm still trying to get my head around this," Kerry replied but with a raised hand Sam stopped her.

Kerry watched as head cocked Sam stood silently then "We've got to move, there's an alien craft coming this way."

"Damn!" Kerry swore as they hurried to catch Neville and Monique.

"This way, quickly," Sam urged them all.

Unslinging her rifle Kerry hurried on behind the others looking to the sky. She expected to see an alien ship any second. Sure enough a few minutes later she heard the unmistakable sound of one of the attack ships. She stopped, scanning the sky but Sam called.

"Kerry, over here."

Turning Kerry saw Sam standing by what looked like an overgrown bush covered in vines. She pulled a handful of vines aside as Neville, now in human form carried Mike through the opening.

Kerry hurried over running through the entrance that Sam held open. Sam hurried in behind her gently lowering the vines, together they crouched silently as the attack craft came closer. They waited for what seemed an eternity but the alien craft seemed to keep going.

"Is it moving on?" Monique whispered but Sam silenced her with a gesture. Kerry strained to hear but the engine sound had disappeared, she looked quizzically at Sam but she still gestured for silence as another higher-pitched whirring sound made itself apparent. Kerry gripped her rifle tighter; she'd not seen one before but Sargent Laurence's people had reported the alien's use of three and six-wheeled ground vehicles that sounded like electric cars.

She watched Sam listening intently for any sign the aliens had found them but as the new sound began to fade, she began to relax.

With the sounds finally gone Kerry looked around but quickly looked back as the still naked Neville was taking his clothes back from Monique who was unknotting them.

"Don't worry, you'll get used to it," Sam whispered smirking at Kerry's discomfort before moving over to where Mike lay.

Sam checked his breathing, she put her pack under his head and began to gather fronds and leaves to cover him.

"Here, let me look at him," Kerry said beside her "We get basic first aid training in case we have to bail out behind enemy lines." She told her.

Kerry checked Mike's pulse and felt for a fever. "No fever, that's good, his pulse seems ok, his blood pressure might be a bit high but I can't check it accurately without the right equipment."

"At least he's stopped fitting," Sam said,

"Yeah, that would really take it out of him physically but he seems to be sleeping naturally now." Kerry agreed. "Now while we wait why don't you tell me about your people." She said settling herself down.

"I think we've shown you more than we should have already."

"Aw come on Sam, cut me some slack! You can't drop all this werewolf crap on me and not tell me the whole story."

"Well, first of all, we're not Werewolf's!" Sam snapped.

"Ok, well what are you then, it can't be that big a secret, seems everyone on this island knows already."

Sam sighed, "not everyone, just a few friends we trust, like Monique and her family."

"The Sargent?" Kerry asked

Sam nodded "but not everyone, we have to stay hidden, there are people who would hunt and murder us if they knew we were here."

"Who? The government?"

"No, we call them the Cabal. They are an ancient organisation with groups in pretty much every country around the world. They keep our existence secret but only so they can hunt us. The Cabal killed my father and many others over the years. Mike's parents helped us escape when the Cabal found us in England but they didn't know what we really were though I don't think it would have mattered to them if they did."

"But what are you exactly? I won't tell anyone about you I promise." Kerry finished.

Sam considered for a moment. "we, my people, are the Therians."

"Are you from here? The Earth I mean."

"Our legends say we came here from our own land which was destroyed by war. In your own legends, our land was Atlantis or Lemuria but if that is where we originally came from, I don't know. Our legends say the survivors fled in clans and settled in every continent where we encountered your people."

"Have your people always been…"

"Skin changers?" Sam asked, "Yes as far as I know it's what we've always been."

"It's incredible, you look so human."

"That's because we are human." Sam explained, "even in our other form, bones, blood organs are all human normal. The only difference is our skeletons are more flexible in parts, our muscle mass is more concentrated which makes us stronger and our hair follicles grow and retract but that's it."

"But you don't speak in your other form"

"We do but only in our own language."

"I thought it was an old childhood dream but it was you in my cell." A husky voice interrupted them.

The two women looked over to see Mike watching them through heavy-lidded eyes.

"Mike?" Sam asked

"Hey, Mike, you back with us buddy?" Kerry added.

"I saw you once when we were kids. I convinced myself it was a dream but it wasn't was it." Mike said to Sam "and then it was you following Engines and me that day in St Theresa."

"You knew?" Sam said taking his hand.

Mike nodded slowly, then letting go of her hand he pushed himself up into a sitting position. He sat back against the wall. "No spasms, well that's an improvement at least." He said half to himself. Then looking back at the women's concerned faces. "I'm ok, honestly, but I could murder a drink."

Kerry reached for the canteen on her belt, "it's only water I'm afraid." She said handing it to him.

Mike's hand shook slightly as he took it and Kerry went to help but he pulled it away and took a drink.

"that's better, thanks, shame you haven't got anything stronger though." He joked but when he handed the bottle back Kerry noticed the tremor in his hand was gone.

"The aliens know about you though." He told Sam "they kept asking about you, where you were but when I couldn't tell them anything... well, let's just say they kept trying to encourage me to."

"Kerry put the canteen back on her belt "Well we'll see what we can find you when we get back to the mountain." She said lightly

"I'll keep you to that, good to see you, Kerry. Nathan?" he asked

But Kerry shook her head, "we lost a lot of good people that day."

Mike looked down, "I'm sorry, Nathan was a good bloke. I wouldn't have made it if he and his flight hadn't turned up when they did. So, what's the plan now?" he asked

"Well, when night falls, we're going to head for the caves in the mountain where we're living," Sam explained.

"The caves? You stocked them as I told you to?"

Sam nodded "Yes, they've saved a lot of lives since this all started."

"Anyhoo, it's been a long night and most of us haven't been able to sleep through it." Kerry said pointedly "So I think we'd best get some rest. I'll take first watch then I'll get Monique to spell me. You and Neville need to rest more n us anyway." Kerry stated.

Mike looked at her questioningly but she just said: "We'll tell you later now get some sleep." She told them as she headed to the entrance.

Sheena sat at her desk, or rather Jeremiah's desk, checking over the inventory report on the levels of stores they had. She frowned at the level of detail. She'd asked Samantha to compile the report and the early part was definitely up to the standard she had come to expect of her daughter but the later parts were not as detailed, it was as if Samantha had passed the job to someone else to complete.

She'd asked Pegra to find Sam so she could ask her but that had been over an hour ago. Sighing she put the report aside, it would have to wait for now. She went on to the next item on her to-do list when a knock at the 'door' made her look up.

"Come in."

Pegra came in and sank heavily onto the chair opposite "Auntie"

"Pegra," Sheena interrupted her "we've known each other a very long time and frankly I find the idea of someone of your experience calling me 'Auntie' ironic in the extreme."

The older woman dipped her head and smiled slightly "Sheena" she corrected herself

"So, have you found my wayward daughter?"

"No, and I must confess it concerns me."

At Pegra's tone, Sheena looked up.

"No one has seen Samantha since late yesterday afternoon, nor it seems has anyone seen Lieutenant Lightningblood, Monique or Neville."

"You don't think...." Sheena began but Pegra interrupted

"I think she is very like her mother who made her way into a Cabal camp to snatch her dying husband and bring him home so he could die with dignity." She finished gently

Sheena looked silently at her hands, folding them to stop them shaking.

"Do you want me to send some pride's out to look for them?"

"No! the council decided we couldn't risk the clan being discovered. We still can't take that risk, even for my daughter." She finished.

"Mike, come on buddy time to wake up." Kerry's voice said

Mike opened his eyes groggily to see Kerry looking down at him.

"That's better, how are you feeling now?"

Mike sat up gingerly and stretched carefully. "Better." He replied

"Do you think you can walk? I'm sure we can get team wolf or whatever they are to help you if you need it."

Mike chuckled "They're not wolves that's for sure. And I know you're only joking Kerry but Sam is my friend." He said seriously. "And to answer your question, yeah I'm a bit stiff but I think I can walk. Is there anything to eat?" he asked

"Sure," Kerry handed him a ration bar and her canteen.

"Thanks." Looking around he noticed only Monique was in the cave with them. "Where are Sam and her other friend?"

"They're out scouting to make sure our alien friends haven't left any nasty surprises for us. They went out at dusk; they should be back soon."

"we'd best be ready when they do," Mike said finishing his ration bar, putting a hand on the wall he gingerly pushed himself up.

Kerry watched him carefully as he pulled himself slowly to his feet, ready to help him if he needed it. Still a bit shaky, Mike let go of the wall and grinned at Kerry saying "There that wasn't too bad was it." Then taking a breath he began to walk slowly around the cave. He managed to make almost a full circuit when there was a rustle at the cave entrance and Sam came in, already transforming back into her human form. Seeing Mike up,

Monique, holding Sam's clothes moved to stand in front of her. Taking that as a cue Mike turned to look directly at Kerry who managed to smother a snigger at the look of surprised embarrassment on Mike's face.

"I thought you'd seen her change before" She whispered.

"I was ten and it was only very brief," Mike whispered back

"Mike, how are you feeling?" Sam asked

Mike turned as she walked over tucking her shirt in, was that an amused look she shared with Kerry? He wondered but whatever it was soon replaced by concern as she searched Mike's face.

"I'm ok, honestly, I'm still a little stiff but walking around is helping." He told her.

There was another rustle at the door and this time it was Kerry's turn to avert her gaze. "So, did you find anything out there?" she asked Sam.

"We found some pieces of equipment; I don't know what they do but we've found a path through them. It'll add a bit of time to our journey but we should still be able to make it back before dawn. Mike, do you think you can walk on your own? Neville can carry you if you need him to."

"It will be my honour to carry you again Commander Mike, you saved uncle and my brother's lives," Neville said as he and Monique joined them.

"I'll be fine, honestly, and I'm glad your uncle and brother made it, they fought bravely." Then taking a breath he continued "I just want to thank all of you for getting me out of there."

"You're worth it," Sam said squeezing Mike's arm "but if you're ok, we'd better get going."

Picking up their meagre equipment they made ready to move. Mike took Kerry quickly aside "Have you got a spare gun?" he asked

"Sure," she said taking out her pistol and spare magazines before handing them to Mike.

Mike sorted them into the pockets of his flight suit then turning back saw both Sam and Neville had changed again and were waiting at the cave entrance. Nodding, Mike and Kerry followed them out into the forest.

"So, what are your plans now you're free?" Kerry asked quietly as they moved through the forest.

Mike looked sideways at her "At some point, I'm going back, there are still other prisoners from the base. Professor Sahota is one of them."

"Sahota? The guy who built.."

"The Rapier, yes." Mike finished for her. I don't think they realise who he is yet but they've got him doing techy work, it's only a matter of time before they put all the pieces together."

"Damn, but they must be more advanced than us, you sure it'll make much difference?"

"That's just it, they aren't that much more advanced. Sure, they can travel interstellar space but their ships weren't better than ours and our weapons were much better than anything they had."

They walked on in silence for a few more minutes when Mike stumbled, he saved himself from falling by grabbing a tree. He held onto it for a few moments while slight dizziness passed but as he went to move, he found Sam next to him holding his arm. "I'm ok," he started to say but another wave of weakness washed over him.

Kerry helped Sam lower him to the floor "We've made good time; we can afford to take a short break." Sam said. She quickly disappeared to get Neville as Monique came back to them.

Monique was handing out some dried fruit to go with the ration bars and water while Kerry checked Mike out as Sam and Neville returned. In deference to Mike and Kerry, they'd taken time to put some clothes on. Sam knelt next to Mike and Kerry "how is he?"

"They really put him through the meat grinder," she said, "I think it took more out of him than we thought."

"I'm fine." Mike replied defiantly "I just need to catch my breath, that's all."

The two women looked at each other grimly.

"Seriously guys, just give me a minute." Mike insisted

"So, are you really planning to go back and get your friends out?" Sam asked, "I heard you talking to Kerry." She said at Mike's look.

"I have to try, if they get the professor to talk it would be a disaster."

"It's a disaster already. Face it, Mike, they've won."

"No, they haven't, we've still got bases, troops and equipment that we're holding for when we're ready to fight back. But if they get the weapons technology in the professor's head it will all be for nothing."

"Are you sure? You haven't heard the radio recently, we have it's the same all over the world. They're taking over."

"But we're still fighting, aren't we?"

"Yes but."

"There are no buts Sam, we've got to keep fighting, all of us." He paused for a moment "Will your people help?"

Sam looked over at Kerry "I don't think so." She said sadly.

Mike looked questioningly at the two women

"The council ruled out doing anything that would risk the aliens finding our hideout," Kerry told him.

"But you're here?"

"Sam wouldn't leave you there, she was coming anyway, we just tagged along."

Mike squeezed Sam's hand "Thanks again, but surely not everyone was against doing something?"

"No, not everyone but there's some conflict among Sam's people, her mom had to play safe and compromise to keep everything together."

"You're mums in charge?" Mike asked

"She's regent until uncle recovers but Marcus, one of the elders, is very protectionist and a traditionalist, he doesn't believe women should have any power. He's got a good size following so she's got to try and keep him happy."

"Well, I'm just going to have to convince this Marcus and his followers. Come on, the sooner we get to the mountain the sooner I can start." Mike said standing.

Chapter 22

Sheena had tried to keep the search for Samantha and her friends quiet but unfortunately, Marcus had gotten wind of the search and wasn't happy.

"It is deliberate defiance!" He roared. "This council made a firm decision, no rescue attempts which could endanger the clan were to be permitted and yet Sheena, your own daughter seems to believe that council edicts do not seem to apply to her. If you cannot control your own offspring how do you believe you are fit to lead the Clan?"

Sheena listened to him rant, she glanced at Marcus's deputies who he'd insisted join him, clearly, they were enjoying the show.

"Marcus!" Pegra snapped "Show some respect, Sheena's is Auntie until uncle returns

"RESPECT! She cannot even lead her own family. But what can you expect from a mere female?" He spat.

"MARCUS HOW DARE YOU!" Gareth cried outraged

"I dare because it is the truth, only your liberal eyes are blinded to it. The decision was taken."

"Excuse me, Marcus," Commander Rosenburg interrupted "but the council decided no sanctioned formal rescue mission would be made but nothing was said about private individuals acting independently."

"Remember your place Commander, you are here on sufferance only. Besides, it appears you can no more control your females than she can." Marcus snapped derisively.

Rosenburg flinched as if physically struck but before he could reply a knock at the door interrupted him. Welcoming the interruption Sheena called "Come in."

A young woman entered "Yes Emily?" she asked but before the girl could answer five other people entered. "Samantha!" she gasped half rising.

"Mother, councillors." Sam began "I heard you were looking for us so I thought we'd best come here straight away."

"So, your wayward brat deigns to make an appearance. Well, 'Auntie' will you have her arrested or shall I" Marcus sneered.

"Arrested?" Sam replied taken aback.

"Marcus, you overstretch yourself." Sheena snapped "You have been rude and insulting to our friends and me. The commander has raised a good point which as leader I will consider in my own time. She said glaring at Marcus who just sneered back. "However, Samantha," she continued turning to her daughter, "you have acted rashly, possibly defying the council so until I have had time to consider ALL points," she continued looking around the table "you will return to your quarters until summoned. Neville, Monique, that goes for both of you as well"

"Mother, Neville and Monique just followed." Samantha began

"You have been dismissed, girl! Consider yourself fortunate it is your mother who dismissed you!" Marcus spat. Sheena just glared at him as he continued "Now next business."

But ignoring him Sam asked loudly "Mother, with your permission may we stop off at the infirmary for a quick checkup?"

"Of course you can, now you may go," Sheena replied. Taking a breath Sheena looked down at her agenda when a cough caught her attention. Looking up she saw Lieutenant Lightningblood and a bedraggled looking man still standing there. The man looked vaguely familiar; she searched his face realising who he must be. "Michael I'm very pleased to see you are alive and finally with us but anything you wish to say about Samantha will have to wait."

"Thank you, Mrs Selkie, but that's not why I'm still here. I believe Commander Rosenburg's is present as the senior military officer, Commander I know we share the same rank but I believe you are a logistics officer? so as the Captain of a warship I believe I am now the senior military officer? Especially as a British officer in a British overseas territory."

Rosenburg blinked in surprise and looked first at Mike then Kerry before saying slowly "Yes sir, I believe that would give you seniority. On both counts." He added rising to give up his seat.

"Thank you, Commander, Mrs Selkie, with your permission?"

"Of course, Michael, and you aren't a little boy at my kitchen table anymore so it's Sheena." She replied watching as Mike took the proffered seat and how Lieutenant Lightningblood hovered near him, clearly, he hadn't had a chance to recover fully from his ordeal.

Rosenburg went to leave but Mike stopped him, "Sheena with your permission I'd like both Commander Rosenburg and Lieutenant Lightningblood to remain as my advisors, they have a far better understanding of your set up here than I at the moment."

"Please Commander, lieutenant, sit," Sheena said eager to get the meeting back on track but a muttered conversation from Marcus's aids caught her attention.

Sotto Voce "That's all we need, another of these Endym scum polluting the air." "Don't worry by the looks of this one he'll be dead soon."

A gasp from Rufus showed he'd heard also heard as both he and Pegra glared at the aides.

"Marcus, you will keep your aide's in order or they will leave," Sheena told him.

"Marcus, ignoring the comment glared at Mike "If any should leave it is those who do not belong.

This is a clan council meeting; I do not believe any Endymion's are members of the clan."

"MARCUS!! Rufus gasped in outrage. But it was Mike's voice which caught everyone's attention.

"I must confess councillor, despite having grown up closely with Leader Sheena and her family I don't speak your language but from the reactions of your fellows, it seems to me that's not a word one uses in polite society. We have a saying where I come from that if you need to resort to insults and profanities you've lost your argument before you even start."

"I have no interest in what is said where you come from but as you are here 'Senior Military Officer' please regale us with your story. Tell us, why we are sitting in a cave under a mountain? Why your own people have to flee their homes and impose themselves upon us. Tell us why you failed our whole world."

Mike sat quietly for a few moments, then looking up he said: "do you really want to know councillor? Do you really want to hear how we went out there, out into space, seven ships and a few fighter pods to face an armada of thousands of alien ships? We were so few but we went out anyway. Do you want to hear how Professor Joshua M'Benga went out in an unarmed space plane to talk to them, to speak peace and how they butchered him and his crew? Do you really want to hear how they kept attacking and how we held for days, weeks and months? How many times we threw them back, a few of us dying each time but how the rest of us stood, fighting to protect you. Do you really want to hear names like Lieutenant Christine Archibald, General Brett Kaminsky, Commander Zhang Mi and her pilots, Commodore Victor Aleshco, Commander Alexander Timoshenko, Oberleutnant Hans Goering and their crews. The ships Yuri Gagarin & Georgi Zhukov who all died defending you and everyone else here. How they died protecting you, destroying dozens of the alien ships before they fell. How about people like Admiral John Greene, Commander Rachel Sinclair, Lieutenant Nathan Jameson and the hundreds of officers and sailors who died fighting the aliens in the first few hours of the invasion. Tell me Marcus do you really want to hear about how those of us with the courage to stand, fought and died?" he paused a moment then looking directly at Marcus, fire in his eyes he continued. "Or do you want to sit there, sneering at us while you complain about how you've been failed proclaiming that you and your people should stay here hiding. Abandoning the rest of the citizens of this world" as he finished he slumped back into his seat spent.

Silence greeted Mike's speech then after a few moments Marcus slowly began to clap. "Bravo Commander, how eloquently you excuse you and your people's failure. But all of your words do not excuse how your people with all your technology and military power have failed. For generations, the Endymions have at best shunned and worst hunted us. Sheena, you call yourself our leader and yet you seek to protect those who have murdered hundreds of us over the centuries, hundreds including your own mate." Standing he pointed at her "You are a traitor most foul!" turning to his aides he shouted, "Seize her and the rest of these traitors and our enemies!"

Mike looked up, while he'd been talking more than a dozen of Marcus's supporters had entered the room, now they quickly fanned out seizing the council members. Rough hands seized Mike, he tried to shake them off but the effects of his ordeal finally caught up with him and he slumped weakly. He tried to gather his strength when there was a roar followed by a pain-filled howl. Mike looked up and Sheena stood, half transformed, two of Marcus's followers standing back, one cradling a blood-soaked arm.

"If you are going to challenge me, Marcus, then come yourself, don't send children to do your work for you." Sheena snarled.

All eyes turned to Marcus "Challenge you? If you were a man, I would happily challenge but you are not worthy of such a trial." He sneered "but your treason must not go unanswered. I call the clan together to judge all of you." With that he let out a mighty howl, Mike felt his blood turn to ice as the howl echoed through the caverns.

As the sound died down Sheena, returning to her fully human form straightened her clothes saying "Very well Marcus, we shall let the clan decide but do not be so sure they will vote with you." Then calmly, gathering Pegra, Rufus and the human delegates she led them through Marcus's supporters out into the caves. Mike quickly made his way to her side "Is this a coup?" he whispered.

Sheena nodded "Marcus doesn't want to rule but he hates your people. He wants to send them back to their homes, to fend for themselves. And the only way he can do that is to get rid of the council" She told him quietly.

Mike nodded. "So, what happens now?"

"Now he has called a gathering of the clan. He thinks he can convince enough of them to follow him. I'm sure he will have his followers scattered among the clan to 'persuade' my people to do just that."

"I don't know many of your people but from what I've seen they aren't stupid," Mike replied.

Sheena looked aside at him "My people are just like yours. they can be deceived; they can be bullied and they are frightened."

Mike nodded "We'll convince them."

"Michael, be very careful, it's unlikely Marcus will allow you to speak and he or his followers will not hesitate to make an example of you." She finished leading them into the largest cavern Mike had seen. The cavern was huge but it was already nearly full of people, most of them members of the clan but a few of the islanders and surviving sailors stood nervously around the edges.

Marcus made to stride towards a stage set up in the centre of the chamber but Mike 'stumbled' into his path allowing Sheena to climb up first. Marcus glared at Mike, talons slowly sprouting from his fingers but Mike just smiled at him as Sheena began to speak.

"Brothers and sisters, I'm sorry you have been summoned here but there is conflict within your council of elders and your decision is required." She announced loudly as Pegra and Gareth joined her. She was just about to speak again when Marcus bounded onto the stage.

"THERIANS!" he bellowed "Fellow Therians I have called you to this gathering because your council has betrayed you! They have betrayed our whole race!

Brothers, for generations we have lived as clans, alone, self-sufficient, wanting nothing from outside. But for generations we have been hunted by, murdered by, Endim hunters. Endim's who have flooded this world, taking everything from this planet sharing nothing. Now, this council has brought these very Endim's to our sanctuary, revealed our refuge our greatest enemy. But this is not the end of their treachery for not only have they revealed our refuge, given the food and supplies we have stored for you, our own people, to them!" he finished pointing at the few islanders standing watching.

"Brothers and Sisters," Sheena interrupted "Marcus would have us abandon our friends to these invaders who have bombed their villages and towns, burned their homes and enslaved their neighbours." She paused for a moment "Some of what Marcus has said is true, the Cabal have hunted us, murdered some of us, my husband among them but these people are not the Cabal! If we abandon our friends and neighbours as Marcus demands we would be no better than the Cabal themselves."

"ENOUGH!" Marcus bellowed "These traitors stand accused and you have been called together to judge." He told the crowd moving to the opposite side of the stage.

Around him, the Therians began to move, some towards Marcus, some to Sheena and the other council members. Mike looked around and saw a number unsure talking quietly to friends but several men approached these groups shoving them towards Marcus, others who looked like they were going to support the council being blocked. "This is a stitch-up!" he said to Kerry as he went to intervene but Kerry stopped him.

"Sheena told me we can't be seen to interfere," she told Mike urgently.

Mike was about to retort when a mighty roar filled the hall. Everyone froze immediately. Mike spun round along with many others to see, standing in the entrance one of the biggest men Mike had ever seen. The man's torso and shoulder were heavily bandaged, next to him stood Sam, Neville and a couple of others.

"It's Jeremiah!" Laurence gasped.

"Sam's Uncle?" Mike asked but before anyone could answer Jeremiah walked slowly towards the stage.

As the big Therian approached the crowd parted around him, Mike went to move as well but Jeremiah stopped in front of him. "Commander James," he said loudly so all could hear. "I'm told it was you who fought the aliens off so my pride could escape. I owe you my life," He stated in his rich deep voice. Then turning to Neville, he took a long parcel wrapped in cloth. "This was later retrieved from the site of our battle. It belongs to you." He said handing it to Mike.

He waited patiently as Mike unwrapped it to reveal "My sword!" he marvelled.

"Please join me," Jeremiah said dipping his head slightly as he moved on towards the stage.

Startled Mike stood and watched as Jeremiah moved off but Sam quickly grabbed Mike's arm pulling him along as they climbed up onto the stage to stand with Sheena.

Jeremiah turned to the crowd "Marcus has accused the council of treason. He has told you they have revealed our refuge to our natural enemy, worse he has accused them of stealing the food from your mouths to give to our enemies. But Marcus is wrong! The people of this island are not our enemy, they are our friends and neighbours." He paused; his eyes wandered over the crowd.

Next, to Mike, Sam gave him a gentle nudge looking at the sword he held. Taking her silent cue, Mike stepped forward. "Sir," he began, "You said a moment ago you owe me your life but the people of St Theresa owe you so much more. It was my honour to join your fight with our mutual enemy." Then on impulse, he drew the Rapier from its scabbard and raised it to the ceiling "My sword and all my people are yours to command!"

He glanced down at Kerry who seemed to wince at the cheesiness of his speech but the approving murmur of the crowd showed their acceptance of his words.

As the murmur died down Jeremiah spoke again "Thank you, Commander, These invaders from another world are the enemies of all the peoples of this planet!" he told the crowd "The decision to bring our friends to our caves was mine." He told them "and all similar decisions since are with my approval. I stand with my Regent and council. Who stands with me?" he finished

In answer there was a sudden surge as people began to move towards Sheena's side of the room, Marcus's supporters who had tried to block people's way were swept aside.

Seeing his victory slip away Marcus cried "NO!" jabbing a taloned finger at Jeremiah he continued "You are responsible for this; you have betrayed our entire race! I will not let you drag our clan down with your shame" he finished, advancing on Jeremiah he tore his shirt off as he began to change but Mike stepped in front of the still wounded leader levelling his Rapier.

"Stand down Marcus, you've lost, accept it."

"I would think carefully if I were you, Marcus, I have seen how well the Commander can use that sword," Jeremiah said but Marcus just snarled in reply. Mike braced himself for Marcus to attack but a hand gently pushed his blade down.

"You have challenged the leader of the clan and as Regent, I accept your challenge Marcus," Sheena said, "Unless you are afraid of fighting a woman."

Marcus roared leaping off the stage.

"Sheena," Mike began

"No Michael, this is a matter for the clan to resolve itself," she replied firmly

In front of the stage the crowd had moved back creating a large ring, Marcus now fully transformed, his body covered in bristly grey hair stood snarling up at them. Slipping out of her dress Sheena quickly transformed and stepped lightly off of the stage. She landed in a crouch then gracefully rose to her full height but no sooner had she stood Marcus charged roaring his rage. He held his arms wide to scoop her up but as he reached her Sheena with the poise of a ballerina pirouetted to the side. As Marcus charged past there was a roar of pain and blood splashed out.

On the stage Mike's grip tightened on the hilt of his sword, next to him Sam watched anxiously her uncle's hand on her shoulder as they saw blood dripping from Sheena's right hand but as the two combatants parted they saw it was Marcus's arm that hung limply, blood pouring from several deep gashes.

"Marcus is the stronger but he is old and your mother is the more skilful," Jeremiah told Sam quietly.

Marcus shook his arm painfully but any hopes Mike had that he was lamed were dashed as he lifted it and began to advance on Sheena. He moved more slowly this time, herding her towards an edge populated by his own supporters.

Seeing what he was doing Sheena feinted to the right pretending to go after his injured arm but as she ducked left Marcus swung his left arm catching Sheena on the shoulder. She screamed as she flew through the air, landing heavily she rolled onto her back. Sensing his advantage Marcus leapt onto her biting at her throat but at the last moment, Sheena brought her arms and legs up. She jammed he left arm into Marcus's jaws saving her throat but his teeth sliced into her flesh, but it was her legs which were important. As Marcus pressed down the talons on her toes tore into his abdomen. Screaming he let go of her arm but Sheena slashed at his neck with her right hand as her feet gutted him.

Marcus pulled himself free and rolled away, unsteadily he rose to his feet, his left arm clutching his belly, holding his intestines in as blood poured from his neck. Sheena stood also, her left arm held tight to her chest she stood side on, right arm poised to slash but as Marcus took a step toward her his legs buckled and he collapsed, Sheena stood waiting but Marcus remained slumped on the ground. Transforming partially Sheena called for Gareth who jumped down and went immediately to Marcus's side. Summoning several of his assistants he stood up. "It's over, he's unconscious."

"Get him to the infirmary and please do what you can Gareth," Sheena told him.

"So, what happens now?" Mike asked warily eyeing Marcus's supporters.

"Marcus challenged and lost, his supporters share his loss and will withdraw their opposition," Jeremiah told him.

"But what about Marcus? What will happen to him?"

"We are not barbarians Commander; Marcus will be treated and unless he wishes to leave will remain with the clan. He will lose his position on the council; it would be untenable after his defeat but that is all."

"And there is no reason why one of his supporters could not replace him," Sheena said joining them.

Mike moved slightly to allow Gareth room to dress her wounded arm. At Mike's surprised look she explained: "Whether the majority agree with them or not they are part of our clan and their voices are entitled to be heard."

"I do understand," Mike said, "And while it's not what I'm used to I do think it very open and frankly brave of you."

"Within the Clan, the council members are appointed not elected. We don't rule as much as lead and all decisions are for the good of the Clan as a whole, not individuals or groups." Jeremiah explained, "Even Marcus's 'coup' was for what he saw as being for the best for the clan, not the promotion or advancement of his ideology."

While he was speaking Neville appeared with two chairs which he put down for Jeremiah and Sheena. Gareth finished dressing Sheena's arm as Sam appeared with a third chair which she placed by Mike. Mike looked at her questioningly but it was Gareth who answered him as he turned from Sheena.

"Sit." He commanded

"I'm sorry?" Mike asked

"I said sit, Samantha has told me about the torture you endured, I want to check you over," Gareth told him.

Mike thought about arguing but the looks both Sam and Gareth gave him suggested that neither would have any problem with physically putting him in the chair if he didn't comply, so he calmly sat as the older doctor began examining him.

"Well, I wanted to talk to you anyway." He began but Gareth interrupted him

"Not now you won't! Samantha, please take your mother to her quarters, she needs to eat and then rest for the remainder of the day. Neville, kindly help Uncle back to the infirmary, you shouldn't be moving around yet and I want to check your stitches again." He told Jeremiah pointing at the fresh blood stains on his dressings. "And as for you Commander, I want to give you a full examination. Don't worry you can talk to the council in the morning but for now, you all need rest!"

Mike starred at Gareth incredulously but Jeremiah's chuckle made him look around

"I find it best to listen to Gareth, he is invariably correct and the repercussions of not doing as he says can be quite painful when he is proved to be so." He told Mike.

Mike grinned back "I think that's common with most good doctors. But please I do need to speak to you as soon as possible." He finished following the Doctor out of the cavern.

Chapter 23

Mike woke up to the sound of voices outside his cubicle. For a moment he wasn't sure where he was but as he came fully conscious the memory of the previous day returned. After the duel between Sheena and Marcus, he had been taken to the infirmary. Gareth had told one of his nurses to take him for a shower then bring him back to the cubicle. When Mike got there, they gave him some clean pyjamas and told him to lay on the bed. A few minutes later Gareth had come in with another assistant and they'd given him a full examination then Gareth gave him some injections. One, Mike realised, must have contained a sedative as that was the last thing he remembered.

He pulled himself up to a sitting position and as if on cue the curtain in front of him opened and Sam looked in. "He's awake," she called over her shoulder before entering fully, she carried a tray in with her which she handed to Mike "Breakfast." She told him.

"Thanks," Mike replied realising how ravenous he was. Sam watched him nervously as he tucked in,

"So ah, how are you feeling?" Sam asked.

"Better, thanks," Mike answered looking up. "What's the matter Sam?" he asked seeing the look on his face.

"Well a lot's happened over the last couple of days, it's a lot to take in," she replied looking away.

Mike took his time chewing his last mouthful before answering, "Sam, I won't pretend it's nothing but your still you, still the girl I grew up with, still my friend." He told her "Is this why your family left?" he asked.

Sam nodded, "The Cabal found out we were living in the town so we had to leave quickly. Your dad helped us, he smuggled us out in his van. We thought we'd gotten clean away but not long after your dad had dropped us off the Cabal hunters caught up with us, they caught my father."

"Did they kill him?" Mike asked gently.

"Not immediately, they tried to get information out of him, about where we were, where the clan was. From what I've heard my mother got into their camp and brought him out. When she was finished the hunters weren't in any position to try and find anyone again." She finished.

"I'm so sorry Sam," Mike said helplessly

"It was a long time ago," she replied smiling sadly "Finish your breakfast she told him but before he could have more than another mouthful the curtain opened again and Gareth entered.

"Good morning Commander, how are you feeling today?" he asked bending down to examine Mike again.

"Uh, much better thanks,"

"Good, glad to hear it, now tell me the truth."

"Well I've still got a slight headache and I'm still a bit achy but I'm a million times better than I was," Mike told them.

Gareth nodded as he shone a light into Mike's eyes checking his pupils. "Well you had a couple of head injuries, severe concussion, bruising to your ribs and I hate to think what those energy pulses did to your nervous system but you certainly seem to be on the mend." He finished handing Mike some pills, "Here take these, they should help."

"Thanks, Doctor, Now I really need to speak to your council."

"Yes, Jeremiah and Sheena have already been pestering me. It's against my better judgement but I've agreed we can have a meeting in Jeremiah's room, it's large enough and it's in the infirmary. I've already summoned the other members; do you think you can walk commander or shall I get you a chair?"

"No, I can walk," he said getting out of the bed, "Um can I have some clothes though?" he asked

"Here we'll give you a few minutes to get dressed," he said handing Mike a bag, "Samantha, Jeremiah and your mother told me to say you may also attend." He told her as they left.

Mike opened the bag which contained his uniform and flight suit which had been laundered and repaired. He quickly put on his shirt, uniform trousers and boots but left the flight suit in the bag.

Dressed he left his cubicle and found Sam waiting for him "Gareth had something he needed to attend to, he said he'd meet us in Uncle's room." She told him leading the way.

"So, is Jeremiah actually your uncle? It's just everyone seems to refer to him as uncle, and your mum as Auntie."

"Jeremiah is my uncle, he was my father's brother but the leader of the clan is considered to be a parental figure so is referred to as uncle or if a woman auntie," Sam explained.

When they reached Jeremiah's room, they found Sheena, Pegra, Sargent Laurence and Commander Rosenburg already there. Sheena sat next to

Jeremiah who was sitting up in his bed, there was another chair next to Sheena's which Gareth who entered behind them ordered Mike to sit in.

"So, Michael, I trust you are feeling better?" Sheena asked as Mike sat.

"I am, thank you Sheena, and thank you all for agreeing to see me."

"To be honest Commander we are just as interested in speaking to you as you seem to be about speaking to us," Jeremiah told him. "What can you tell us about this invasion, who are these creatures? Do you have any idea about what they want?"

Mike thought for a moment before answering. "Well as for who they are I can't tell you; we've known about them for over a year now, a space probe encountered them near Neptune. It managed to send some footage of their ships before they destroyed it. After that, we monitored their progress in-system and the UN began preparing our defences."

"What defences did you have?" Jeremiah asked, "We noticed your base and the 'satellite' launches."

Mike nodded "Yes those satellites were actually Atomic bomb pumped X-ray laser mines which were controlled from several manned control modules. We used nearly every warhead available in those constellations. We also had three warships, my ship, the Rapier, and two converted Russian Missile subs plus two squadrons of Chinese space fighters and their support modules. The ISS was converted into the main orbital defence command station."

"That does not seem a very large force." Sheena voiced

"It wasn't but we held them, we held out for over two months. We killed dozens, of their warships, damaged over a hundred more but there were just too many of them. If the UN had deployed more ships we might even have beaten them back, made it too expensive to try and invade but the UN Space Command decided we didn't have enough ships to make much of a difference and it was too risky to reveal our hidden bases by launching while they were so close."

"You certainly did well holding these aliens as long as you did but surely a few more ships would not have made any difference, the technological gap between yours and their ships must have been astronomical," Pegra said.

"That's just it ma'am, it wasn't. Clearly, they have been in space longer than we have but they travelled in vast motherships with enormous engines. Their warships engines were not much better than ours functionally and our weapons were far better than theirs."

"I see, Well thank you for enlightening us Commander but you wanted to speak to us as well, what is it you wanted to ask?" Jeremiah asked

Mike composed his thoughts for a few moments "Well sir, I need your help. As I just explained our weapons were superior to the aliens and if we are to have any chance of winning this war, we need to keep that advantage."

"Yes, I can see that but how does that involve us?" Pegra asked

"The weapons on the Rapier were designed over on the base by a specialist team. This team was led by Professor Madhu Sahota, he probably knows more about our weapons systems than anyone on the planet." Mike paused and looked around as the realization began to register on the faces of the assembled council members "And the last time I saw him was when I was a prisoner in the Alien base."

"My God!" Rosenburg exclaimed, "Do they know who he is?"

"I don't think so, at least not yet but they have figured out he is a technical specialist. When I saw him, they had him working on a translator device so they could communicate with us. I think it's only a matter of time before one of them starts wondering what he did before."

"And with a translator device, they'll be easily able to ask," Rosenburg added

"And you want our help in rescuing him," Jeremiah said plainly.

Mike looked at Jeremiah Directly "Yes sir. If they start interrogating him, I don't think he'll be able to hold out for long."

"But how?" Laurence asked "My people have been all around the outside and we've even managed to speak to someone who was inside. They have cleared a kill zone all the way around their base and the walls and pens are filled with both manned and automatic weapons. A direct assault from any angle would be suicide!"

Mike glanced at Sam briefly before answering "No, I've always thought direct attacks were overrated, a frontal assault is out of the question, but as they say there is more than one way to skin a cat."

"Do you have an alternative plan, Michael?" Sheena asked

"I do," Mike replied looking again at Sam he outlined his plan.

Three days later Mike stood waiting while his 'Strike Team' assembled. It had taken that long to form and brief the individual units then find enough weapons to equip them. Mike had begrudged the length of time it took but he had to admit he'd actually needed that long to heal properly. While he waited, he mentally reviewed the plan again.

There would be five strike teams in total, three small 'infiltration' teams he would lead team 1 with Sheena leading team 2 and a Kerry leading team 3. Mike would have liked to have had Kerry with his team but they were very short on qualified officers.

The two 'Main Assault' teams would be led by Sargent Laurence who had had time in the Army before joining the Police and an American Marine 2nd Lieutenant named John Barclay, one of the very few Marines who had survived the destruction of the US task force.

"Mike?" Sam said shaking him from his thoughts "we're all ready, Mum asked if you want to address the teams before we head out."

"I suppose I should, it is traditional after all" Mike replied ruefully. He followed her on to the stage in the main cavern where Jeremiah, Sheena, Kerry, Laurence and Barclay waited. Pegra, Gareth and Rosenburg were also there even though they would not be going.

"All ready?" he asked.

"All of the teams are ready and we are ready to either lock down the caverns or disperse our people if the need arises." Jeremiah told him.

"It is not a Therian tradition but we thought perhaps you would like to say a few words," Sheena said gesturing to the assembled teams.

Mike just nodded and stepped forward. He looked over the expectant faces that looked back at him, some calm, some excited, many more nervous but determined. As he looked at them many more faces came to his mind, friends, colleagues, comrades in arms. Some he might not see again, some gone forever. The taking a breath he began to speak.

"There have been many battles both big and small in our worlds history and tradition has it that some General or Admiral always gives a stirring speech. Well, I could do with one of them being here now!" he said.

There were a few chuckles and grim smiles at his joke. "But far more common is that those armies are made up of people just like us, people who until recently led normal lives but when faced with adversity, a threat to their families, their friends and the normal lives they cherished they stood up and did what was needed." He paused a second to see the reaction to what he was saying.

"And we are the same! These aliens have come to our world, our home. They threaten our families, our friends. They threaten everything we and our ancestors have built and in this, we ARE the same! Be we Human or Therian-Human, British, American or St Theresan. Soldier or civilian, we stand together today and we will go out and do what is needed, we go to show them we will not give in, we will not hide and if they want this world then there is a price they will have to pay and that payment starts now."

As he finished speaking Sam strode next to him her arm raised and her fist clenched, she had extended her claws and they bit into the flesh of her palm and blood dripped slowly from the cuts "Our blood and the blood or our world is shed, let the blood of these aliens wash it clean" she cried.

The cheers that had started from the humans were now joined by the cheers and howls of the Therians and the cavern shook with them. Mike let them go on for a couple of minutes before raising his arms for silence. "You all know your units and objectives, form up on your commanding officer. Good luck and may your God go with you. Let's get this done" he finished. Turning to the council and officers he said: "Good luck to you all, if everything goes well everyone will be back here in a day or so."

The others all bade him good luck as they filed off to join their teams but Sheena stopped him "You don't intend to come back, do you?" she asked

Mike shrugged "Well no plan, no matter how good, ever survives contact with the enemy but they have ships at their base and if I get chance to grab one and can fly it, then I'll try and get it and the professor to our base at Antarctica." He told her.

She considered what he said, "If that is what you need to do then you should try but if you get chance take Samantha with you, she may be more helpful than you realise." She finished. Then squeezing Mike's arm, she left to join her unit.

Chapter 24

 The five units all headed off into the forest in slightly different directions, Mike led his unit out roughly in the centre of the loose formation. They quickly lost sight of the others as Mike led them towards their objective. His unit kept a steady pace through the night until with Neville in the lead scouting they reached the clearing they had been making for. Mike did a quick check Sam was quietly talking to the four other young Therian women who would carry out the first stage Neville and two of his friends were checking the perimeter for alien devices which left Mike with two American sailors, Kowalski and Myers, and one of Laurence's constables Marie St Jacques. Like Mike, all three were armed with light submachine guns. Mike waved them over and they all went to one knee. "You all ok?" he asked quietly.

At their whispered and nodded assents he continued "Ok Sam and her friends are going to start tunnelling in a few minutes, We'll give them time to make a start then we'll go through after them, I'll go first followed by Neville, then Kowalski and Myers alternate with Neville's friends with you Marie bringing up the rear, Laurence tells me you've got an uncanny sense for trouble so I want you to keep an ear out in case anything follows us through the tunnel."

St Jacques nodded her understanding as Mike continued "Now remember these aliens have armour which a quick burst won't touch but a good burst will take them down. If you're close your knives are sharp enough to cut through it. Remember though they aren't human so they don't have the same weak spots as us. If you take one down finish them through the neck, they definitely breathe the same way we do."

His words were met with grim nods, Myers asked quietly "How do those ladies know they are heading to the right place?" he asked

"Don't worry about that, their sense of direction is incredible when Sam rescued me, she dug right up into my cell first time."

"But we don't know where the Professor is," Kowalski said

"No, we don't but we do know the layout of the old Governor's house so we're going to come up in the basement and work our way up. Sheena and Kerry's team are going to come up near the boundary walls and take the sentry weapons out from the inside so the two main groups can attack. That should create enough noise and distraction to cover us as we work our way through the building."

As he finished Sam and Neville came up beside them.

"The perimeter is clear Commander," He told Mike

"Thanks, Neville, Sam, good to go?"

"We're ready, we'll build the tunnel two across and alternate between the five of us so we can keep a good pace. We should reach the base by first light." She told him.

"Good, well if you're ready let's get started," Mike told them.

Sam was as good as her word, Mike couldn't believe how fast the Therian women dug, Sam had told him that is was a natural instinct for them but he hadn't appreciated the natural skill they had until he saw them in action. Sam rotated them one at a time so they kept their momentum all the way and just under three hours later Sam stopped them. Mike waited patiently as Sam made her way back to him, transforming as she came.

"We've reached the basement but Cara who is leading said she could hear some activity. We've stopped for the moment. Do you want us to try somewhere else?"

Does it sound like regular activity or just someone passing?"

"She said it sounded like someone moving things around."

Mike thought for a second "It might be a storeroom or something, can you get us to behind what it sounds like being moved? If it's crates or something like that, we could use that as cover when we come up."

Sam said they could and headed back to her team. fifteen minutes later she came back. "We're ready to break through," she told him

Mike followed her to the front where Cara was poised to open the tunnel. Mike listened but couldn't hear anything. "Is there any movement up there?" he asked Sam

She listened and the quietly growled to Cara who said something back in their language. "Cara said there is some but it's back over that way." She told him gesturing behind them.

"Ok, open her up but I'm going out first." He said drawing his sword.

Cara started digging up and soon a dim light filled the tunnel. The Therian woman moved aside as Mike crawled past, poking his head through the hole he saw that they had indeed come up in a storeroom and a row of barrels was just next to him. Pulling himself up he eased over to behind them and looked through the gap. A party of three prisoners were busily moving crates of stores around, two guards lazily watched them sitting with their backs to Mike.

Mike felt a presence next to him as Sam crept up to him. Mike gestured to the guards but Sam gestured him back down as she changed into her Therian form and moved away. Around him, four more silent shadows silently crept forward. Mike crept forward himself, one of the prisoners, a naval rating by his uniform, glanced over and saw him. Mike put his finger to his lips. The sailor nodded and moved slowly to his companions quietly passing the message.

Then as if on cue the five silent figures leapt from the shadows, claws slashing and jaws biting, it was over almost before it started, Mike moved forward but the guards were already dead, their throats torn out. Mike quickly went to the three prisoners who stared at the bodies in horror. "Come on sailor, snap out of it." He said sharply to the rating who'd seen him.

The sailor flinched at Mike's tone looking up "What the hell sir?"

"Never mind that now, what's your name sailor."

"Sorry sir, leading seaman John Hernandez. This is technician Jackson and Mr Durie, one of the islanders." He said indicating the two others, Jackson looked at Mike expectantly while the civilian just stared at the dead guards.

Mike sensed the rest of his team joining him and by the looks on the three ex-prisoners faces some of the Therians were in their other form. "Ok, now you're going to see a lot of pretty weird shit so you'd best get used to it now. All you need to remember is these people are on our side ok?" the two sailors nodded while Durie stared open-mouthed.

"It's alright Mr Durie, it's me Samantha Selkie," Sam said reassuringly next to Mike.

Mike glanced around, Sam and the others were all there, dressed to Mike's relief, in Bikini's and shorts though Neville and his two friends were in Therian form.

"I, I'd heard the stories but I..." he stammered as Cara gently led him to sit on a barrel.

Turning back to the sailors Mike asked: "Have either of you seen Professor Sahota, do you know where they're holding him?"

"Yes, sir I have," Jackson replied, "They've got him and a few others holed up in a couple of rooms on the second floor, they've turned them into a workshop. They've got them working on some machines and other things."

"Good lad," Mike said, "Look I know you've been through hell recently and if you want to sit this out, I understand but are either of you up for a bit of payback?" he asked

"Yes sir, you bet I am!" Hernandez said as Jackson agreed.

"Good lads!" Mike said smiling as Kowalski and Myers came up, they'd stripped the guards of their weapons and equipment.

"I'm not sure if we can use these Commander but I thought we'd better take them," Myers said

Mike took one of the rifles "The handgrips a bit awkward but I've seen them use them." He said demonstrating the firing action. Myers had a go but his hands weren't big enough so Kowalski took the rifle. Hernandez said he's also seen a rifle used and managed the second. Jackson taking Kowalski's machine gun nodded he was ready.

"Ok, here's what we're going to do." Mike said, "Sam I need one of your friends to stay here, who would you recommend?"

"Cara did most of the tunnelling, she could do with a bit of a rest."

"Ok, Cara, I want you to stay here with Mr Durie if we find any more prisoners, we'll send them here when you feel you can, I want you to send or take them out through the tunnel. Kowalski, you stay here to keep watch for them. The rest of us will get the professor." He finished nodding to Jackson to lead the way.

Checking the corridor was clear Jackson lead them out of the cellar Mike close behind him "There's a guard at the top of the stairs but the foyer has normally got at least two or three aliens in it as well."

"Ok," Mike said looking at his watch, "If the other teams are on schedule things should get a bit lively soon enough." He said as they climbed the stairs.

Third Drojun Greshh stood at duty stance by the door that led down to the storerooms and looked around the foyer of the people's command base. Dorm how he hated this planet, or at least this part of the planet! He'd heard that in other sectors the natives resisted and his comrades there achieved great glory but the creatures here seemed to just hide and skulk in this nest of weeds! At least Sedeksh and Nal were guarding the slaves down in the stores, there was always a small chance they may try to escape. This sentry duty was so boring if only something would happen, he thought when the explosion tore through the dawn silence. Greshh's reaction would have done his instructor proud as he quickly raised his weapon scanning in the direction the explosion had come from. Unfortunately, he was so fixed on that he never saw the thick black fur-clad arm as it shot round the door behind him.

Neville waited patiently by the door to the foyer when as Commander Mike had promised an explosion echoed through the building, he glanced through the slightly open door as the guard lifted his weapon. Jackson yanked the door fully open as Neville reached around, his huge hand grabbed the guard round the mouth and he yanked him back. As the sentry's head spun there was a mighty CRACK! Neville's other arm was raised to strike as he dragged the alien through the door. Jackson just looked at him in amazement as the alien's body hung limply its head at an impossible angle. Neville just looked down, then glancing at Jackson, shrugged his shoulders as he dropped the dead alien and charged through the door.

Mike charged after Neville and Jackson without sparing the dead alien a glance, in the foyer there were four more aliens all looking towards the sound of distant fighting. Mike raised his weapon but six of the Therians raced past him and pounced on the distracted aliens making quick bloody work of them.

"Fuck me!" Hernandez muttered from behind. Mike glanced back as the seaman blushed "Sorry sir, but I'm glad they're on our side."

"You and me both!" Mike replied. "Jackson, which way now?"

"This way sir" Jackson replied indicating one of the staircases.

"Right St Jacques and Jackson upfront with me, Hernandez, you and Myers take the rear, let's go," Mike ordered as they raced up the stairs.

They'd almost reached the top when a squad of alien troops appeared at the top of the stairs, Mike's vanguard opened fire instantly taking the first four aliens down, the remaining troops fell back briefly then returned fire as Mike's team reached the top. Mike hurdled the fallen troopers, sword in hand with Jackson Firing behind him, St Jacques was next to him and he saw her fall as he careered into the alien squad, he slashed out in a wide arc as the rest of his squad joined him. Some of the alien's, too close to use their weapons pulled wicked-looking combat knives while the others tried to use the butts of their rifles but they were no match for Mike's team. The fight was vicious and bloody, one alien charged Mike, thrusting at his gut, Mike used his gun to pare' the thrust as he sliced down with his sword taking the trooper in the throat. Out of the side of his eye he saw another alien raising his rifle to strike one of the women, he raised his gun but the combat knife had broken the barrel so he threw it instead. It caught the alien on the arm as it clubbed the downed woman. Looking up at Mike the alien brought his gun round but the woman managed to kick out at its leg and the shot went wide. Mike leapt at the trooper driving his blade through its chest with his first thrust. As the alien fell Mike looked around but the fight was over.

Mike took a quick check, of his team St Jacques was the only fatality but Simone, the woman who'd been clubbed had a broken arm and Jonas, one of Neville's team had a bad flesh wound. He quickly sent them back to the storeroom, Jonas carried St Jacques body with him.

"Come on, move, all hell's going to break loose now," he said urging his team on but Hernandez called him

"Sir! Look at this"

Mike crossed to the window where Hernandez was pointing. Outside the wire was down on one of the pens and the prisoners were charging out, overwhelming their guards.

"Those are our guys! Go on lads give it to them!" he cried

"Good stuff!" Mike said "but come on we can help them when we've got the professor. "Which way now Jackson?"

"Just up there sir," he said pointing at another staircase across the landing.

Mike led them over at a run but stopped them short. "If they've got troops up there our little scrap just now will definitely have given us away," Mike said.

"This will tell us Commander," Neville said as he walked past Mike, carrying a dead alien trooper. Stopping at the foot of the stair he threw the dead alien. As it flew up the stairs rifle fire barked knocking the body down.

"Well, that worked I suppose," Mike said,

"Have we got any grenades" Jackson asked.

"Unfortunately, no," Mike responded

"What about this?" Sam asked handing Mike a fire extinguisher "It's a carbon dioxide one I think"

"There was another at the other end of the hall as well" Another of her friends added

"Go and get it, Hernandez, do you think you could hit one of these if Neville threw it up there?"

"Yes sir, no problem."

Sam's friend brought the other extinguisher over and handed it to Neville. Mike, who'd taken one of the alien guns, and the rest of the team crawled up the stairs as high as they dared and he signalled to Neville who threw the first extinguisher up. As it sailed over the top of the stairs Hernandez fired and the canister exploded.

Mike quickly ran up the last steps and threw himself onto the top landing firing as he went. Neville threw the second canister and it bounced once in front of Mike as it flew towards the aliens. Mike took aim and exploded it right in front of them. With a cry, Mike charged firing from the hip as the rest of his team joined him.

Seeing the doors of the workshop/prison Mike kept going while his team finished the guards. Firing as he ran he shot the lock off and kicked the door in, he pulled back as the door flew inwards and several shots answered him. Ducking down he leant in seeing two guards, he quickly fired taking the first down as he rolled into the room.

The second guard brought his weapon round tracking Mike but Jackson had followed him and gunned the alien down. Jackson flinched back behind the door as two more shots splintered the doorframe by his head. Mentally Mike tracked the shots backwards, calculating the angle he popped up from behind the cabinet he was hiding behind and froze. Over there lined up in the corner were Professor Sahota and his team, standing behind Sahota, his arm around the professor's neck was the alien commander.

The alien stared directly at Mike; its head tilted slightly in recognition. "Commander James! Surrender or this one will die" the translator's voice came.

Mike glanced down and saw the translation device held tightly in the professor's hand. "I don't think so chum, you kill him and your shield is gone," Mike replied. "No, I don't think you're that stupid, I think you're stalling hoping your troops will get here but I think you should know MY troops are already here taking your base apart at the seams. We've already released the military prisoners and all my force is now inside your walls. Now I'm going to give you just one chance to give up. Surrender and order your troops to stand down and I'll let them all live."

The alien just watched Mike head still tilted "He's listening to something." Mike realised then he noticed Sahota's other hand was pointing to the right, Mike glanced across to see another door along the wall.

"How about we make it a bit more interesting?" Mike said suddenly. "You know who I am, you know you couldn't beat me even when you had me tied up and half a dozen guards helping you, how about I give you one last chance, just you and me one on one. You win and my troops will let you go."

"What will you require if you are victorious?" the alien asked.

"If I win, I doubt you'll be able to give me anything," Mike replied standing up

"Accepted" The alien commander replied shoving Sahota aside he stepped forward and holstered his weapon then reaching behind him he drew one of the alien's long combat knives.

Mike put his rifle down on the cabinet and drew his Rapier as he walked around it to the centre of the room. The alien looked down at Mike's sword then reaching back drew a second knife.

"MIKE!" Sam's voice came.

The alien stopped, looking towards the door. Mike glanced around "Stay back." He ordered, "This is between the two of us." He said moving cautiously forward waving Sahota and his team towards the door.

Seeing Mike's team stand down the alien moved forward in a crouch, both knives held outstretched.

Mike watched the alien advancing cautiously, he'd had some classical fencing training but the commanders' approach was nothing like he'd ever seen so he kept his sword loosely in-front ready to block any attack. The alien commander tried a couple of feints's trying to force him back but Mike held the centre answering each feint with a block. Seeing he couldn't move Mike the alien began to circle, slowly extending one leg to the side first then sliding over. Mike let him move a couple of times then swiftly launched a probing attack, the Alien quickly blocked with one knife and slashed with the second but Mike had already withdrawn. The commander circled, seeking out any weakness, Mike continued to watch before launching a feint to the right but it was what the alien had been watching for. It immediately struck at Mike's flank which he barely parried in time, the alien followed this strike up with a series of slashes and thrusts forcing Mike back a step but the fight was now on and Mike countered parrying the thrusts and launching a new attack of his own. His Rapier was a blur but each thrust was met by a block and an attack of the aliens own. Then sensing an opening, the commander thrust with both knives, Mike slashed down to block the first and spun around dodging the second but instead of just dodging Mike turned the spin into a roundhouse kick catching the commander just above the wrist. There was a loud crack and the alien dropped one of its knives as it staggered back.

Mike continued to spin all the way coming back to face the commander, he raised his sword into an on-guard position. The alien, holding its clearly broken wrist protectively, screamed it's hate and hurled its last knife. Mike ducked bringing his sword up to block as the door along the wall burst open and a squad of alien troops burst in weapons blazing. Mike hurled himself back towards the cabinet he'd hidden behind before as Jackson, Hernandez and Myers returned fire from the doorway. Mike crawled back into cover as the gunfight raged, grabbing his gun he looked round the cabinet to see the alien commander being hauled through the door. Mike took his chance and made a dash for his own squad as alien rounds whizzed past him.

Running low, he reached the door where he was grabbed by Neville and pulled through and plopped down behind a desk, "thanks" he gasped catching his breath. He quickly looked around taking stock, the aliens had pulled back for the moment and his shooters grimly kept watch at the door, Sahota and his team were huddled in a corner where they stared at the Therians with a mixture of awe and terror.

"Mike are you ok?" Sam asked crawling over to him.

"I'm fine but we've got to move, I don't think the commander will hold off for much longer and if they get a team behind us, we're finished." He replied crawling towards to exit. Poking his head out quickly he checked the hallway was clear. "Jackson, take position upon the stairs. Neville, you go with him." He ordered before going over to the professor and his team.

"Professor?" he asked gently

Sahota looked at him bewildered "Commander? I thought they'd killed you." Then looking past him, he said, "Who, what are these, people??"

"There's no time to explain now professor but they are our friends. Now we need to get out of here, do you know the quickest way out?"

The professor nodded "If we go left out of here and down the back staircase, we'll come out at the rear of the building but that's where their attack ships are."

"Perfect, I want to have a look inside one if we get a chance," Mike told him.

"You want to?" Sahota started to ask before turning to his assistants he said: "Johanna quickly bring me the tablet and the other item from cupboard A."

The young woman jumped as she heard her name, quickly recovering she ran over to one of the wall cupboards then returned handing the professor an obviously jury-rigged computer tablet.

"This is the latest version of the translation device they made me build." The Professor explained, "They wanted to use it to connect into our computers and equipment to translate everything into their language but it will just as easily plug into their computers and translate into English."

"Fantastic, grab that and anything else you need now," Mike began but Sahota interrupted him. "Wait a moment Commander," Sahota said taking a rucksack from his assistant, "It's also connected to this." He finished handing the bag to Mike.

Opening the bag Mike's eyes widened in surprise "My helmet!"

"They recovered it after you were captured, it was kept here with any other pieces of technology they found."

"This is really good professor," Mike said looping the rucksack over his shoulders "but we've really got to go, everyone follow me. Hernandez, bring up the rear." Mike ordered.

"Aye aye, sir." The sailor replied from behind Mike.

Surprised Mike turned to ask why the sailor wasn't guarding the door but the answer was apparent, while he'd been talking to the professor Sam had told her people to block it. The doorway was now completely blocked by assorted furniture.

"Good thinking." He started to say when an almighty crash followed by several shots interrupted him. "Jackson?" he called charging out into the hallway

"They're coming up the stairs sir, but Neville here just chucked that dresser down at them." The technician reported proudly patting his companion's arm.

"Well done, keep their heads down for a couple of minutes, Sam?"

"On it!" she replied before growling a few words at her people who quickly grabbed the remaining furniture and carried it over to the stairs.

"Myers, Hernandez, check out the back stairs and make sure they're clear. Professor?"

"We're ready." Sahota replied while watching the Therians barricading the top of the stairs "My goodness they're strong!" he exclaimed

"You've no idea professor," Mike replied as Myers's voice came back

"Clear Commander!"

"Right, Professor?"

"Yes, of course," he said ushering his assistant's towards the rear stairs when another crash echoed through the hall as Neville chucked another cabinet down the stairs.

"That should hold them," Sam said as suddenly a crash sounded from the other doorway.

"Sounds like the Commander wants another go." Mike said, "come on time to move." Urging the last of his people after the professor's team.

Leaving Jackson and Neville as rear guard, Mike quickly ran to the stairs where Myers was waiting.

"Still clear Commander, Hernandez is on the next landing."

"Right, come on everyone." He said charging down to the next landing where Hernandez waited.

"Sir." He said as Mike joined him.

"Keep an eye on that hallway, then join Jackson and Neville as they come past. I don't want any nasty surprises." Mike told him as he passed. As he headed down the sound of fighting grew slowly louder. At the bottom of the stairs, Mike found a fire door, he gently pushed the locking bar down and opened the door a fraction. The noise of the battle suddenly filled the stairwell, glancing out Mike saw the liberated prisoners and islanders were engaged in a desperate fight with the aliens, as he watched a squad of alien soldiers jogged past carrying what was clearly a crew-served weapon of some sort. They stopped about fifty yards away next to a small wall and began setting the gun up.

"Bloody hell sir, we can't let them set that thing up" Jackson whispered behind Mike.

Glancing back "We're not," Mike replied, "Myers, stay with the civilians, Hernandez, Jackson, with me." He said but Sam's hand held him back.

"Mike, give us two minutes." She growled.

Stepping back Mike watched as the Therians quickly slipped past and disappeared silently into the night. Giving them the two minutes Sam had asked for Mike watched impatiently as the alien squad efficiently set the gun up. Fearing time was running out Mike waved his men forward taking up position in the centre. "Make sure of your aim, we won't get a second chance" he whispered then sighting along his own rifle he mouthed a quick prayer. "FIRE!"

The sailors loosed a quick volley taking down two of the aliens, the rest of the squad quickly dived for cover, scrabbling for their own guns.

"Hit the deck!" Mike hissed as he waited for the return fire but no rounds came. Instead, a series of roars and howls filled the air, Mike glanced up as a number of dark shadows fell upon the alien troops and screams joined the noise.

"Come on let's give em a hand!" Mike said rising quickly but his headlong run was halted by a shout.

"MIKE!"

Looking over Mike stopped his team as leading a group of fighters Kerry ran up to him.

Mike waved everyone down as Kerry joined him

"Sheena told me to wait till they've finished before joining them." She told him "She said it probably wouldn't be safe while they dealt with them." she trailed off nodding to the gun emplacement

Glancing over Mike paled at the thought of what he was going to lead his team into.

"Ok, What's the situation out here?"

"Well it's pretty confused, we've managed to liberate all the prisoners, the Sargent is getting the civilians out into the forest. Most of the Military prisoners are either helping her or have stayed to fight, quite a few of them have plenty they want to get even for." She said gesturing to some of her people.

Mike looked and quite a few of them held captured or makeshift weapons.

"Who's your number two?"

"Olsen, he's a Lieutenant JG." She replied

The young man she pointed to looked over expectantly, he looked somewhat battered, his uniform torn and a freshly healed gash on his forehead. A black eye was an indicator of hidden bruises. Mike waved him over.

The young man crawled over to where Mike and Kerry crouched, even through the dirt and bruises the lieutenant looked painfully young. "Lieutenant Olsen?"

"Sir, yes, Lieutenant Junior Grade Frank Olsen sir."

"So, tell me, Mr Olsen, what was your speciality?"

"Sir, I was stationed aboard the USS Hanson, I've covered Engineering, Navigation and weapons control."

"Weapons? Tell me, lieutenant, do you think you could take a crew and that gun there and use it to do these aliens a bit of no good?" Mike asked.

Olsen looked over at the now unmanned gun and a hungry look came into his eyes. "Sir, yes sir!"

"Good lad," Mike said patting the young man's shoulder. Then turning to his own team "Hernandez, take a couple of Lieutenant Lightningblood's people and get the professor and his party. We'll meet you over at the gun."

With the battle still raging around them Mike led his people quickly to the gun emplacement when two figures appeared out of the darkness. "Michael?"

"Sheena, Sam," Mike greeted them

"Did you find your scientist?" Sheena asked

"We did, there just coming." He told them

"Do you still intend to try and capture one of the alien ships?"

"Yes, that's the plan."

"Then we will come with you, I spoke to Jeremiah and he agrees, Antarctica is the ancient home of our people, we should be present."

"Sheena, I can't authorise that and I don't have time to argue." Mike began

"Good, then don't argue." She cut him off "I believe their ships are this way." She finished starting to head off.

"SHEENA STOP!" Mike ordered.

Sheena spun and glared at Mike growling deep in her throat

"Mike, Antarctica is ours, and this is our fight as well." Sam soothed stepping between them.

Mike looked at the Therians and waiting humans. "Ok," he said resignedly "But we will do this properly. Kerry, I need you to leave all of your people here with Mr Olsen and his gun crew, Sheena, Sam, I need you to leave most of your people with them. There just won't be room in the ship. We'll take my team, the professor and his people."

Taking a calming breath, Sheena said: "We will take half of my people to the ships, they can re-join Lieutenant Olsen after we have left."

"I've got a few good trigger pullers who'd be good to have too, they can head back with Sheena's guys if we can't fit them in," Kerry added.

"Ok, that makes sense. Olsen, it's your command now, use that gun to support the attack but don't let yourself get outflanked. Kerry, you've still got your flight helmet, yes? Good, go and see the professor he's got a translation unit that can connect to your HUD. Sheena, send your scouts out towards the attack ships but they are to scout and report back, they are not to engage without support. Alright people what are you waiting for?" he finished.

As his troops sped off to their duties Sheena led her scouts away and Samantha handed Mike some spare magazines for his rifle. "Mum didn't mean any disrespect Mike," she said quietly "but our hunting instincts are very strong and she is one of my people's leaders."

Mike looked over as he re-loaded "Can she control those instincts?"

Sam smiled showing the tips of her canines "You're still alive, aren't you? Yes, we can control them but sometimes it's hard, especially with the smell of so much blood around and while she knows you are in command her instincts tell her she is an Alpha and you challenged her."

"Ok, I'll try and bear that in mind but she has to realise Sam there can only ever be one commander."

"She knows that Mike and I'll talk to her as well, just don't slap her down too hard in future."

Mike nodded as Kerry returned with the Professor and the rest of Mike's team.

"Ready Mike?" Kerry asked

"Right let's go, Professor, you and your people keep back and keep your heads down. When we call you move quickly ok?" he said leading the team off.

With Mike leading the humans in the middle and the big Therian Males flanking they moved quickly towards the landing field. Up ahead Mike saw a small dog-like figure running towards him. Mike halted his force as the therian reached them, next to him Sam barked a few words and listened as the young female replied.

"Mother has found an ammunition store at the edge of the landing strip but they have also seen several of the aliens heading towards some of the ships, she fears they are going to launch them to attack us."

"Take us to that ammo store first then we'll deal with those aliens." He ordered.

They followed the young scout across the grounds through a hole in the fence to where Sheena and several of her women were waiting by a small prefabricated building.

"Michael," she greeted

"Is that the ammo store?"

"Yes, there appear to be a large number of munitions and weapons in there, I thought you would want to see them."

You're right I do. Prof, come with me, I want you to look at what's in there, see if you can figure out what's what."

Mike led the professor inside with both Sam and her mother following. Ignoring the rifles and guns stacked along the walls, Sahota quickly began opening crates and boxes. "These appear to be the rounds their ships use," he said moving onto the next box, Ah, these might be more useful, I've seen the enemy troops training with these, they're small explosives, they can be used individually like hand grenades or attached to others like this." He demonstrated "and be used for demolition."

"Sheena, how many of these joined together could your people throw?"

Sheena looked at the device Mike handed her, "Three or four quite easily."

"Right, Prof, I want you to get your team in here and make as many bunches of four grenades as you can. Sheena, we need to get these guns and ammunition out to your people."

"We do not use weapons other than those nature gave us." She told him

"Tooth and claw won't fight off an attack ship Sheena." He replied

"No but there are others who can use them, we will take them for the islanders and your people." She said ducking out.

Mike followed her out as a procession of the Therian's in human form began to empty the hut of weapons.

Summoning Sheena, Sam and Kerry over he quickly explained his plan. "We need to disable as many of those ships as we can, that's your people's job, Sheena,"

"With the explosive devices the professor is making, yes I understand." She said nodding

"Kerry, we'll grab one of the ships, did the Prof hook the translator up to your HUD?"

"Yeah, I'm good to go Just tell me when and where we're going."

"Excellent," Mike replied as Sahota came over to them.

"We have made a few dozen bombs and distributed them to er, our friends" he finished unsure of what to call the Therians

"Thank you, professor, my name is Sheena Selkie and this is my daughter Samantha. We call ourselves Therians." She said graciously offering her hand.

Mike smothered a grin as at Sahota's expression as he took the hand of the half transformed, Bikini-clad Therian Matriarch.

"Ok, I'm afraid the rest of the introductions will have to wait," he said, "Looks like they're fuelling those ships there to launch." He continued pointing "we'll take the one on the right. All the others get a bomb ok?"

Sam quickly passed Mike's orders to the rest of her people.

"Ok, let's go fast and quiet till they see us then it's gloves off ok? Right, GO!"

Mike led the way towards the line of waiting attack ships with Kerry and Sam beside him and the Therians fanning out behind. Ahead of them, a number of alien technicians were busily preparing some of the attack ships. Hearing something one of the technicians looked up and gave a shout but it turned into a gurgled scream as one of Sheena's scouts who had crept forward pounced but it was too late. Alerted by their comrades cry the alien guards turned as one.

Rising from his crouch, Mike shouted "They're onto us! GO GO GO!"

A chorus of howls answered Mike as Sam and her mother, followed by all of their people, charged ahead.

Mike and the rest of his squad charged behind firing as they went, their first volley took several of the guards down but the rest, focussing on Mike's group quickly returned fire. Beside Mike two people went down, he didn't have time to see who they were as he kept charging but that one volley of return fire was all the guards had time for as the Therian's tore into them.

"Leave the guards for Sheena's people, keep going for the ship!" Mike ordered.

Mike's team began to run for the ship he'd indicated as around them the Therian's ran amok, slender females and younger males pulling down and slashing guards and technician's while the bigger males tore doors and hatches open throwing their makeshift bombs in. Already three of the alien ships were crippled and ablaze. A fourth ship exploded causing Mike to duck when.

"MICHAEL!"

Mike spun round to see Sheena pointing across the field but as he looked where she indicated he saw an alien lurch up behind her.

"SHEENA! Behind you!"

Reacting like lighting, Sheena spun round but it was too late, wrapping his arm around her neck the guard plunged his combat knife into her side. Mike raised his rifle but he couldn't get a clear shot. Sheena screamed as the guard pulled his knife out for a killing stroke but suddenly there came a furious scream and a red blur slammed into him. Mike ran across to help as the guard tried to cut at Sam but vicious claws slashed through muscle and tendon while with her other hand, she tore the arm out of its socket and threw it away. The guard screamed once but it died on his lips as her jaws clamped down on his throat, silencing him forever.

Mike dropped to Sheena's side, the wound was deep and blood poured onto the ground. Grabbing a field dressing from a pouch on his suit Mike stuffed it into the wound. Trying to stem the bleed Mike sensed other's next to him.

"Commander, please Miss Chang here is a medic." Sahota's voice came.

Mike quickly moved as one of the Professor's assistants knelt and examined the wound.

"MOTHER!" Sam's anxious cry made Mike look up. He quickly got up and intercepted the young women, gripping her shoulders.

"Sahota's assistant's a medic, let her do her job." He said soothingly but Sam just stared at her mother's prone body.

"Michael," Sheena called weakly

Letting go of Sam, Mike knelt beside the wounded matriarch.

"Over there, she said raising her arm, a ship." She finished, her arm flopping back down.

Looking over Mike saw at the opposite end of the field a ship was almost ready to launch, on the boarding ramp a figure starred across at Mike, a figure with one arm in a sling.

"It's the base commander!" Mike said, behind him, he heard Sam growl low in her throat.

The alien commander quickly turned and headed up the ramp of his ship. It was too far away Mike realised for any of his people or the Therians to do anything about it. Turning he called out "Kerry, Professor! Get the ship ready to launch. Miss Cheng, can Sheena be moved?" he finished quickly

The young medic looked up "I've managed to stop the bleeding but it's a bad wound and she's lost a lot of blood. She needs a hospital sir."

"Sam, can your people get her back to the mountain?" he asked but Cheng interrupted him

"Sir, if they try and carry her any distance, she won't make it. We need an ambulance or something."

"Mike?" Sam begged

"Ok, get her into the ship and strapped in, Sam, get Neville and whoever else you're bringing. Professor, get your people aboard. We've got to go now." He ordered, then taking one last glance around the battlefield he sped after them.

Mike raced up the ramp into the body of the attack ship, Jackson, Myers and Hernandez were already strapped in Sam was helping Chang strap, Sheena, down while Sahota's other assistants were making last-minute checks.

"Is everybody aboard?" Mike asked

"Almost." Came a voice behind him. He turned as four more Therians trotted up the ramp, transforming back into their human forms as they came with Neville bringing up the rear.

"Get strapped in, this is going to be rough," Mike told them as he went through to the cockpit.

Mike pulled himself through the hatch to the cockpit, it was much larger than he'd expected, in the middle were three duty stations, one raised slightly behind the two in front, with four more stations at the side. Kerry had strapped herself into the right-hand front station while the professor was busy working on the third, raised station.

"Ah, up here please commander," Sahota said as he saw Mike

"I'm just configuring the command station, the forward two are helm and navigation while the four around the sides are weapons, communication and engineering. I've transferred weapons to the command console."

"Good work professor," Mike replied before shouting through the hatch "Myers, Jackson, come forward" he called.

"Professor, can you put some basic labels on the engineering and communications consoles?"

"Yes of course," he replied finishing the settings on the command console.

Myers and Jackson came through the hatch together "You wanted us, sir?" Jackson asked

"I did, the professor is just putting some labels on those two consoles, Jackson, you're rated in the engine room aren't you and Myers, Commander Rosenberg said you were a communications specialist."

"Yes sir," the two ratings replied together.

"Good, take your places. Kerry, are we good to launch?"

"All good Mike," she replied but the words were barely out of her mouth when through the cockpit window there was a flash of rockets as the base commanders' ship blasted into the sky. Moments later a second ship followed.

"Everyone strap in or hang on," Mike yelled through the cockpit door before leaping into the command seat. "Kerry, GO!"

Chapter 25

Mike fought to strap himself in as Kerry punched the launch control and G forces hammered him into his seat.

"Man, this bitch has some kick!" Kerry called as she desperately gripped the control stick.

"Commander, the second ship's banking round for an attack run, "Jackson called

Mike brought the targeting system up on his console, the second alien ship was banking around while the base commanders ship was accelerating away.

"Damn!" Mike cursed, "He's sending the second ship to hit our people while he gets away."

"They get a good strafing run in it'll be a slaughter," Kerry said.

"You reckon you can take him dogfight?" Mike asked

"Damn straight I can!" she replied hauling the attack ship around

"Myers, get on the radio and tell anyone you can get that we're coming in behind the enemy ship, it would be a real pain if we got taken out by friendly fire."

"Hang on!" Kerry called as looping she brought the ship up and then angled down bringing them quickly behind the enemy ship.

Mike activated his guns bringing up the weapons lock when a second window caught his attention. "Kerry! These things have rear guns" he warned

"Rear guns? CRAP!" she exclaimed spinning the ship away just in time as a hail of tracer rounds tore past them

Mike held onto his console desperately as Kerry hauled the attack ship through a series of manoeuvres as like lightning the alien swung after them.

Kerry rode through the turn and banked hard to bring them back but the Alien pilot had anticipated her move and she had to throw her ship into a nosedive as a hail of fire flashed past them.

"Damn this monkey is good! Mike is there any play on those guns?" Kerry shouted as she spun into another turn

Bringing up both targeting windows he checked all of his controls, "It's no good Kerry, the guns are fixed, I've only got a degree or two firing arc."

"Ok hang on this is going to get funky," she said banking steeply.

On his screen, Mike watched as the alien ship veered around again. The alien pilot was good, no doubt and he knew his ship better than Kerry. But Kerry was a graduate of the US Navy top gun school and a veteran of three combat tours in the middle east. "Come on Kerry get me a shot," Mike whispered to himself as Kerry threw the ship into another tight turn.

"Mike, I'm gonna bring us down past his centre, you'll only get a short window," Kerry said suddenly

"I'm ready!" he replied

Kerry yanked the control column back and down, on Mike's screen the alien ship appeared veering away. Mike jammed his thumb on the firing stud and tracers blasted from his guns. Seconds later they were clear, Mike started to search for the enemy when.

"YEEHA! You got him! Kerry crowed

On his screen the alien ship appeared in his rear gun window, smoke trailing from its side. Mike quickly thumbed the rear gun firing stud and a second hail of tracers wracked the stricken alien ship. More smoke and flame erupted from its side quickly followed by an explosion which tore the craft into two.

Tearing his eyes away from his domed opponent Mike quickly scanned the sky. "Where's the commander's ship?"

"There commander," Sahota replied pointing up "I have been monitoring him, his ship is on an orbital trajectory, I don't think we will be able to catch him."

A movement behind him caught Mike's eye as Sam pulled herself into the cockpit "Mike, mother's not good, we've got to get her to a hospital." She began worriedly.

"Sir, I've got a transmission incoming." Myers interrupted them.

"Can you transfer it to me?" Mike asked

"No sir but I can put it on speaker."

"Do it," then at Myers nod "This is Commander Mike James, who is this?"

Mike's blood froze as from the speaker the alien's translator spoke.

"Commander Mike James, you have achieved nothing, all you have done is secured the destruction of your land. Then when all is destroyed, I will return and find your body and it will be displayed for your whole race to see what befalls those who challenge us."

Sam's eyes widened in horror but Mike waved to be quiet and nodded for Myers to transmit.

"Drop your bombs but you won't destroy us, and when you land your people will only find their own deaths and I won't be there but remember this. I fought your fleet in space and you couldn't destroy me, you captured and tortured me but you couldn't break me and I have fought you here and you lost. I promise you now, if you murder innocent civilians, I will come for you again and it will not be just you but your whole race that will pay." He nodded to Myers to cut the connection.

Taking a calming breath, he continued, "Myers, get a message to St Theresa, tell them to get everyone into shelter, I wouldn't put it past them to bomb the island out of spite. Kerry, I'm sending you some coordinates, I need you to set a course for them straight away."

"But Mother," Sam began but Mike interrupted her.

"I'm sorry Sam, I really am, but if he sees us go back to St Theresa, he can convince his bosses to go through with his threat. But if they see us heading away, his bosses are going to be more concerned about finding out where we've gone with their ship and what we can do with their technology."

Rising from the command station Mike took Sam's arms "Go back to your mum and do what you can, I'll try to get us to medical help as quickly as I can." He said gently guiding her back through the hatch.

"Myers, I need the radio," he said shooing the rating out of his seat. "Kerry, take us down low and go as fast as you can." He finished.

Kerry keyed in the coordinate Mike gave her and taking the ship down to sea level pushed the throttle to go as fast as she dared. Mike sat at the communications station but he'd connected it to his helmet, ten minutes later he lifted his visor, "Myers, take over, Kerry, I'm sending you some revised coordinates, we need to get there as quickly as we can." He said rising.

"Got em," she said keying them into her console, "At this speed, I reckon we'll be there in a little under two hours but that's still in the middle of the ocean."

"Yes, I know, just get us there. I'm going to check on our passengers."

Mike walked through into the main cabin, most of the passengers who were still strapped in looked up at him expectantly, "We're heading away from St Theresa now, there's no pursuit at the moment but that could change so keep strapped in if you can." He told them

He kept going back to where Chang was treating Sheena, as he neared, he saw Sheena lying on the bench with Sam looking very worried next to her, a small flexible tube linked their arms.

"How is she doing?" he asked

Chang looked up, "She's lost an awful lot of blood Commander, Samantha and I have managed to put a transfusion kit together with odd bits and pieces, it's helping but we really need to get to a facility."

"We're going as fast as we can." He assured her then sitting next to Sam, he put his arm around her shoulder "How are you holding up." He asked gently

"I'm ok," she replied tiredly

"I'll get her to help, I promise."

Sam looked at him a tear in the corner of her eye "I can't lose her Mike, please I can't"

"I know, but your mum's a fighter, she'll hang on."

"Samantha?" Chang interrupted, "I'm sorry but I'm going to have to take you off the transfusion, you've given two units already."

"No, she needs more." Sam protested.

"Miss Chang, I believe I'm the same blood group as Samantha and Auntie." A deep voice came from behind them.

Mike looked up as Neville came over.

Chang looked up at him, "Ok, let me unhook Samantha and then take her seat."

Neville changed places with Sam and Mike guided her to a seat. Sitting her down Mike handed her a water bottle and a ration bar. "You need to eat and drink, with your mum wounded your people here need you so you can't afford to get sick." He told her sitting beside her.

"I never thanked you properly for getting me out of that cell." He said as she ate.

Sam looked up, and smiled "Do you remember when we were ten and I found that little cave in the cliffs? I went in to explore but you didn't like the look of it."

Mike frowned as he thought back "And you caught Vince Barratt and his mates smoking cigarettes."

"That's right and you heard something and came running into the cave to get me."

"Ha, yes I seem to remember getting a black eye but Vince came off worse if I remember though knowing what I know now I probably did him a favour!"

"Well you didn't leave me then and I couldn't leave you in that cell."

Mike hugged her gently "I really missed you when you left." He began but just then Jackson poked his head through the hatch.

"Sorry sir but you need to come forward."

Squeezing Sam's arm Mike rose and followed the rating back to the cockpit.

"ok, what's going on?" he asked as he sat in the command station.

"Well, we got good news and bad." Kerry replied, "First the good, Myers?"

"Well sir, I managed to get a signal through to St Theresa, I spoke to Sargent Laurence, she confirmed all allied forces had successfully disengaged and were heading back to base. She said they'd managed to destroy all the remaining aircraft and a large portion of the base and they'd released all the prisoners."

"Outstanding! Did you pass on my warning?"

"Sir, yes I did, the Sargent said she's got everyone in to cover."

"And that's not all, this tin can, can really shift. We're about ten minutes ahead of where I thought we'd be by now."

"Even better, so what's the bad news?" Mike asked

"I'm afraid they are," Sahota said highlighting several icons on Mike's console. "It looks like four attack ships, they're still high up in the atmosphere and I don't think they've seen us yet but.."

"But it's just a matter of time and there may be more of them." Mike finished.

"Ok, if they find us, they find us we'll just have to be ready." He said bringing up his targeting screen. "How long till we get to those coordinates I gave you?"

"We're doing better than I expected but still at least forty minutes, more if I have to go to evasive."

"No, keep going straight for now. Professor, keep an eye on those scanners and let me know if you see any more ships or if you think they've spotted us." He finished settling into his station.

The minutes seemed to drag slowly as Kerry, managing to get even more speed from her engines, flew them onwards. Mike tried to relax and checked his guns again when Sahota cried out

"Commander, the aliens are altering course, they've seen us!"

"Mike, I got two more dead ahead," Kerry called out

Mike checked his screen and quickly calculated how far away their pursuers were compared to the ships in front.

"Ok, keep going Kerry, let's see if these beggars have ever played chicken!" Mike ordered.

"Game of chicken huh, alright let's do it."

Mike grinned as on his screen the alien attack ships closed. the two alien pilots, clearly unsure of flying so close to the waves, were a good fifteen to twenty feet higher than them. "Kerry looks like these guys don't like the water."

"Yeah, you want me to take us up then dip down as we pass?"

"keep dodging up and around then yep, dip low, their guns won't be able to track down that far."

"You got it." She replied with a feral grin.

Kerry took them up twenty-five feet then kept jigging left and right as the two aliens opened fire. Mike let loose a couple of bursts in answer but kept them short as he counted the distance down. "KERRY NOW!"

Kerry quickly brought the ship almost to the level of the waves, underneath the aliens, realising they couldn't target Mike's ship the alien pilots tried to rise away but Mike had them in his sights. Tracers wracked the two aliens as they tried to evade. Mike quickly switched to his rear guns as they sped past stitching more rounds into the aliens. One desperately clawed for the sky, smoke billowing from its hull but the second crashed into the waves breaking up as it hit.

Now they sped on towards the coordinates Mike had set but behind them, four alien attack ships slowly gained on them.

"How long Kerry?" Mike asked

"Too long," Kerry replied we're still at least twenty minutes away and those puppies will be all over us in fifteen."

Mike checked his ammunition "Over half our ammo's gone as well," he said to himself, he thought quickly then closing his helmet he opened a channel to Kerry's helmet. "Ok Kerry, when they get here I'm going to try and hold them off as long as I can but I need you to do something, it might seem crazy but it's our only chance."

Kerry didn't look back but closing her own visor she replied: "Ok, but why the cloak and dagger?"

"because what I need you to do really is crazy and I don't want anyone to hear and panic." He said then laying out his plan he explained what he wanted.

"You crazy Limey bastard," she said when he finished.

"Don't you mean 'you crazy Limey bastard sir." Mike teased

"Yeah, ok I see why you didn't want everyone to hear but are you sure it'll work?"

"No, but it's the best chance we have and if it doesn't we're dead anyway."

"Ok, but we'd better make sure everyone is strapped in."

Just then a light on Mike's HUD flashed, "They're here." He said then opening his visor he called out "EVERYONE STRAP IN, THIS IS GOING TO BE ROUGH!"

Keying his targeting windows Mike opened fire, short bursts but it was enough to throw the first pursuer off and it veered aside but the next two fanned out away from his guns and angling themselves slightly they opened fire. Rounds tore around them, several pinged off the armour and there were screams from behind as a couple pierced the hull.

Mike swore but just then one of the aliens flashed into his target zone and he snapped off another short burst. The alien ship banked away but two more replaced it with the third coming around again. Mike pressed the firing stud but nothing happened, he quickly checked his ammunition but a pulsing red light told him his guns were off-line.

"Kerry, the guns are out, do it now!" He ordered.

"Oh crap, here goes nothing! Hold onto your seats guys!" She called as banking around she angled the nose down and dived towards the ocean.

"COMMANDER!" Sahota cried shocked

"Just hold on," Mike called back as the ship plunged into the water. Instead of cutting power and letting the ship level off Kerry kept the thrust on full pushing the ship deeper into the ocean.

"Keep us going down Kerry, right to the bottom." Mike said, "Myers, get back there and help seal any holes, we need to keep the cabins airtight" Mike ordered

"Jackson, keep an eye on those engine readings, I don't know how they will react to water."

"Mike, I'm losing power" Kerry called suddenly.

"It looks like the engines are shutting down and sealing themselves," Sahota said studying the readings.

"Are we still sinking?" Mike asked

"Yes, we'll keep going down till we hit bottom now," the professor said.

"Ok, good. Well, there's nothing more we can do here so we might as well all go back to the main section." He said rising.

Mike led the cockpit crew into the main body where Sam and the others met him.

"What's happened, are we in the sea?"

Mike waved for calm, "Settle down everyone, yes we've come down in the ocean and are heading to the bottom but there's no need for alarm, it's all under control. Has anyone been injured?"

"Rene was hit by some splinters when the bullets came through but she's the only one." Sam told him "So what happens now?"

"Now we settle down and wait. The alien ships are still up there so we need to sit down and be quiet." He told them.

Mike followed Sam over to the bench where Sheena lay still unconscious. Sam sat next to her and took her hand. Chang sat opposite her monitoring her condition. "How is she doing?" he asked.

"Commander," she acknowledged "Well she's stable at the moment, she's had four units of blood so far, I've stopped the main bleeding though I can't tell if she's bleeding internally or not but I daren't take any more from Samantha or Neville." She told them.

Mike nodded, "Thank you If there's anything more you need just call me." Squeezing Sam's shoulder, he said, "I'd better check on everyone else but I'll come back." He promised

Mike made his way around the cabin, he went over to Sam's friend Rene' first, she was lying on the bench with Neville sitting next to her. "How is she, Neville?"

"Some splinters went into her shoulder when some bullets came through the hull. Miss Chang managed to get most of them out. Then she gave her something to make her sleep after dressing her wounds."

"How are you holding up?" Mike asked

"I am ok Commander." He replied,

"Well you're tougher than me then, it was very good of you to donate your blood for Sheena. I wanted to thank you personally for that"

"It was my honour; Auntie is very important to our clan."

"Well I know Sam is grateful as well. It's an honour to have had you under my command." Mike said patting the big Therian's shoulder.

Mike moved on speaking to everyone in turn till he reached Kerry. "How are you holding up Kerry?"

"Oh, I'm just peachy," she said tiredly

"That was some pretty spectacular flying back there."

"Oh, that was nothing, took me a little bit to get used her but she's not a bad tub."

"Well at some point I hope to get another ship, how would you feel about flying something bigger."

"Are you offering me a job Mike?" she asked with a laugh

"Well the Rapier was supposed to have three pilots but we were down one so I've got a vacancy."

"But you don't have a ship, Mike,"

"Not at the moment but I will get another ship, even if I have to steal one of theirs, I could do with a good pilot."

"Well unless wherever we're going has a few spare F35s lying round I guess I'm free."

"Consider yourself hired then, now get some rest," he said

Mike turned to leave when suddenly a loud thud sounded from the hatch.

At once several people started calling and shouting.

"EVERYONE QUIET!" Mike bellowed then moving quickly to the hatch he grabbed his gun and using the butt hit the hatch three times.

He waited a few seconds then another three thuds came, there was a pause then a series of thuds followed.

"Hey, that's Morse code" Myers announced.

"Yes U.B.E A.T.T.A.C.H.E.D" Mike translated

"Tube attached?" Myers asked

"Don't the new Jersey class subs have DSRV's attached?" Kerry asked

"Yes Ma'am, they do" Myers replied.

"ok, let's see if it's safe," Mike said as he started hammering S.A.F.E T.O. O.P.E.N H.A.T.C.H"

There was a slight pause then the tapping resumed S.A.F.E

Mike waited a few seconds and no further message came. "Right let's get this open." He said as he started to pull on the hatch lever. "It's stuck!"

"Excuse me, Commander," a deep voice said and Mike stepped aside as one of the big Therian men politely edged past him Evan, Mike remembered. He seized the lever and pulled gently while he studied it. "There are some metal splinters jammed in here. Can someone pass me a knife or something?"

Jackson handed him a small utility tool and holding the lever with one hand gently teased the splinters out then handing the tool back said: "There are still one or two in there but they should come out on their own, but please stand back in case they come out quickly." He said then gripping the lever with both hands he pulled. Several small splinters flew out but the lever moved and with a squeal, the hatch finally opened.

There was a small shower of water but on the other side of the hatch a sailor grinned down at them, several faces could be seen behind him "Is Commander James there?"

"I'm James," Mike replied, "we've got wounded do you have a doctor aboard?"

"Yes sir," the sailor said moving aside as the people behind him moved forward.

"Commander, I'm Dr Elijah Ben Josef, these are my assistants," The man behind the sailor said.

"This way please Doctor, we've two wounded, Mrs Selkie here has a stab wound and Rene' over there has a shrapnel wound. Miss Chang here is our medic; she's been treating them." Mike explained.

Ben-Joseph sent one of his nurses to check on Rene' while he examined Sheena.

"Ah Commander," The sailor from the DSRV had followed them "I've been ordered to bring you back to the USS Sea Tiger."

Mike turned "lieutenant?"

"Lieutenant Junior Grade Anthony Curtiss sir."

"Well Lieutenant Junior Grade Anthony Curtiss, I will be delighted to accompany you to the Sea Tiger when I'm happy my people are all alright."

Turning back, he waited while Ben-Joseph finished examining Sheena.

"Doctor?" he asked.

"Miss Chang here has done a good job but my concern is moving the patient. We need to get her to the Sea Tiger so I can operate on her wound but we'll need to move her carefully. We have some equipment in the DSRV that I'll need. But we should move her as quickly as we can."

"Ok Doctor, do what you need to do, Lieutenant Curtiss, how many people can you transport in your sub?"

"Sir, we can carry twenty-four casualties, sir."

"Very good Lieutenant, we'll start by evacuating the wounded,"

"Commander?" Ben-Joseph interrupted "when we move Mrs Selkie, we will need to get her to the Sea Tiger immediately, in my opinion, we should move her last."

Mike thought for a moment "Alright," then turning to the cabin said loudly "ok everyone time to move. Neville, Evan can you get Rene' onto the DSRV, then I'll need you back, everyone else follow them." He ordered

"I think we should get Neville and Evan to carry Mrs Selkie, no one will be as careful as them," Mike told the Doctor.

"Lieutenant, you get aboard your ship and get ready to leave," Mike ordered

"Yes, sir!"

Mike waited while his crew boarded the rescue sub until only the Doctor, his assistants, Neville, Evan and Sam were left. Then with a nod to the Doctor, he said: "Come on Sam, we're next."

Sam went to move but a weak voice stopped her.

"Samantha?"

Sam quickly moved back "Mother?"

"Samantha? Did we win?"

"Yes mother, we won! We're just moving you to a hospital, hold on it won't be long." She said

"Samantha, remember, it's important when you get to Theria, remember the legends of Mulamuria."

"It's ok mother, you can show me, you're going to be alright," Sam said

"Samantha, listen" Sheenah began but Mike moved in taking her hand,

"No auntie Sheena, you listen. Sam and Neville have given you their blood to keep you alive. Now you just do as the Doctor tells you and heal. D'you hear me?"

Sheena looked up at him blearily, "I suppose it would be a shame to waste such effort." She said weakly.

"Bloody right it would." He replied squeezing her hand.

Mike led Sam into the DSRV closely followed by Neville, Evan Sheena and the medical team.

Twenty minutes later the DSRV docked with the USS Sea Tiger, Curtiss moved to open the hatch and Dr Ben Joseph led the medical team quickly through the hatch with Sheena and Rene'

Mike followed with Sam "Go on Sam, I'll see you soon, ok?" Mike said. Sam squeezed his hand as she followed her mother to the sickbay.

Mike watched her go as his crew slowly disembarked from the DSRV.

"Commander James?" a voice said behind him.

Mike turned and found a short thick-set man "Yes?"

Commander Bart Sherman sir, welcome aboard the sea Tiger. It's an honour to have you aboard sir."

"Thank you, Commander. I need to arrange the recovery of the attack ship."

"All in hand Commander, we've got two more subs heading in to tow it to Antarctica. My orders are to stay here till they arrive then to transport you and your people to redemption base."

"Thank you, Commander, umm as you may have noticed, my people are somewhat lacking in possessions."

"Don't worry sir, we have accommodation and clothing available."

"Thank you again, Commander, now I really must see to my people."

"Of course, sir, Chief of the boat!" Sherman called to a nearby Chief Petty Officer. "Chief Ramirez will show you where you and your people are bunked then he'll take you to the sickbay." Sherman finished.

Mike followed Ramirez to make sure his people were accommodated then followed the Chief to the Sickbay where Sam was waiting.

"How is your mum Sam?"

"She's out of surgery, Dr Ben Joseph says the operation went well and she should recover."

"That's great, we've been allocated a block of bunks but I agreed with Commander Sherman that you can stay with your mum. They're going to drop some clothes off for you as well."

"Thanks, Mike, I'd like to stay and be with her when she wakes up."

"No problem, um I'd better go and make sure everyone else is settled but I'll come back."

She touched his arm anxiously "Mike, I had to tell the Dr about us. I don't think he believed me till he started operating, our physiology is slightly different to yours"

Mike nodded "I'll speak to Commander Sherman; he seems a decent enough bloke. I'll tell him everything you've done, make him understand you're on our side."

Sam smiled appreciatively, then pulling him closer kissed him on the cheek, "Thank you. Now go and do what you need to." She said as she turned and went back to her mother.

Mike watched her go then turning went back to make sure the rest of his people were alright.

The voyage in the Sea Tiger took another eight days but on the last day, Mike was talking to the Sea Tiger's Captain when Sam joined them on the bridge.

"Miss Selkie" Sherman greeted her.

"Sam, how's your mum doing? I heard she was in a coma" Mike asked

"She's sleeping while her body heals." She replied, "Commander, I just wanted to thank you for the way you've treated us all while we've been aboard your ship."

"Well I'll be honest ma'am when Dr Ben Joseph told me about what he'd seen I was somewhat concerned but Commander James here put me straight and your people's behaviour after all you've been through has been inspirational. It's been an honour to have you aboard."

"Thank you, Commander."

"Ah, I should tell you that I had to include some information about you in my report to the commander of Redemption base. Though I took pains to include Commander James' full report and support as well as my own." Sherman added nervously.

"I understand Commander, we'd already decided we couldn't hide our true nature and were going to present ourselves to the base's commander when we arrived."

"Well, we've just surfaced and Commander James and I were just going up to take a look, would you like to join us in the conning tower." He said handing them a pair of warm jackets. Sam, like the rest of the Therians, had been issued standard Navy jumpsuits while Mike wore his uniform shirt and trousers. They both donned the jackets and followed Sheridan up to the conning tower.

They emerged into a tunnel made of ice. "This is the approach to Redemption base," Sheridan explained. "We'll come out into the base proper shortly."

Mike and Sam starred about them in awe as the Sea Tiger sailed through a tunnel made entirely of ice. Around them the sea and ice sparkled like precious gemstones with all the colours of the rainbow, ahead there was a bright glow where the tunnel ended.

As they reached the end of the tunnel Sheridan said: "Commander, Miss Selkie, Welcome to Redemption base."

As they came out of the tunnel, they found themselves in a wide valley, ahead of them the river flowed clear and fresh. The valley was awash with green grass, trees and other plants. In the distance, two small volcanoes smoke drifting lazily from them provided warmth. Above them instead of the sky a roof of crystal white ice. The Sea Tiger headed slowly to a dock and sprouting out from the dock sat the base. Further up the river they could see construction docks where ships like the Rapier and the Gagarin were in various stages of construction.

Sam gasped as she looked around "Mulamuria" she said quietly.

"Sam?" Mike asked looking across at her

Sam smiled self consciously

"Mulamuria, it's what our ancestors called this place. According to our legends Mulamuria was where the survivors of my people fled from when this land was destroyed." A voice behind them said.

"MOTHER!" Sam cried turning.

"Sheena, you should be resting." Mike added

Sheena smiled tightly, "I'm much better, if a little weak," she told them "And I couldn't miss our arrival here."

"Well I don't know anything about what this place may have been called but to us it's Redemption base and it's where we're going to kick those alien's asses all the way back from where they came." Sheridan promised. "Now if you'll excuse me, I need to get back to the control room. Please stay up here as long as you like." He said heading toward the hatch. "I'll send a blanket and chair up for Mrs Selkie." He told Mike quietly

Sherman was as good as his word and a few minutes later a sailor appeared with a camp chair and blankets. With Sheena made comfortable Mike and the two Therian women watched as the Sea Tiger slowly approached the dock.

"There is a group of people gathering over there." Sam observed.

Noticing a tightening around Sheena's eyes as she followed Sam's gesture Mike looked the through the observers' binoculars. Sure enough a group appeared to be gathering at the point the Submarine was due to dock. He wasn't sure but some of them were carrying tools and other items.

"The Cabal!" Sheena spat.

"We don't know that for certain." Mike cautioned "But just in case I'll go first when we disembark."

Mike led Sheena and Sam back into the sub where he sent them to prepare the rest of the survivors from St Theresa to disembark. Sherman was waiting for him in the control room.

"Commander, there's a group waiting on the quay, have you received any messages?! Mike asked

Sherman looked at his radio operator who shook his head. "No nothing's come through apart from our berth and docking instructions" seeing the worried look on Mike's face he went over to a monitor and switched on the external camera feed. On the screen they could clearly make out a large group of mainly men armed with an assortment of tools and pipes. He looked worriedly at Mike "Any idea what that's about?"

"I think news about my friends may have reached the wrong people. If they try and board, can you hold them?"

Sherman studied the mob "I dunno, the Sea Tiger has only a small crew and no marines. I could break out some sidearms." He replied doubtfully.

"I'd rather avoid a confrontation if at all possible. I'll go out alone when we dock but if you could put a call through to the base command and tell them we need a security contingent, I think that would be a good idea."

A few minutes later as the Sea Tiger docked Mike made his way to the hatch where, as he expected Sherman waited for him. What he didn't expect was that Kerry, Jackson and Myers along with both Neville and Evan. Sherman had a pistol which he offered to Mike.

"Thanks Commander but a gun could provoke them." Then turning to the others, he continued "I believe I said I'd go out alone."

"Yeah, we heard that, aint gonna happen Mike." Kerry told him.

"Look if they are the Cabal." Mike began,

"We've thought about that Mike," Kerry interrupted him. "We know if they see Nev and Evan they'll kick off, so they've agreed to stay just inside but they are our insurance. Besides you're the hero who held the aliens in space and the three of us as back up might just make em think twice."

Mike thought for a second then, "Ok but no one does anything unless I say so, and for god's sake keep those out of sight." He said gesturing to the pipes Jackson and Myers carried and the knuckle dusters Kerry wore.

Kerry smiled slyly as she put her hand nonchalantly into her jacket pocket while the two others hid their own makeshift clubs. Satisfied, Mike ked the way down the gangplank, behind the group crowding the dock Mike could make out a jeep and what looked like an officer arguing with some men blocking their way. At the bottom of the gangplank a couple of the military policemen were attempting to stop the leaders of the mob from boarding the submarine. Just behind the men shouting at the MP's stood a large man wearing an elaborate uniform. Mike strode down the gangplank then with a gentle touch on each MP's shoulder "officers" he said as he eased between them. Ignoring the front row Mike locked eyes with the big man behind them.

"Let the officer through boys, he's human enough." The large man said in a southern United States drawl.

The front row parted as Mike moved forward, at a gesture from his hand Kerry and the two ratings waited behind the MPs. Mike stopped in front of the American who was clearly the leader of the group. The bigger man tried to intimidate Mike by leaning over him but Mike just lightly crossed his arms without breaking eye contact and raised an eyebrow. Then making a show of looking round he said

"It's normal for civilians to welcome those who've actually fought the enemy with a parade rather than a gathering but thanks for the effort anyway. Now you and your friends are blocking they quay, so I think you'd better move on now don't you." He finished dropping his arms loosely at his side.

The big American sneered "You want us to move on? And just who the hell are you to tell us to move?"

"I'm Commander Mike James."

At the mention of his name there was a low murmur from the crowd. The American glanced round quickly and the murmuring stopped.

`Well Commander Mike James, me and the boys are always happy to give our warriors a heroes welcome but that ain't why we're here. You see we heard there was a vermin infestation on this here sub and we aim to clean it out."

Mike took a forceful step forward, making the Cabal leader flinch slightly before trying to lean forward again but before he could move Mike said "The only vermin I can see is on the dock." Then raising his voice he continued "Now move on before I have to do something you'll regret!"

"Now then Fella, you heard what the Captain said. Move along, NOW!" a strong Irish voice sounded.

Mike glanced toward the sound of the voice where a group of sailors led by Duffin had infiltrated the crowd. Next to Duffin stood Raj Singh, with Jess, Mike's Steward, on his other side. Behind them were what looked like most of the Rapiers crew. One the American's followers went to put his hand inside his jacket but a hand grabbed his wrist and Joanne Isaacs leant in to whisper in his ear. The thugs face drained of colour and he quickly put his hand back dowm

Behind him Mike could hear a number of the Sea Tigers crew were on the gangplank with Kerry and her two companions. Behind the cabal group two MP cars were just pulling up. An MP wearing Lieutenant's bars got out of the lead car, the two MPs that got out with him could almost have been the twins of Neville and Evan.

Mike glanced around nonchalantly then turning back raised an eyebrow at the Cabal Leader. The MP Lieutenant was looking at the two groups and conferring with his senior NCO hurriedly.

"Time for you to be going I think." Mike said as Duffin made his way to his side, who was quickly joined by Kerry.

The big American, regaining his composure, looked down at Mike and coolly removing his dark glasses said "We're just concerned citizen's making sure no, undesirables, turn up unwanted like. But I see such fine officers like yourself 'Commander' have things under control. Just keep your dogs on a leash!" he finished then raising his voice said. "Come on boys, we got places to be."

Giving Mike a last hard look the American turned and walked away, his entourage slowly following.

Mike watched them go as Sam and the rest of the St Therese survivors joined him.

"Gobshite!" Duffin said as he watched them go.

Mike laughed out loud "God I've missed you engines" he said clasping his friends shoulder. "I missed you all." He said turning to his crew.

Duffin grinned back at Mike, "It's good to see you back Mike, we thought..." he said.

"I know mate,"

Duffin nodded then looking at the retreating gang "Do ya think we need to keep an on them?" he asked.

Surrounded by his crew, both of his crews Mike said, "We'll deal with them in due course but we've got a bigger job to do." Taking Sam's hand "The fight back has already started, for the first time in history, all of the peoples of the Earth are united. We've shown these aliens we won't go down, that they try to take our land they will pay the price. It may not be today, or even this year but we will make them regret ever coming to our world."

Slapping his best friend on the shoulder he started walking towards the docks saying "Now engineer, where did you park my ship?"

Printed in Great Britain
by Amazon

23254418R10136